The Seed of Empire by Fred M White

Fred Merrick White was born in 1859 in West Bromwich in the Midlands of England to Joseph White and Helen Merrick who had married the previous year.

Joseph was a solicitor's managing clerk, who by the time the family moved to Hereford a few years later, had become a solicitor's article clerk.

Little is known of White's early years but what is known is that he followed in his father's footsteps and worked as a solicitor's clerk in Hereford. His father by now had also become a solicitor and times seemed quite prosperous for the family.

However in the late 1880's something went badly wrong for his father and he was imprisoned.

White had by now decided that writing was a more preferable career for him than the law. By 1891 Fred M. White, now 31 years old, was working full-time as a journalist and author, earning enough to support himself and his mother, Helen. By this time Fred's younger brother, Joseph A. White, had left home and working as a glass-blower.

In 1892, White married Clara Jane Smith. The wedding took place at King's Norton, Worcestershire, and the couple went on to have two children; Sydney Eric White (1893) and Ormond John White (1895).

As the century closed Fred's father had been released from prison and was living as a "retired solicitor", together with Helen, in Worthington in West Sussex.

By the time of the 1911 census, Fred M. White, now 52 years old, and his wife Clara were living at Uckfield, a town in the Wealden district of East Sussex. As the ominous shadows of the First World War gathered White had established himself as a popular and extremely prolific author. Indeed whether it was novels or short stories they flowed from his pen with a startling speed and many of them were initially serialized in the popular weekly and monthly magazines. His clever use of science to create imaginative and highly adventurous story lines was a particular talent of his.

During the First World War, both of his sons served as junior officers in The Royal Inniskilling Fusiliers.

The titanic struggle of the First World War and his sons' war-time experiences in it greatly influenced this phase of his writing. His novel The Seed of Empire (1916), describes early trench warfare in great and gritty detail. He went on to describe how the social changes after the war created many problems for returning soldiers as they attempted to fit back into a now peaceful society.

Fred and Clara spent their twilight years in Barnstaple in Devon, an area which also provided the backdrop for his novels The Mystery Of Crocksands, The Riddle Of The Rail, and The Shadow Of The Dead Hand.

Fred Merrick White died in Barnstaple in 1935.

Index of Contents

CHAPTER I - Black Monday
CHAPTER II - Ragged And Tough
CHAPTER III - A Friend In Need
CHAPTER IV - All For The Flag
CHAPTER V - Shoulder To Shoulder
CHAPTER VI - The Thin Brown Line
CHAPTER VII - "England, Home, And Beauty"
CHAPTER VIII - "Tipperary"
CHAPTER IX - "The Girl He Left Behind Him"
CHAPTER X - Boot And Saddle
CHAPTER XI - The Shadow Of Mons
CHAPTER XII - Fog Of War
CHAPTER XIII - After The Guns
CHAPTER XIV - By Telephone
CHAPTER XV - Saved!
CHAPTER XVI - The Lonely Farm
CHAPTER XVII - Back With The Guns
CHAPTER XVIII - Women's Work
CHAPTER XIX - Something Attempted
CHAPTER XX - In Clover
CHAPTER XXI - Ginger's Odyssey
CHAPTER XXII - The New Republic
CHAPTER XXIII - In The Vernacular
CHAPTER XXIV - News From The Front
CHAPTER XXV - Plain Words
CHAPTER XXVI - The Old Spirit
CHAPTER XXVII - Light In The Darkness
CHAPTER XXVIII - Back To The Front
CHAPTER XXIX - Sticking It
CHAPTER XXX - A Mystery
CHAPTER XXXI - To The Rescue
CHAPTER XXXII - "Savoy Hotel"
CHAPTER XXXIII - A Staggering Task
CHAPTER XXXIV - The Deadly Grip
CHAPTER XXXV - A Cheerful Tommy
CHAPTER XXXVI - At The Base
CHAPTER XXXVII - The Musketeers At Play
CHAPTER XXXVIII - Tommy's Little Way
CHAPTER XXXIX - The End Of The Game
CHAPTER XL - The Red Cottage
CHAPTER XLI - Inside The Cottage
CHAPTER XLII - The Hidden Battery
CHAPTER XLIII - Homeward Bound
CHAPTER XLIV - The New London
CHAPTER XLV - Home, Sweet Home
CHAPTER XLVI - The Deeper Meaning

CHAPTER XLVII - Back To The Front
CHAPTER XLVIII - Neuve Chapelle
CHAPTER XLIX - The Early Morning
CHAPTER L - The Good Young Stuff
CHAPTER LI - The Day's Work
CHAPTER LII - The Next Day
CHAPTER LIII - And After?
FRED M WHITE – A CONCISE BIBLIOGRAPHY

CHAPTER I - BLACK MONDAY

The scrap of paper lay on the counter of Europe, and the honour of more than one great Power trembled in the balance. And accordingly the greatest nation of them all would be compelled to act. Not that she had ever hesitated; not that she would swerve one inch from the path that she had pursued for nearly a thousand years; and perhaps because of this, from the north to the south, and from the east to the west, anxious hearts were beating and anxious eyes turned towards the storm centre that hung so black and threatening over Central Europe.

Would Germany respect her word? Would she hold by the compact she had entered into so many years ago? There were those who declared that she would, that the fear of Germany was no more than the exploitation of a certain school of journalism; but there were others who knew better than that, who knew for a certainty that Belgium was merely a pawn in the game of chess that Germany had played incessantly for the last 40 years. And so England waited.

The storm had gathered all too quickly. Seven days before, outside the charmed circle of European diplomacy, not a score of people had seen a sign of the gathering tempest. All England had been looking forward to its playtime, hundreds of thousands of honest toilers in the workshops and the offices were joyfully anticipating the holiday month. Eyes were turned eagerly towards the sea and the moorland, and now it seemed as if all that was forgotten. There had been trouble threatening on the Thursday and Friday, and then Black Monday had come with the most fateful Bank Holiday since holidays had first begun. And now to all practical purposes Germany had cynically flung her honour into the melting pot, and already had broken her solemn promise to Belgium, and England was at war with Germany, and the greatest conflict in the history of the world had begun.

It was a strange, weird holiday the Londoners were spending, a combination of holiday and funeral. It was as if some great nation was suddenly in the grip of mortal plague just at the moment when work had been flung aside with no heed for the morrow, a decorous mute festival with the shadow of some dire misfortune looming behind it.

So far there had been no outbreak of passion or emotion, no waving of flags, no outburst of patriotism from a million throats. For the thing had gone too deep for that. Early as it was, the nation was beginning to realise the stupendous task that lay before it. It seemed almost incredible that this quiet, sombre-eyed London was the same capital that had gone into the Boer War with noise and tumult, the wagging or flags, and the loud bray of brass and cymbals. For already deep down was the feeling that this ghastly business had been inevitable from the first, and that the future of the Empire was in peril.

Some such thoughts as these were passing through the mind of Harold Bentley as he walked through the streets of London on that Black Monday, without in the least knowing where he was going and what end he had in view. Here were crowds and crowds of people wandering about more or less aimlessly and discussing the great question with bated breath. Here and there somebody laughed, and the mirth seemed to be strangely out of place—almost an outrage. Here were some carelessly and light-heartedly making their way into places of amusement; some who did not understand, and probably never would understand, the full weight of the blow that had fallen. Here and there people were gathered in groups, and at the foot of the Nelson column a Socialist orator was raving and ranting to a detached and uninterested audience, who listened to his poisonous treason with a certain stolid apathy. It was one of those amazing sights only to be seen in London; it would be impossible in any other European capital. And that, too, under the very shadow of the Englishman who did as much as or more than any son of the Empire to make Britain what she is to-day.

Bentley paused almost involuntarily. He had nothing in his pocket; he had no object in life for the moment, except to kill the time, and he paused rather cynically to listen to the frothy rubbish that came so glibly from the man's lips. The speaker was a big man, heavy and red of face, and he spoke with the hoarseness which is always suggestive of gin and fog and the beery dissipation of the common pothouse. He was appealing for some cause, too, for there was a collecting box at his feet, and now and again some good-natured passer-by dropped a coin into it.

But it was only for a moment that Bentley listened with a smile upon his lips. Then he edged a little closer to the speaker, and his fists clenched instinctively. He was standing shoulder to shoulder now with the crowd, listening without betraying the slightest emotion, and just for a moment he felt a certain contempt for his fellow-countrymen. He did not quite realise that their attitude was one of benevolent toleration, due to the Englishman's instinctive love of fair play and his desire to give the meanest outcast a chance.

"I tell yer it's all in our hands," the speaker vociferated. "It's all in the hands of the working man. If you chaps like to put yer foot down you can stop this war now. The working man of Europe could stop anything. Do you suppose those people in the House of Commons and at Whitehall care a hang for Belgium? D'you suppose they'd lose a moment's sleep, if Germany annexed Belgium to-morrow? Not they, my lads. Because why? Because this is a war got up by capitalists to put money in their pockets. It means millions and millions dragged out of your pockets in the way of taxation, and it will be all spent on the employers of labour, who'll be living on the fat of the land, whilst you chaps can hardly get bread, to say nothing of beer."

"And you wouldn't like that, guv'nor," a voice from the crowds jeered. "Is that wot you're collectin' for?"

"Ah, you can laugh," the speaker went on. "But who's going to do the fighting? Who's going to lay down their lives on the blood-stained fields of Europe? Why, the working man. When he finds himself without food and wages he'll take the shilling in sheer despair and go and fight for what he calls his country, whilst the nobs will stay at home with their champagne, wine, and their golf and their shooting. When I see the gentlemen, as they call themselves, coming forward to fight then I'll say no more about it. But just let me know when you catch 'em at it. Why, there's one of 'em there now—that chap with the blue suit as is sneering at me and you and every other honest son of toil. There he is, him in the straw hat."

It seemed to Harold that every eye was turned upon him in an instant. For the first time he was conscious of the hot anger that filled him, conscious of the tingling in his finger-tips, and a mad desire to jump forward and dash his fist into that red, drink-sodden face, and take the consequences. Where were the police, that they permitted an outrage like this to exist at the very base of Nelson's Column? And Harold was conscious, too, of the little knot of powerful-looking loafers—friends, no doubt, of the speaker, and potential shareholders in the collecting box at the orator's feet.

"Are you speaking of me?" Harold asked.

"Well, what if I am?" the orator demanded. "Since you put it to me like that, I am."

"It's a lie," Harold said hotly. "It's as much of a lie as it is for you to call yourself a working man. You've never done a day's work in your life."

"That's the style, Mr. Bentley," a hoarse voice said. "Rub it into the swine. I'll back yer up."

CHAPTER II - RAGGED AND TOUGH

Harold turned a surprised glance on the speaker. He saw a little man, short and squarely built; a man with fiery red hair, and whose impudent face was deeply marked with orange freckles. His clothes were dingy and dilapidated, his toes were working through his broken boots, and to all appearance fortune had not smiled his way of late. But the impudent blue of his eyes and the audacious swaggering smile on his lips seemed to have been born there and ready to defy every misfortune that came his way. He might have been any age between 19 and 25, but in the case of the typical pariah of the London streets it is always difficult to tell. This was not the question that Harold was asking himself—he was wondering how this ragged and tough specimen of humanity knew him so well by name.

"I think I can manage all right, thank you," he said coldly.

"Don't you be put down, Mr. Bentley. Don't yer let 'im 'ave all 'is own way, I'll back yer up. There's a bloke astandin' be'ind the Socialist, that cove with the long nose. An' I don't mind tellin' yer as I'm a-dyin' ter punch 'im."

Harold edged the speaker on one side. By this time some of the crowd, bent on mischief, were egging him on. The orator had ceased speaking, conscious, perhaps, that he was getting the better of the argument, for he turned sneeringly to Bentley, and demanded to know if he had any more to say.

"Only this," Harold cried hotly, "that you are no working man. Work is a thing that loafers of your class don't believe in. In any other country but this you would be pulled off that pedestal and drowned in the nearest fountain. Yes, I've a great mind to save the police the trouble of hanging you."

The crowd tittered and then broke into a hoarse laugh. The Socialist's face turned a deeper red.

"And what about yourself?" he asked. "You're one of the nobs, you are, you of the nuts. Pap-fed at a public school, and then swaggering at Oxford College. Oh, I know your sort. Catch you doing anything for your country! You've enlisted, of course? Did it this morning, may be."

Bentley said nothing for a moment. For it was a question he had not anticipated. He wanted to explain; he had an insane desire to tell the now interested spectators the reason why he had passed one recruiting office after another without a glance to the right or left. But the thing was impossible. He could not stand up there before that little knot of fellow-creatures and explain to them that, though the speaker's guess as to the public school was correct, he was merely a city clerk more or less fortunate in the possession of 30s a week, and with a mother and sister entirely dependent upon him. No doubt, later on, a grateful country would do something for those who had given up everything to follow the flag, but meanwhile the call of those nearest and dearest to him drowned the trumpet call of patriotism and country. And it would have been so easy to lie to the red-faced spouter, and thus escape the jeers and sneers of those around him.

"No," he said, "I have not enlisted. It is no business of yours, but I merely tell you the truth. My father died for his country, and if circumstances—"

He broke off abruptly and bit his lip. What a fool he was to lose his temper like this, how childish to betray these sacred confidences to callous strangers who were merely seeking a few minutes cheap recreation! He would have turned away and edged through the crowd had not the next words of the speaker arrested him. He pulled up quivering in every nerve.

"There what did I tell you? He ain't going to fight, not he. Ain't got pluck enough. Hiding himself behind a woman's petticoats. Now, look here, young fellow, I've had enough of you; you just hop off, else I'll come down and make you."

The little man with the red hair by Harold's side chuckled joyfully. The light of battle gleamed in his eyes.

"E's fairly arskin' for it, Mr. Bently," he whispered, "Now, don't yer go an' fly in the fice o' Providence. Don't yer lose a charnce as is fairly stickin' aht at yer. You tike 'im on, and I'll go for the melancholy bloke with the long nose. Lor' bless yer, sir, many the time as I've stood a-watchin' yer in the gymnasium of the old school when you've 'ed the gloves on with some o' the other gents. Why, that left punch o' yourn't ud 'ave made a champion of yer if you 'adn't been one of the toffs with pots o' money. I don't suppose you remember me, sir, but at one time I was boot-boy in Mr. Seymour's 'ouse when you was at Rugby. Nime of Ginger Smiff."

In a hazy way Bentley was beginning to remember. But there was little time for questions now, for the red-faced bully, feeling more sure of his ground, was advancing threateningly to the attack. Already Harold could feel the man's hot breath on his face; he was conscious of the thrust-out jaw and the cruel anger in the blurred grey eyes of his opponent. No doubt the assailant had calculated upon the moral support at least of the crowd, for he lunged out viciously, his one desire to hurt and maim his opponent before the arrival of the police.

Harold was cool enough now. The joy of the fight was on him. Here was the chance to let himself go, to relieve his pent-up feelings, and strike a blow for his country, even if only an oblique one. Out of the corner of his eye he could see the little man with ginger hair wriggling his way through the crowd until he was face to face with the long-nosed Socialist, who promptly made a dash for him with a stick. Bentley was conscious of the fact that Ginger Smith's opponent was suddenly brought up all standing with a vicious body blow, and then he went down, to rise no more, before a vigorous left on the point of the jaw. And then Harold saw his chance, too.

It was a cruelly uneven contest from the very first, for the fat and flabby Socialist was no kind of a match for two-and-twenty years of perfect condition and muscular manhood trained fine as a star and rendered hard as nails by outdoor exercise. In the language of the ring, Harold was all over his opponent; it was mere child's play to him, and his one regret lay in the fact that it was over all too soon. The man collapsed, a blubbering heap at his feet, yelling and cursing and calling for the police. From somewhere in the distance a whistle blew, and it was borne in upon Harold that this generous impulse of his was likely to get him into trouble. He snatched the money-box and crushed it in fragments under his feet. Then he scooped up the contents and scattered them amongst the crowd. By this time Ginger Smith had completed his work and was back by Harold's side.

"Come on, sir," he panted. "Let's get out of this. It's been a bit of a beano so far, but yer don't want ter be run in and fined five pahnds fer spilin' a swine like 'im. Come on, sir, 'ere's the bloomin' coppers a-comin'."

Ginger burst his way through the crowd and darted across the square in the direction of Whitehall. Harold was alive to the peril now, and followed rapidly. It would never do for him to find himself figuring before magistrates over this wretched business. His employer was a cold, austere man, a money-grubber, and selfish bachelor, and an worshipper of the conventions, who would have discharged him without compunction had anything of this come to his ears. And Harold knew only too well how hard it was to earn the bread of life in a city office.

He saw Ginger dart and twist under a policeman's arm and vanish down an entry. Then he was conscious of a motor car pulling up by him alongside the pavement.

"Well, this is a nice game, Harold," a cheery voice said. "I was just in time to see the end of it. Jump in, old chap—I suppose you don't want to find yourself in Bow-street. And now, where have you been hiding all this long time?"

CHAPTER III - A FRIEND IN NEED

With a deep sigh of relief, Harold dropped back against the luxurious cushions of the car, only too thankful to escape from the folly of his recent adventure. It was some little time before he spoke, not indeed until the car paused before a block of flats in Campden Hill, and the rescuer led the way up the stairs to the first floor. Here he put his latchkey in the lock, and a few minutes later Harold was seated in a deep armchair, with a choice Turkish cigarette between his lips. It was the first time he had smoked for weeks.

"Now, what on earth do you mean by it?" his friend demanded. "What excuse have you got to make for turning your back on your friends in this fashion? I suppose you know it's two years since we last met? Now explain yourself."

"Oh, I daresay you'll think me very ungrateful, Ronnie," Harold said. "But try to put yourself in my place, old man. When the poor old governor was killed in that little affair on the Indian frontier we were under the impression that we were going to be fairly well off. As a matter of fact, there wasn't a penny left. My father had muddled everything away in all sorts of mad speculations. Of course, my notion of going to Oxford was knocked on the head, and instead I had to turn to and get enough money to keep my mother and sister. And weary work it's been, too. You see, my mother is not capable of doing anything but manage a house, though she can do that to perfection. My sister is in a fair way to becoming a successful artist, but meanwhile she has to be kept, and I can assure you that 30s a week doesn't go very far."

Ronald Kemp was duly sympathetic. He had never known what it was to lack anything. He had a fine place of his own out Harrow way, where he spent a good deal of time with his sister and her elderly companion, and he kept up his luxurious flat in London as well. It was a popular fiction that he took an active part in the great firm of which his father had been the head, but it was seldom indeed that the handsome presence and cheery laugh of Ronnie Kemp were ever seen and heard in the city of London. For the rest, he was a clean-limbed, clean-lived, and healthy type of young England, as moulded by a public school, than which the whole world can present no finer type of high-minded and wholesome humanity. Furthermore, he was generous and large-hearted and loyal to his friends, and there was a frown on his face as he listened to Bentley's story.

"Well, at any rate, you might have come to see me," he protested. "You know jolly well that what is mine is yours. It makes me downright mad to think that the best pal I ever had at school should be starving on a few shillings a week, whilst I'm literally flinging the stuff about. My dear old chap, just try and remember that we shared the same study for three years, and never had a misword the whole time. Here, fill your cigarette case out of that box. And, how much do you want? Will you have a couple of hundred to go on with?"

"That's just like you, Ronnie," Bentley said unsteadily. "Always ready to do a kind act. But it won't do, it won't indeed. Don't you see I can't take it? Would you take it if you were in my place? If it wasn't for the sake of the mater and my sister, I wouldn't care a scrap. I'd enlist like a shot. But I can't, old man, I can't. I shall have to go about with everybody turning the cold shoulder on me; I shall have the girls in the omnibuses handing the white feather to me. It's infernally hard, old son, but I shall have to put up with it. I hear already that lots of men in the city have offered men in my position a full salary if they join the colours. But not my old blackguard, selfish old bachelor. I put it to him on Saturday, and he told me I could go if I liked, but if I thought he was going to do anything for the mater and Nettie I was jolly well mistaken. Upon my word, I am worried about the thing until I'm unable to sleep even. But what's to be done?"

Kemp nodded sympathetically. He was evidently turning over some project in his mind.

"You want to enlist, of course?" he said.

"My dear chap, I'm aching to do something. I suppose I've met a score of the old lot since Saturday, and there isn't one of 'em who isn't doing something. And you?"

"Oh, I'm all right," Kemp explained. "I joined the Hon. Company of Musketeers as soon as I left school. On and off I've been three years in the corps. We're all old O.T.C.'s, as you know, and I don't suppose there's one of us who can't show a Certificate A. With any luck, we shall be at the front in a month. And you see, without boasting, we are to all practical purposes regulars. We're full up now, but I was down at headquarters this morning, and I heard that they were well on towards a second battalion already. Sort of 'let 'em all come,' arrangement: 'Duke's son, cook's son, son of a millionaire.' We're going to have the cream of London, my boy—the chaps who come first without waiting for the call. I tell you we shall make up a brigade to be proud of. And, what's more, I'll bet you a sovereign we're full by Wednesday morning. Ah, well, I know it's the fashion to laugh at us and call us nuts and make fun of our socks, and accuse us of hanging about all those dear little flappers, but the stuff's there, my boy, it's there all right.

Waterloo was won on the playing fields of Eton, and the freedom of Europe is going to be won by the flanneled fools and muddied oafs, and good old Rudyard Kipling will be the first man to acknowledge it when the time comes. We're going together side by side, the navvy and the nut and the Gaiety boy and the miner all side by side, and we're going to win out with the old flag. We're going to show the country what it never dreamt of; I can feel it in my bones. But what a beastly selfish chap I must be to talk like this to you. But I've done it with a purpose. You've got to put your beastly pride in your pocket. It isn't the time to think of that sort of thing. You've got to come with me into the trenches; you've got to lie down side by side with Tommy from Whitechapel and Bill from Shoreditch; and you've got to forget that there's any difference between us, because, as Kipling says, 'The Colonel's lady and Biddy O'Grady are sisters under their skins.' And we're brothers under our coats, though one is cut in Bond-street and the other is a reach-me-down sold for a tanner in Petticoat-lane. Now, I only ask you one question—Are you coming with me, or are you not?"

"If I could," Bentley groaned. "Oh, Lord, if I could."

"Well, you can," Kemp cried. "It's as easy as kiss your hand. Now, listen. This is all arranged by Providence. You know that my sister lives in that big place of mine until I get married or make an ass of myself in some other way, and that she has a kind of companion-housekeeper and chaperon who looks after her. Now, Miss Hochkess wants to go and join her sister, who runs a big school in Eastbourne, and needs her very badly to assist there. For nearly a year Miss Hochkess has stayed on to oblige us, merely because we can't find anybody good enough to take her place. Your mother would be ideal. She's a lady, and I know how capable she is—I ought to, considering the times I've stayed at your place. It's not a difficult post to fill. Dorothy used to be very fond of your mother, and she and your sister were great pals till you went and hid yourselves in that mysterious fashion. And it's a two hundred-a-year job. And I'm dashed glad I've got that bit out. Now, what do you say? Mind you, I should have made the same proposition if there'd been no war."

It was some time before Bentley could find his voice. Then he put out his hand and murmured something under his breath.

"So that's settled," Kemp cried. "Hurrah for the old flag, and here's to the King, God bless him!"

CHAPTER IV - ALL FOR THE FLAG

Kemp bustled about the room with the matter-of-fact air of one who has settled some commonplace piece of business, but he was careful not to look at Bentley just then. Harold was grateful enough, but he was feeling just a little unmanned. He was disposed to blame himself for not having looked up some of these good pals of his before; he could see now that it had been foolish pride on his part; at the same time, he had not the slightest intention of accepting any of Kemp's money, but this new offer was a different matter altogether.

"I don't know how to thank you," he said.

"I'm jolly glad to hear it," Kemp laughed. "You'd have done just as much for me. Now, look here—I'm no end anxious to get you into our first battalion. Of course there's no chance at present for either of us to get a commission, but there are certain to be a few vacancies in the ranks, seeing that we are dead sure of being at the front in a month's time. A goodish few chaps who are all right for ornamental work won't pass the doctor now, and that's where you come in. Now, sit down and scribble a letter to your mother, and say you won't be back till some time to-morrow. Say I'm giving you a shakedown for to-night, and that you have got some good news for her. Then we'll pop down to the depot early to-morrow morning and clinch this business."

Kemp called down the stairs to the porter and asked if he had a messenger in, one of the class of men who hang about big blocks of flats in want of a job; Bentley looking up from his letter presently saw his old acquaintance Ginger Smith standing in the doorway. There was a grin on his face, and he appeared to be perfectly at home.

"I knowed you was all right, sir," he said. "I see you 'op it inter Mr. Kemp's car, so I jest jumps on the back, an' 'ere we are! I runs lots of errands for Mr. Kemp, and 'e's werry kind to me, 'e is. I'd do anything for 'im, I would."

"Except work," Kemp smiled. "Ginger is quite a handy man, but work frightens him. He thinks nothing of walking ten miles from here to a golf club and back and lugging half a ton of clubs round a long course, but that's because he doesn't think it's work. I've offered to take him into my employ, but it's no use. He'll never be good for anything."

"Oh, yes, 'e would," Ginger grinned. "Because 'e's got 'is charnce. I never told you, sir, did I, as my father were a Tommy? Served seventeen year, 'e did, an' died in the Boer War, and 'e wasn't shot in the back, neither. I was only a bit of a nipper in them dyes, an' mostly I've storved on an' off ever since, but 'ere in a little bag wot I carries rahnt me neck I've got three little silver things as belonged to the ole man wot 'is country give 'im, an' I never pawned none of 'em yet, though many a dye I've known wot it is ter go wifout a mouthful o' grub, An' now I'm goin' ter arsk you, sir, ter give me one more charnce. You may call me a loafer an' a wister as is good for nothin' except sellin' pipers an' 'anging abaht a golf club, but all the sime I believe as I've got the right stuff in me ter make a soldier. An' if you would be so kind as ter get me in that there regiment o' your'n then I'll never forget it. An' I'll do more'n that. I've bin caddyin' this mornin'. An' when I come in an' drawed my money, the caddie master 'e says ter me:—'Don't let me see any o' you chaps 'ere agin as is between the ages of eighteen and thirty-five.' O' course, I knowed wot 'e meant, an' I say's, 'Wot o, ole pimple fice. It's me for the flag to strike a blow for me King an' to keep a roof over the head o' you an' yer ole missus.' Then we shakes 'ands, an' parts like two ole pals. An' I ain't goin' back no more. An' I'll tell yer wot, sir. I knows as you wants recruits for that second battalion o' your'n, and if you'll 'elp me to shove meself in khaki and fight shoulder to shoulder with two gentlemen like you, then it'll be a real proud moment for me an' the other chaps."

"Regular orator, isn't he?" Kemp laughed. "What other chaps are you talking about?"

"Nearly all the rest o' the caddies. We come back together this evenin', over 70 of us, an' we all made up our mind as we was out for the flag. But we didn't jest know wot ter do till I 'as wot yer calls a Hinspiration, an' I says, 'Leave it ter me,' I says. An' they did. An' if yer don't mind, sir, I'm comin' rahnd ter yer 'eadquarters ter-morrow mornin', an' I'm goin' ter bring abaht eighty more wif me. We ain't much ter look at, but you feed us up an' treat us like men, an' you'll find as 'wot we are men. I dare say you'll think as I'm doin' a lot o' gas wif me mawth—"

"Here, shake hands, Ginger," Kemp cried. "My good fellow, I'm delighted to hear you talk like this. It's the good old British spirit bred in the stock that Drake and Nelson and Wellington came from, and it shows that the old country is still sound to the core. I'll go out of my way to get you into our first battalion, and I don't mind telling you that you will be the first working man who ever belonged to it. It may sound rather snobbish to talk like that just now, but still—"

Ginger held his head high as he took Bentley's note and swaggered from the room. In some subtle way his rags seemed to have taken on a certain dignity, his powerful shoulders were drawn back, and there was a keen look in his eye.

"Here, just half a moment!" Kemp cried. "I'll tell you what. There's plenty of room here, and if you like to bring those pals of yours round here to breakfast to-morrow morning I'll be proud to welcome you as my guests and shake hands with you. Now then, off you go."

Ginger clattered importantly down the stairs. Through the open windows came the cries of the newsboys yelling the very latest sensation. Belgium had already been invaded, and there was nothing for it now but to see this thing through.

"I haven't grasped it yet," Bentley said. "It only seems a few hours since I was wondering how I was going to spend my bank Holiday. You can't get much fun on a solitary half-crown, and my idea was to take a long country walk. And here we are with the biggest job in history before us, and we are actually looking forward with pleasure to-morrow morning to breakfasting with a choice assortment of golf caddies. Now, what would you have said if anybody had told you that a week ago?"

"I don't know," Kemp confessed. "Advise him to go and see a doctor, probably. And yet, by Gad, it's true! I don't mind telling you that I shall be downright proud to march those chaps into our quadrangle to-morrow morning. And, mind you, I don't underrate the seriousness of this job. We can see now that the Kaiser and his gang have been getting ready for this business for over thirty years, and many a good fellow will be down and out before we are in sight of Berlin. The question is, shall we be in time to save Paris? Personally, I doubt it. Those brutes will be through Belgium almost before we can stir. In all these years Lord Roberts has been no more than a voice crying in the wilderness. Well, I suppose we shall muddle through somehow. We always have, and we always play the game and give the other fellow the benefit of the doubt till the last moment. And we've paid for our generosity in blood and tears. Half an hour ago I was going to suggest that we cheered ourselves with an hour or so at a music hall. But in some funny way I seem to have grown about two years older. I seem to have lost my taste for all sorts of pleasure, even my cigarettes don't smoke quite so pleasantly. How could they, with those words ringing in one's ears?"

For down below strident voices of the newsboys were pitched in another and more ominous key.

"Germans across the frontier. Heavy fighting in Belgium. Dreadful slaughter, Official."

CHAPTER V - SHOULDER TO SHOULDER

With the morrow and the morning's papers the full meaning of that vile treachery was apparent to the most credulous Englishman who had ever been fooled by the shallow pretence of German friendship. Certain German writers had been preaching the doctrine of German world supremacy for years, but the Kaiser had always posed as the apostle of peace. Every child knew now what the whole thing meant. The Kaiser's pose was assumed in order to dull fools and visionaries into a false sense of security. And he had done his work well!

At the same time, it was beyond question that the participation of England in the strife had come as a rude shock to the conspirators in Potsdam. To a certain extent they had been visionary, too, dreamers too prone to believe what their spies had told them: England would never come in; she would never abandon her slothful attitude; even if she did, her pampered, over-civilised population would never permit her to strike a blow; and, again, if she did there would be civil war in Ireland, India would rise like one man, and South Africa would pass away from beneath the flag.

But all these hopes were destined to be dashed to the ground. England had no army, it is true, except what Germany contemptuously regarded as a handful of paid mercenaries which would never be augmented by a real fighting force.

But England knew different. It was easy for Germany, with her population in the grip of the military party, to drag her children into the firing line whether they liked it or not, and oblige them to make a virtue of necessity. But Germany knew little of the real sporting spirit that brought recruits by the hundred thousand even before they had been called. At that moment business was forgotten; nobody heeded the Stock Exchange and the City, for there were more vital interests at stake than mere money. The streets looked different, there was a different spirit in the air, and with it all a quiet assurance that everything would be well when the time came. The very newspapers were transformed. No longer was any heed taken of the trivialities of life. For the Germans were over the Belgian frontier, and already the mighty fighting machine had encountered its first check.

Every line of this was eagerly absorbed by Kemp and Bentley as they sat waiting for Ginger Smith and his friends.

"It was happy chance that brought us together last night," Bentley said. "I don't know what I should have done if I had not met you. Fancy jogging along to the office this morning by the tube, and sitting at a desk all day adding up columns of figures! The mere thought of it makes me shudder. I should have had to go, and I should have been miserable. And now everything is different."

"What are you going to do about it?" Kemp asked.

"Oh, I'm not going back if that's what you mean. I'll ring up my old patriot on the telephone presently and tell him he can look out for another prisoner. I hope within an hour or two to be wearing the uniform of the Musketeers."

Anything Kemp would have said in reply was cut short by the intrusion of the hall porter. He seemed to be struggling between annoyance and amusement.

"Beg your pardon, sir," he said. "But that there Ginger Smith's jest turned up with about a hundred wot 'e calls recruits. 'E says as you've arsked them all ter breakfast. I should jest 'ave sent them off, only down in the 'all a lot o' waiters from Harrod's is turned up an' a van full of provisions. Of course, sir, you know your own business best, an' if so be as Ginger's tellin' the truth, why, then, sir, I suppose I'd better tell that lot as they can come upstairs. If not, it seems ter me I'd better send for the police."

"Oh, that's all right," Kemp agreed.

"Might 'ave come off a racecourse. Class o' stuff wot you see 'anging around the National Sporting Club when there's a big fight on. If I was you, sir, I'd put all them nick-nacks away."

"I'm ashamed of you," Kemp said solemnly. "Do you know you're libelling sons of the Empire? Do you know that all social distinctions have been swept away, and that to-day we are all brothers? My good man, those chaps are recruits. You won't know them in a fortnight. Show 'em up. And tell those people from Harrod's to get the breakfast ready in the dining-room as soon as possible. By Jove, this is something like life, isn't it? And only last week I couldn't make up my mind which was the least boring way of spending August."

They came shuffling noisily up the stairs, a ragged, unwashed and dilapidated crowd, following more or less shyly on Ginger's heels. It was quite evident that some of them at least regarded the whole thing as a hoax on Ginger's part. But Ginger led the way with a cheery grin on his pleasant face, his natural audacity not in the least abashed by his surroundings. His greasy cap was cocked over his left eye, and with his right eye he winked familiarly at his host.

"'Ere yer are, sir," he said. "Abaht seventy of us altogether. An' a nice job I 'ad ter get 'em 'ere. It's lucky for me as they all 'ad a good dye yesterday, an' so they was travellin' dahn ter Richmond by the nine-five instead o' walkin' as usual. So I cops the 'ole lot. Now, chaps, was Ginger a liar or did 'e tell yer the truth?"

"Beg pardon, sir," an agonised voice in the background addressed Kemp. "I don't know if yer knows Ginger as well as we do, but 'e says as 'ow 'e know'd a cove, wot's yerself, sir, as 'ud given us all a invitation ter breakfast. We was goin' caddyin', but seein' as 'ow we ain't wanted any more—well, it's like this, sir. Someone's got ter put them bloomin' German swine in their right plice, and there ain't one of us wot isn't ready ter do 'is little bit. 'An if you'll be good enough ter give us a bit o' bread and cheese—"

"My good chaps, you shall have the best breakfast that money can buy. And I shall be proud to march with you afterwards down to the headquarters of the Musketeers. Now make yourselves at home. There isn't over much room, but we'll manage somehow. You'll finds some cigarettes on the table yonder, and you can smoke till the food is ready."

"This is very refreshing, William," a languid drawl came from the back of the crowd. "Who says that the spirit of romance is dead? Show me the man who dares to say that England is a decadent nation. But yesterday, William, I should have said that our esteemed host was a pampered son of luxury, a sort of human lily who toils not, neither does he spin."

"What have you got up in the corner there, Ginger?" Kemp laughed. "Who's the aristocrat in the flannel shirt? And the gentleman named William in the blue serge?"

"I don't know, sir," Ginger said, "Two toffs, I think. They comes up to me at the station an' arsks wot's goin' on. Then the cove in the flannel suit, 'e says 'e was out o' work along with the war, an' 'e up an' says 'e was comin' along. An' the other bloke 'e says ditto. 'Ope you don't mind, sir."

"Oh, Lord, no," Kemp exclaimed. "The more the merrier. I think I must have a few words with William."

"Quite right, old chap," the man called William drawled as he screwed a glass into his left eye. "Bit of a liberty, of course, but I didn't think you would mind under the circumstances. Fact is, me and my friend are stockbrokers, at least we were yesterday. To-day we are unemployed. We'd like to join those musketeers of yours, and if a couple of pretty useful motor cars are any assistance to you, well, they're yours. Funny sight, this, isn't it? But it's one to be proud of all the same."

CHAPTER VI - THE THIN BROWN LINE

It was a strange gathering. There was almost a touch of nightmare in it: it was like a fantasy of Stevenson's, a page from some modern Arabian Nights, and yet it seemed the most natural thing in the world. And when presently the motley gathering filed down the stairs, and turned in the semblance of a company into Kensington High-street nobody laughed, and a few people on the pavement stopped and cheered. Women waved their handkerchiefs, full of understanding, and indeed it did not need any vast intelligence to know that here were a handful of men anxious to do something for the flag. The man with the eyeglass disappeared for a moment into a shop and came back presently with his arms full of red, white, and blue ribbons, which he gravely handed out to the caddie squad, who as gravely put them in their caps. At the head of the procession walked the man with the eyeglass and his friend, together with Kemp and Bentley, as if they were doing the most natural thing in the world.

"By Gad, it's a sort of disease," the man with the eyeglass said. "Now, if anybody had asked me to do this a week ago, I wouldn't have said yes for a thousand pounds. And yet here am I at the head of all these chaps, and dashed proud of the chance. I tell you what, we'd better make a long march of this. If we'd only got a band, we'd gather the men by the hundred. A banner wouldn't be a bad wheeze!"

True enough, as the procession straggled along towards Blackfriars, where the headquarters of the Honourable Company of Fusiliers were situated, it was augmented by scores of other men who were merely waiting for a lead. There was something striking in the idea, a simplicity about it and a streak of humour that appealed to the crowd. And then one of the caddies with a natural tenor voice struck up some familiar song that carried them on jauntily till they came to Blackfriars Bridge. They had fed well, too, probably the best meal that any of them had ever tasted. It was fun of the wildest, maddest type of course, the fun that Tommy loves on the march or in the teeth of danger, but behind it all was a grimness of purpose and tenacity of grip that was not lost upon those who had the eye to see beyond the apparent madness of it.

"My word," Kemp exclaimed. "We're not the only pebbles on the beach. Why, the quadrangle's full of men."

It was even as the speaker said. Here was a big open barrack square with buildings all around, and it was packed with perspiring humanity, all eager and anxious to be doing something for the flag. They had come from all parts of London, knowing the reputation of the Musketeers, and all grasping the fact that through them lay the way swiftly and surely to the front. These were not the men who waited to be asked, not the men who required to be spurred on by platform appeals or to be bribed to do their country's work.

Here and there were men in uniform, a sergeant or two keeping the surging mob back, and inside one of the big whitewashed rooms half a dozen doctors in shirt-sleeves, hot and perspiring as they examined one recruit after another. At a sign from Kemp, Bentley and the other two men turned down a stone-flagged passage and entered a room where the captain in uniform was busy writing at a desk.

"Could you spare me five minutes, Crighton?" Kemp asked. "I've got three likely recruits for you, that is, of course, providing you've got any vacancies left. It must be in the first battalion. Now, do you happen to know what proportion of men have been rejected by the doctors this morning?"

"Well, a goodish few," the captain said. "And mostly old athletes, I am sorry to say. That's the worst of overdoing it. A man keeps himself in strict training by violent exercise; then he drops it, and his heart goes rocky. I can fix up your pals all right. Have you got any more?"

"Yes, one," Kemp said. "And a rare character he is in his way, too. But perhaps you may object to taking an ex-golf caddie? By the way, he has managed to get hold of over 70 recruits, and bring them down here this morning—"

"Oh, that sounds good," the captain said. "I shouldn't mind making room for one or two of that type. The fact is, we must make up a battalion to-day. If we do, we can get right away under canvas at Harrow to-morrow and start training. I've no doubt most of our chaps will get commissions, but that's a secondary consideration for the moment. I've had a tip from the War Office that if we can lick ourselves into shape, as we ought to do pretty quickly, we shall be in France by the beginning of September. Between ourselves, we've got over 50,000 men in France already. It's the smartest bit of work that the Transport Service ever handled. And it will be a nice little surprise for that Potsdam scoundrel when he runs up against us. But introduce me to your friends."

"Name of Allen," the man with the eyeglass drawled. "Winchester and Cambridge. Until yesterday, Stock Exchange. Now, nothing doing, or likely to be. This is my friend Garton. Also Winchester and Cambridge. Ditto Stock Exchange. One of the unemployed, and anxious to do his bit. And if you want a couple of good motor-cars they are at your disposal."

"Oh, you'll do," the captain said approvingly. "You're the type we want. I had a good few men round here yesterday, but too many after commissions. I suppose you know that you'll have to rough it unless you are on the same game."

The man with the eyeglass grew serious.

"Well, we ain't," he said, "Don't know that I'd have one even if you offered it me. Only last week I refused a chance of joining a shooting party in Perthshire because a man was going who always makes a point of tucking his table napkin under his chin. That's the sort of chap I was seven days ago. But the call is in my blood now, and something has wiped all the snobbishness out of me. I want to go and fight those German swine, and I'm not the only one of my kidney by the hundred thousand. In a month's time you can go all over England, and you won't find a single one of the nuts who isn't doing his duty. Yet a little time back, if anybody had asked me, I should have said that we'd all got a bit flabby. Well, it would have been a lie. I'm ready at the present moment to lie down on the bare ground with any man who can call himself an Englishman. I don't care a brass farthing whether he comes from Cambridge or the New Cut. We're all brothers in arms now, and one man's as good as another. Them's my sentiments, old cocky, and you can make the best of 'em. I suppose I shall have to salute you and call you 'sir' in an hour or two, so I'm just going to cheek you as long as I have the opportunity. It's all made of the right spirit."

The captain nodded approvingly.

"Oh, I quite understand," he said. "And your sentiments do you credit. I'll just take your names and see that you are shoved well forward, and then you must excuse me, for really I am tearingly busy. You may have to stand in that yard for hours before you pass the doctor, but I don't think that's going to discourage men of your stamp. You ought to get your uniforms by this evening, and I hope we shall be able to ask you to report to-morrow at Harrow. If you take my advice, you won't lose sight of Kemp, and he'll pull you through. And now I must wish you all good morning."

"Monty, my boy," Allen exclaimed, as he smote his companion on the back, "my prophetic soul tells me we are going to live. Hitherto, we have only existed. We are going to lie on the bare ground, instead of rose leaves; we are going to eat bully beef instead of Murray's famous suppers; but, by Gad, it is good to feel that life is keeping its best for us yet."

CHAPTER VII - "ENGLAND, HOME, AND BEAUTY"

The long, sweating afternoon was drawing to a close, and gradually the patient yet light-hearted crowd in the quadrangle grew less. There had been all sorts and conditions of men there, from the gilded youth who came rolling up in his thousand-guinea car to the ragged nomad whose lips had tasted no food that day, and yet who was as willing and eager as the rest of them. It was strange to see young Oxford fraternising with Whitechapel, and exquisites of the city comparing notes with the man who yesterday had left the morning's milk in the area of their town houses. It seemed as if in one blast all social barriers had been blown away; it was as if a dozen streams had intermingled to make one vast sea of eager humanity. One by one the units passed in through those big doors, only to emerge a little later, openly exulting or correspondingly depressed. But these eager spirits formed the cream of the nation's manhood, and the tally of the rejected was pleasingly small. And as the crowd, dressed indifferently in purple and fine linen and greasy rags, grew smaller, so, almost imperceptibly, the khaki began to assert itself. In these very early stages of the war, there was no lack of uniforms and belts and side arms, and Harold Bentley's heart beat high as he surveyed the eager crowd. It came to his own turn presently to face the doctor, and a quarter of an hour later he was surveying himself in a long looking-glass, a soldier of the King and a defender of his country.

Outside in the quadrangle Kemp and the other two were awaiting him. There was a broad smile on the faces of them all, and an assumption of ease that deceived nobody. Up to them presently swaggered Ginger Smith. The little man was transformed almost out of knowledge. He carried himself proudly, for he was a born mimic and an actor of humorous parts, and he might have been a veteran by the way in which he wore his uniform.

"It's all O.K.," he said. "I put the 'ole o' my little lot through, and we're to report ourselves at 'arrow in the mornin'. But we ain't done yet, no bloomin' likely. We're goin' ter meet to-night an' march through the streets down our way wiv a band and everything proper."

"Good for you, Ginger," Kemp said. "Is it the Grenadiers' or the Coldstream Guards' band you've got hold of?"

"Lor, bless yer, sir," Ginger grinned. "We ain't relyin' upon that sort o' music. Perhaps you never 'eard o' Whistler Jordan. 'E's the champion wiv a mawth organ. We've got four of 'em down our wye wot can knock spots off any other performer in the Sawf o' London. An' you'll see us turnin' up tomorrow mornin' with a regular harmy."

There was nothing to wait for now, nothing to be done before morning, and Bentley began to turn his thoughts homewards. Apparently Kemp could see what was passing in his mind, for he took his friend by the arm and led him towards the Embankment.

"Well, it's all good so far, isn't it?" he asked. "You've done the right thing, and you're in the right place. And now, don't you think it would be just as well if you allowed me to go with you and see your mother and Nettie?"

"I was just thinking the same thing," Bentley confessed. "I suppose after tomorrow we shall see little or nothing of our people till we go to the front. And I should like my mother to feel that she has nothing to worry about in the future."

"Well, it'll be her own fault if she does, old chap. But come along. By the way, where do you live?"

Harold and his mother occupied a sitting-room and two bedrooms in a small house out Willesden way, in a dingy road near the station. There was something dreary and depressing in the neighbourhood; it was so suggestive of genteel poverty that Kemp was almost afraid that Bentley might read his feelings in the expression of his face. But he forgot all that presently, forgot the tiny sitting-room, with its horsehair furniture and hideous chimney ornaments, when he found himself face to face with Nettie Bentley. It was two years since they had last met, two years in which she had grown from a child to a beautiful young woman. Care and privation and the stress of life had laid a light hand upon the perfect oval of that beautifully tinted face, and the blue eyes were soft and thoughtful, the droop of the mouth a little pathetic. But all the old daintiness and sweetness and refinement were there, and her environment had left Nettie herself untouched. She might live in a street of workmen's cottages; she might travel to town early each morning in the train devoted to the white slaves of London, but she stood out from the rest of the girls like a thing apart. There was a dainty touch of colour in her face as she held out her hand to Ronald Kemp.

"It seems a long time since we last met;" she said. "It seems years since we left the dear old house. I suppose you have not forgotten it? Those were happy days."

"They were happy days to me," Kemp exclaimed. "Do you recollect—but I suppose I must call you Miss Bentley now."

"No, please don't," the girl said. "I always think of you as Ronald. And I am so glad that you and Harold have met again. It was so silly of him to drop all his old friends. It did not matter so much for mother and myself. But what have you been doing? Harold, do you mean to say—"

"You're not displeased, Nettie, are you?"

"Displeased! Why, I'm proud of you! I'd rather see you in that uniform than—well, you know what I mean. My dear boy, you could not stay away. And I am so glad that you have not stopped to consider us. We shall manage somehow. I feel quite sure that there will be plenty of work for women before long. And I shall be proud to go behind the counter to take the place of a man who has gone to the front. It will be almost as good as fighting oneself."

"As a matter of fact, he was thinking about you," Kemp said. "Now, shut up, Harold, shut up. This is where I come in, and I'm not going to be interrupted. You can't make Harold really respectable, you know. What do you think he was doing when I met him? You'll never guess. He was having a punching match with a greasy Socialist in Trafalgar Square. I literally dragged him out of the hands of the police and took him off to my flat, where I made him tell me everything. Now I'm going to make a suggestion to Mrs. Bentley which I hope won't offend her. You see, Harold has done it now, and he's got to fight, whether he wants to or not. He's a full private in the Honourable Company of Musketeers, and within a month's time he will be doing his little bit in France. So shall I for that matter. But he doesn't want to leave you all alone, and I happen to have a sister that I'm fond of, too. Unfortunately, it happens that her housekeeper-companion-chaperon has had to leave, and I am at my wits' end to find someone I can rely upon to take her place. That's why I regard my meeting with Harold last night as providential. When he told me everything, I said to myself that Mrs. Bentley was absolutely born for the part. There is not much to do, and—and—help me out, Harold."

"It's a jolly well-paid job," Bentley, said curtly.

"Thanks, old chap. Thank goodness we've done with that part of it. Now, Nettie, do you think your mother will be good enough to take this anxiety off my mind? It's a nice house, and I remember that you and my sister Dorothy used to be great chums. She's always regretting the fact that she's lost sight of you. If this comes off, you will have plenty of time for that artistic work of yours—"

Nettie's eyes were bright with tears.

"Oh, it will be glorious," she cried. "Mother will be more than glad—she will be grateful. And I shall be able to do something I've been longing to ever since the war broke out. I must—I must get to the front as a nurse."

CHAPTER VIII - "TIPPERARY"

They had come from the north and south, from the east and west in their thousands at the first sign of danger. Not that any one of them admitted that the Empire was in peril, for such a thing was incredible. Was not Britain the mistress of the sea, and had she not been so for centuries? And did she not possess the finest navy that the world had ever seen? It was a hard thing to make the typical Englishman believe that within thirty years Germany could build up a fleet to compare with ours. To begin with, her people had not the right blood in their veins; they had no traditions, and practically no seaboard. Where were the men coming from, to cope with sailors who were the sons and grandsons of the men descended from the followers of Hawkins and Frobisher and Drake?

And again, at the very outbreak of hostilities, the German fleet had been carefully shepherded in the North Sea, and driven behind the shelter of Heligoland. If anything happened now, it would be from the fact that England was too confident.

Still, he national anger was aroused, for the callous betrayal of Belgium had sunk deep into the hearts of the people in whom the love of honour and fair play was instilled from childhood. And England exulted in the staggering blows which little Belgium had dealt the great bully in the early days of the campaign. All London rocked with excitement; the name of King Albert was cheered to the echo in every place of amusement, and the sons of Britain came rolling in. They came so fast at first that they taxed the resources of the authorities to the uttermost. England became one armed camp, and the tents of the fighting men were as pebbles on the seashore.

A month had passed by as if it had been no more than a breath. Out Harrow way the men of the Musketeers were working side by side without distinction. The man who a week or two before had been in authority over scores of fellow-creatures was now content to stand at attention before the young subaltern who a little time ago might have been taking down his letters. But it is all part of the great game, and even professional humorists like Ginger Smith forgot to smile.

He had taken to his work as if he had been born to it. In a month he was a smart soldier in a smart regiment, and he thrilled with secret pride as he heard the general who inspected them pronounce them to be the equal of any line regiment of the country. He was keen on getting recruits, too. Few days passed without one or two of them coming along at Ginger's instigation. He had developed, too, a certain rugged eloquence of his own, half-humorous and half-pathetic, that went a long way at meetings where his own class were concerned. He had rather a good voice, of which he was sufficiently proud, and he was not modest in the use of it. He grinned from ear to ear at Kemp's suggestion that he should motor over to the latter's place for a recruiting meeting one evening and address a few remarks to some of the labourers in the district, who were somewhat slow in appreciating the situation. For some little time now Mrs. Bentley had been established at The Keep House, and Nettie Bentley was on the high road to gratify her darling ambition.

"Now you come, Ginger, and give us a song," Kemp suggested. "And my sister shall play your accompaniments for you."

"You does me proud, sir," Ginger said, smilingly. "Ah, I've heard the lady play accompaniments before. A regular dab at the gime she is. Only give 'er a charnce ter look at the music and she's on it like a bird. What shall I sing, sir?"

"Well, what were you singing last night just before you turned in?" Bentley asked. "It was something with a real lilt in it. Ripping good chorus, too."

"Oh, you means 'Tipperary,'" Ginger cried. "It was in last year's pantomimes, and didn't seem ter catch on no 'ow. But it's wot the Yanks call the goods. Cully—which I mean, sir—and no mistake abaht it. It's the best marching song as we've 'ad for many a dye. And, you see, there's wot them writin' blokes calls a halegory; means it's a long, long wye ter Tipperary, which yer can call Berlin if yer like, and whilst the blokes ain't making too light of the little job afore 'em they're goin' ter get there all the sime. And fer all I say it as shouldn't, I can sing that little ditty a fair treat. Me an' the lidy'll rope 'em in properly between the two of us."

Ginger turned out to be no false prophet. For the first time a mixed and crowded audience heard 'Tipperary' sung as it should be with its humorously pathetic touch, heard it sung by a British Tommy, a soldier of the King proud of his uniform, and the task that lay before him. The song is a classic now, and will go down to posterity as such, but it was new then, and it gripped the audience as it has gripped the sons of the flag in every quarter of the globe many a time since then. Long before Ginger had finished he had the sons of the soil roaring the chorus with all the fervour of a national slogan. His voice was just a little unsteady, but the cheery impudence of the little man never deserted him for a moment. He turned with a friendly wink to the slim dark beauty in evening dress who was at the piano. Ginger had a fine eye for a dramatic effect.

"Don't you stop, miss," he whispered. "You go on 'ammerin' at that there chorus for all you're worth, and I'll give yer brother the tip ter get the 'ole bahnder in the chair to invite recruits up on the platform."

Dorothy Kemp nodded graciously. She could see what was uppermost in Ginger's mind, and her fingers crashed out the inspiring chords of the chorus. Almost before the chairman opened his mouth there was an eager rush for the platform. It was Ginger's hour, and he knew it, the first of many triumphs he was to win alongside those friends of his who had picked him up in the gutter and given him the chance to show the splendid manhood that was his.

"That's a smart move of yours, Ginger," Bentley whispered.

"Yus," Ginger said modestly. "That was a bit of alright, that was. 'An if you can get these blokes in the recruitin' offices to work 'Tipperary' for all it's worth you'll 'ave the chaps tumblin' over one another ter 'ave a smack at them 'Uns as yer call 'em. You leave it to us. There ain't nothin' the matter with our little lot if you treats us the right way."

Down at the back of the hall a lean, brown-faced man with captain's stars on his sleeve was watching the proceedings with deepest interest. He made his way to the platform presently, and called Kemp and Bentley on one side.

"How did you three manage to get leave to-night?" he asked.

"Oh, that's all right, sir," Kemp said. "We've got to be back at 10. The chairman is rather a pal—I mean a friend—of the colonel's, and therefore—"

"Well, never mind that," the captain said. "I want you to forget just for a moment that I am your company officer, and that you are two of my men. I believe your mother's here, isn't she Bentley, and I think that is Miss Kemp at the piano? Now, would you be good enough to just go and say good-bye to them, and ask them not to say a word about it to anybody."

Bentley's eyes gleamed, and Kemp caught his breath eagerly.

"Good man!" he whispered. "Oh, I think we understand. Here, don't be captain just for a minute. Do you mean that we are on the move, Crighton, on the way to the—"

"Steady, steady," the captain whispered. "If I am doing wrong, don't give me away. At half-past ten to-night we start for Waterloo in the clothes we stand up in. And by this time to-morrow we shall be—somewhere else."

"Off to the front," Kemp whispered. "Think of it, Harold! My aunt, what a bit of glorious luck!"

CHAPTER IX - "THE GIRL HE LEFT BEHIND HIM"

The glorious news seemed almost too good to be true. It was incredible to believe that only a month ago scores of the Musketeers had been slaving over a desk, or at the best looking forward to a month's vapid holiday at the seaside. Only five weeks ago their minds had been intent on socks and tennis flannels, on golf clubs, and, in more sentimental mood, their thoughts had been of the moon and the sea and a cosy seat at the end of the pier. Now all this was wiped out as if a gigantic sponge had been drawn across the mind of the nation. It all seemed so futile and so small by comparison.

For the great adventure had come, and some day, when the history of it is written, the world will begin to understand the true inwardness and force of the uprising of the young blood of the British Empire almost before the bugles had been heard calling. Slackers there were, no doubt, but Bentley and Kemp had seen none of them; so far as they knew, everybody had responded to the cry for men.

It was glorious to think that the desk and the sweat and toil of the city had vanished when the first shot had been fired, and that the rest would be a breathless struggle to the end. Yet, at the same time, Harold Bentley could not shake off a certain vague, uneasy depression. It was not fear; he was not shrinking from what lay before him; on the contrary, the desire to be up and doing gnawed at him like the pangs of a fierce hunger. He wondered what it was, and why he should feel like this.

And then suddenly it came to him.

He glanced down the hall towards the doorway, where he could see Dorothy Kemp's slim, graceful figure and the light gleaming on her dark, beautiful features. She was talking interestedly to a thin, effeminate-looking man with pale features, a man whose eyeglass made him look still more womanly. He was beautifully dressed and beyond all question exceedingly good-looking. And it seemed to Harold that those two were perhaps a little more than friendly. The man was a stranger to him, but he was conscious of a tinge of jealousy all the same. And in that moment he realised that there was going to be something still more painful than the parting with his mother and Nettie. It was only a short walk from the Musketeers' camp to The Keep House, and, in spite of a lot of hard work, Harold had contrived to put in a good deal of time there in the evenings. And he knew now, as if somebody had opened up a book before him, that he had given his heart to Dorothy Kemp, without, so far, seeking anything in return.

"Who is the man talking to your sister, Ronnie?" he asked.

"Oh, that's a chap called Paul Venables," Kemp explained. "He's an American. No end of a clever fellow, but just a bit too sarcastic for me. But, in spite of his childish appearance, he's no end good at sport, and a splendid shot. He seems to have plenty of money, and I understand that he represents two or three American newspapers."

"Have you known him long?" Bentley asked, carelessly.

"About a year, I suppose. He's got a bungalow in this neighbourhood. He's rather a favourite with Dorothy."

Harold would have liked to ask further questions, but wisely refrained. If Dorothy and the American had been more than friends, Kemp would have been sure to have mentioned it.

"Look here," Bentley said suddenly; "there's no reason to say good-bye here. Let's go up to your place for half an hour, and we shall be able to tell them quietly what's going to happen. Then we can run over to the camp in one of your cars."

It was a good suggestion as far as it went, but it was not an easy matter to shake off the American. He strolled calmly alongside Mrs. Bentley, chatting casually to her, and he entered the house with them with the air of a man who has no doubt on the score of his welcome. It was some little time before Bentley contrived to detach Dorothy from the others with the suggestion that it was too lovely a night to stay indoors. He saw Venables raise his eyebrows, and the gesture somewhat irritated him; but he could afford to ignore it, since he had obtained his own way and was at last alone with Dorothy in the moon-flooded garden.

"Do you know, I am sure you have something to say to me," she said. "I have never seen Ronnie so absent-minded before. I do hope there is no trouble."

"Well, I should hardly call it that," Harold murmured. "But the fact is, we are going to the front."

It seemed to Harold that his companion's face changed a little in the moonlight.

"Do you mean at once?" she whispered.

"Yes, to-night. It is an absolute secret, of course. That is why I was rather sorry that your friend, Mr. Venables, came back with us. It was impossible to get rid of him without appearing to be rude, but we were specially cautioned not to breathe a word to anybody about it. Naturally, we should tell you and my mother and sister, but no one else. I believe, though the country knows nothing of it we have nearly two hundred thousand men in France already. It has been a marvellous bit of work. And I wanted to tell you before I told anybody else."

"That was very kind of you, Harold," the girl murmured. "Of course, in a way I'm glad and proud to think that you're going, but now that the time has come it is a terrible wrench. It makes me feel as if some weight is pressing on me—oh, I know it sounds cowardly, but we have been such friends all these years—"

Dorothy broke off abruptly, and turned her head away. On the impulse of the moment, Bentley stooped and took her hand in his.

"You make me feel like a coward, too," he said. "I felt just the same when Crighton told us just now that we were going. I did not know why at first; and then I found out. It was because I am going to leave you."

"And your mother and sister. I understand."

"No, I don't think you do," Harold murmured. "It isn't the same thing. A man may be very fond of his mother and sister, but there comes a time when somebody else gets in front of them. That's what you've done, Dorothy. And I am selfish enough to want to know before we go out whether I'm leaving behind me a friend, or something more. Very greedy of me, isn't it? Most men would be satisfied to be able to boast of the friendship of a glorious girl like you. They would say it was infernally selfish to ask for anything more at a time like this. And, really, it does seem a blackguard thing to try to tie a girl up to a man who might never come back again, But if you understood my feelings, I am quite sure that you would forgive me—"

"Stop!" Dorothy cried. She was facing Harold now, and her dark eyes were full of tender purpose. "It would have been selfish had you not told me. Oh, my dear boy, do you think I have not seen? Do you think any woman could be blind to the knowledge of the love that is there before her eyes? And do you think I, as a girl who loves my country, wouldn't really be happier to know that she has a man out there who was risking his life and young manhood for the Empire? Why, I should boast of it, I could not keep the knowledge to myself. I should be sorry for other girls less fortunate than myself. And if you never came back, and if you had never spoken at all, I should still have grieved for you as sincerely as if—"

She broke off and laid her hands upon Harold's shoulders. Then she raised herself up, and pressed her lips to his.

"There," she said, unsteadily. "Perhaps now you understand. And after that I'm not going to keep you from your mother and sister for another minute."

And Harold followed her without another word.

CHAPTER X - BOOT AND SADDLE

The word had gone round the camp, and every tent there hummed like a swarm of bees. There was no fuss or bustle or confusion, only the knowledge that the time for action had come, and that the morrow would see the Musketeers on the soil of France. It was some time before midnight when the first company marched out in the direction of Harrow station. Then another and another followed until the tents were deserted and ready for the next battalion to come along, and it was not long past 2 when the whole regiment, in four darkened trains, slid out or Waterloo station on its way to Southampton. There were many units amongst them now who had come from the dockside and the workshops on the Thames, for there had been a heavy call on the Musketeers to find officers for the new army. Bentley and Kemp might have reckoned themselves amongst them had they not set their face against all temptation. They were too keen to fight for that. They knew that promotion meant many months in some English camp whilst the rest of the battalion was upholding the honour of the Empire in the trenches.

It was a hot night, and the moon was lifting high over the waters long before Southampton was reached. With its drawn blinds and its six men crowded on either side of the carriage, the compartment in which Kemp and Bentley found themselves was horribly stifling. Here were all sorts and conditions of men from the 'Varsity type to Ginger Smith squeezed up in the corner, and making night hideous with his mouth organ. And yet they were all friends together, all on perfect equality, no man asserting his superiority. The chaff was fast and furious; it was more like a bank holiday crowd at Margate than a choice selection of the cream of England's manhood going out to face the reeking hell of war. Still, Bentley and his friend drew a breath of relief as the train pulled up in the dock siding, and it was possible to breathe the pure atmosphere again.

Just a few yards away lay the long black transport, already packed with troops. There was hardly a man there who had more kit than he stood up in, for all this had been promised them on the other side. In the dim distance, riding in the water, were the half-dozen destroyers told off to accompany the transports on their voyage.

It was all so new and exciting that few indeed had the slightest desire to go down below. Soon after daybreak they would be somewhere in France, so they lay on the deck in the moonlight, chattering to one another with the zest of schoolboys engaged in some new adventure. Ginger Smith had procured a bucket from somewhere, and was using it as a seat. There was a cigarette in the corner of his mouth, and a smile of deep content on his impudent, freckled face.

"Now, this is what I call a bit of alright," he said. "It's very nice to think o' the Government goin' out o' their way ter send us on a little 'oliday trip like this. I never 'ad one before, 'cept once when I went dahn ter Morget for the day on one o' them steamers from Tilbury dock. It was the time wot I picked up a toff's purse on the golf links, an' 'e give me a quid for wot 'e called me honesty."

"How much was in that purse, Ginger?" Bentley asked.

"Fifteen bob," Ginger grinned. "Per'aps if there'd 'ave bin more there wouldn't 'ave bin so much honesty abaht. Well, I gives myself a treat, an' off I goes 'on a beano ter Morget. An' when I gets there a cove offers me a 'ole bathin' machine ter meself for a bob. So I bithed in style and catched a cold as larsted me for three months. It's all wot ye're accustomed to. I don't so much mind it now, but it was a very painful shock at the time."

All this with a perfectly grave face and not so much as a twinkle in Ginger's blue eyes. He was perfectly at home, as indeed he would have been anywhere. There were many who gathered round to listen to Ginger's nonsense and unfailing flow of spirits that nothing could damp and nothing could undermine. And the time was coming when his airy nonsense was destined to brighten many a cold and bitter night, and make those in retreat before the German host forget for the moment the bitterness of defeat. But no cloud hung over the Musketeers just now. They were humming across the sea in the direction of the fight, and on either side of them, like sinister shadows, the black destroyers crept along. And so the hours passed until the dawn came and Boulogne Harbour was reached.

"I suppose we shall get some breakfast presently," Kemp suggested. "Not that I can see any sign of it."

But breakfast was not yet. There was a long, hot march over the hill and the long sand dunes on the other side before an halt was called and a biscuit per man served out. As far as the eye could reach were the rolling sands, and just inside them long stretches of vivid green, with here and there turf still finer and greener than the rest. On the rising ground flanked by a clump of trees stood a long, imposing pavilion. Ginger rubbed his eyes as he lighted a cigarette and struggled to his feet.

"Well, if this don't make me fair 'omesick," he said. "'Ere, you blokes, wot d'yer think o' that? Ever see anything like it before, Bill? Konky, what's that place yonder wif a tarpaulin roof? What price Richmond?"

"Why, strike me if it ain't a caddy shed!" the man addressed as Konky exclaimed. "Fairly brings the tears in me eyes, it do. Why, I can shut me peepers an' feel the 'arf crohns droppin' inter me fist. Two rounds an' a 'arf, I says, an' he gives me four bob. Say, mate, it is a golf course, ain't it?"

"That's right," Kemp laughed. "I suppose you've heard of Le Touquet. Well, this is Le Touquet."

"Yus, an' 'Arry Vardon laid it aht," Ginger said. "Good course, ain't it, sir? Blimme, if them bloomin' French ain't gone up in my estimation."

"It is a good course," Kemp said. "Probably the best on the Continent. Ever played here, Harold?"

"It's little golf I've played the last few years," Bentley said. "But it looks all right."

"Yes, and it is all right. I had three weeks of it at Easter, and never played better in my life. Who would have thought then that we should be here on such an errand now? A month or two ago golf was the only game I was really keen on. And now, if you put a club in my hands, I wouldn't take the trouble to drive a ball with it. I seem to have lost all my taste for that sort of thing. But it is a good course."

A bugle sounded somewhere in the distance, and once more the battalion were on the march again. They passed along in the baking sunshine over the hard, dry roads like a piece of living machinery. They were tired and hungry, but not one man fell out, not one dropped by the way. There were those amongst them, too, who a few weeks before had been mere weeds, flotsam and jetsam of the great city, half-starved, and weak and incapable of anything in the way of exertion from the sheer need of food. And now here they were, strong and well set-up, alert and eager, clear-eyed and clean-skinned, real live men, better for the storm that had broken over Europe. It was quite late in the afternoon before the battalion reached the village, where they found billets in a score or two of barns, and lay there on the clean straw waiting the arrival of the supply wagons. A major came along, and his eyes gleamed with satisfaction.

"Nothing the matter with this little lot," he said to his subaltern. "By Gad, the old regiment is going to keep up its reputation. Not one man left behind after a 12-mile march, and the sun at least 90 in the shade! We'll show those chaps presently how far it is to Tipperary!"

CHAPTER XI - THE SHADOW OF MONS

It had been a long and bitter day, and the little force known as the Honourable Company of Musketeers had been sorely pressed, and, though no man confessed it, they were praying for the darkness. They had come up a week or two before, and had been thrown directly into the firing line. It was trying them high indeed, a terrible ordeal for young, unseasoned troops, to thrust them headlong against the cream of the German infantry, but there had been no help for it. Over in England, people were rejoicing in successive victories, and some, indeed, were obsessed with the idea that the German flood was broken, and that the crisis was past. Heaven alone knows why the authorities at home were wrapping the people in the cotton wool of optimism, but those at the front knew better; they knew that every man was needed; they knew that if that line was broken Paris was doomed.

They knew how unprepared we were, and that France was not in much better case than ourselves. And so a harassed general, who hardly knew which way to turn, had welcomed the advent of the Musketeers as something like a godsend. He did not want to do it; he hated the necessity, but there was no alternative.

"It's got to be done," he told the colonel of the Musketeers. "Now, here's the map; there are the trenches, and you have got to hold them for 24 hours. And, what's more, you must hold them at any cost. You know what that means, and you know your own men better than I do. Good morning."

"Better make it good-bye, sir," the colonel replied. "That's about what it will come to. As you say, I do know my men, and they'll stay where they are told till the last one is left."

It was no idle boast. All that day the Musketeers had stuck grimly to their task under a hell of shot and shell and unprotected by their own artillery. They had seen the Prussians advance to the attack again and again in close formation, only to be mown down by the rain of lead and the hail of machine gun fire till the grey corpses were piled up in ghastly heaps out there in the open, and some of the Musketeers, more daring than the rest, were firing with red-hot barrels behind a rampart of the dead. The line was thinner now by something like 25 per cent of the battalion, but still they held on, black and grimed and bloodshot, tortured by thirst and racked with the pains of hunger. But they held on.

They were fighting now with one eye on the foe and the other on the sinking sun. They could expect no slackening in the attack, no mouthful of food or water for their parched lips, until darkness fell. Now and again a handful of the foe in advance of the rest slopped over into the trench like grey foam blown on the gale, only to find themselves bayoneted with savage thrusts and trampled underfoot. To the left of the trench the Germans had managed to establish a machine gun in a little hollow, half-enfilading the defenders, and rendering some of the younger men jumpy and unsteady. And yet they held on, these boys who only a few weeks before had been living in the soft lap of luxury or starving in the slums. And they were up against the pick and marrow of the Kaiser's troops. They were fighting desperately, hanging on with teeth and eyebrows, opposite men trained to the moment, men who had played the war game for years. It was a case of each for himself, for most of the officers were down now, and every one of the Musketeers had only himself to think of.

In the corner of the second trench Bentley and Kemp, together with Allen and Garton, had established themselves. Ginger, crouching at their feet, had made himself a porthole, through which he was firing grimly. Then came a shot from that accursed machine gun and smashed the rifle in his hand; then another that lifted his cap from his head.

"'Ot work, guvnors," he said. "That's wot in polite circles they used ter call 'a little bit off the top.' 'Ot work, boys, but it's goin' ter be 'otter where we sent them Germans to. 'As any gent got a gun 'e don't want?"

But there was no lack of rifles. Half a dozen lay at Ginger's feet for the asking. He shook his head angrily, like a terrier tormented by flies, as the machine gun bullets rattled round him; then he dropped the rifle he had snatched up and rose to his feet.

"'Ere," he said, "I'm going to stop that gime. Mr. Bentley, I knows you've got a revolver in yer pocket."

"I have," Bentley said. "What do you want it for?"

"Well, I'm goin' ter do in the bloke wot's playin' that trombone. If I don't get 'is number 'e'll get mine. An' I'll be just as sife wrigglin' on me belly aht yonder as doin' the livin' statuary busness 'ere."

There was logic in Ginger's remark, and in any case there was no officer by to say him nay. He edged his way cautiously over the corner of the trench, and crept along like a snake between two rows of beetroot. It was a mad action, rash and hazardous to the verge of insanity, but there were many such that day, and the dark days that followed, of which there is no record, and never will be now. And none knew better than Ginger, despite his cheery optimism, that the odds against him were as a thousand to one. But still he thrust his way forward with a cheery smile in his eyes and the familiar grin upon his parched and blackened lips.

Nearer and nearer he came till he could hear the bullets screaming like a telephone wire in the wind over his head; nearer and nearer he came till the discharge from the gun was hot upon his cheeks. He was fairly safe now, as far as the maxim was concerned, but the crux of his task had yet to come. He had to get behind that machine and take the three men working it. Inch by inch he crept on till the muzzle of the gun actually seemed to rest on his shoulder. Then he leapt to his feet and pushed the murderous weapon over sideways. He was looking so close into the eyes of the gun crew that he could see the colour of their lashes and their grinning teeth. Their rifles lay behind them, so that they were practically at his mercy. He stifled a cry of exultation that was bursting on his lips; then the revolver spoke three times, and three grey corpses lay in the sandy hollow. And then Ginger went mad.

He simply couldn't help it. He was so full of the insanity of triumph that he would have faced the whole of the German army at that moment. With a yell of defiance he jumped to his feet and lifted the Maxim upon his shoulder. Then he staggered coolly along with his burden and threw it down in the trench close to where Bentley and his friends were standing. He dropped lightly down under cover again, and wiped the dripping moisture from his eyes. He was absolutely untouched; it was one of the marvels that do happen on the field of battle.

"'Ere,'" he gasped. "Anybody got a birfday? Cos, if they 'ave, I've got a present for 'em."

"You'll hear more of this, my friend," Kemp said grimly. "I've seen some plucky things to-day, but nothing to touch that. Here the devils come again."

Once more the grey flood was beaten back; then as the darkness fell the attack gradually died down, save for an occasional shot from a big gun in the distance. Utterly exhausted, the Musketeers lay there waiting for the food and drink of which they were in such dire need. It came presently in the shape of a wagon or two and a relief of Army Service men, and with them a man in civilian dress, a dapper man with a glass carefully screwed into his eye, at the sight of whom Bentley gasped with astonishment. He forgot his thirst for the moment.

"D'you see that?" he asked Kemp. "Now, how on earth did he get here? You see who it is, don't you?"

"By Jove!" Kemp exclaimed. "Why, it's that chap Venables. Just think of the utter cheek of it!"

CHAPTER XII - FOG OF WAR

The American appeared to be as much at home there as if he had been passing weeks in the trenches. There was something almost supercilious in the way in which he glanced about him; he might have been seeking acquaintances in Hyde Park. Then all at once his manner changed, and he advanced with outstretched hand in Bentley's direction. But their curiosity was fleeting, for, now that dusk had fallen and the attack was beaten off, they were utterly worn and weary, done to the world, and conscious only of the wild hunger gnawing at them. They lay in the mud with their backs to the trench, with eyes only for the little knot of men who had pushed through the precious food.

"How did you get here?" Kemp asked languidly.

"In the metaphor of my country, search me," the American said. "I am too old a citizen of the world to be surprised at anything. But I don't mind telling you that I am supposed to be with the German forces. I came from the lines behind Mons with half a dozen swagger staff guides to see the contemptible English wiped out. But something went wrong with the little programme, and all those pretty boys found themselves mixed up with some of your Highlanders, who were too dense, I guess, to know when they were beaten, and, when I'd sorted myself out of the fog, I was kind of a prisoner. But they were decent boys and quite good friends as soon as they understood what had happened. Then they got busy again, and I drifted about till some of your A.S.C. men took me in tow, and here I am."

It all sounded quite plausible, the more so as Venables dipped his hand in the pocket of his big coat and produced half a dozen packets of cigarettes, which he distributed with fine impartiality. He was complimentary, too, and made no secret of the way in which his sympathies lay.

"Oh, you jarred them up all right," he said. "They were talking about you chaps this morning. Couldn't make out how it was that you were holding out. I guess they thought that, as you were little bits of recruits—"

Kemp and Bentley were no longer listening. They had eyes only for the beef and biscuit which was being handed out none too liberally. A big man with his arm in a sling and a bandage round his head limped painfully along the trench. Bentley and Kemp struggled to their feet, but the other held up his hand.

"Don't get up," he said. "I have come to see how you men are getting along. You've done splendidly to-day, and I shall see that your good work is not forgotten. What's all this I hear about a German Maxim? Did any of you see it? Unfortunately, you seem to have no officer left."

"I'm afraid that's true, sir," Kemp said. "That's the man over there, the man with the red hair."

Colonel Lord Hailsham had dropped down on an empty cartridge box and listened with a grim smile to the story of Ginger's achievement. He listened perhaps a little suspiciously to Venables' account of his adventures.

"Very fine," he said. "Very fine indeed. And do you mean to say that you haven't got a sergeant left?"

"I don't believe there's one, sir," Bentley replied.

"Really. Well, it can't be helped; you in this trench must do the best you can with what you've got. I'm sorry to tell you that we are absolutely cut off, with no chance so far as I can see of any relief. The other half of the battalion may manage to force their way through, but they will be very fortunate if they do. And there is worse than that. We are absolutely without ammunition, either for the machine guns or the rifles. And two of our batteries have been abandoned on the hill yonder, with all their ammunition and ours, too. If I had a map I could show you exactly where—"

"Excuse me, my lord," Venables interrupted. "But I happen to know the place you mean. I was there this morning. I saw those abandoned guns as late as at four o'clock this afternoon. They are in the spur of a wood, and I don't believe the Germans know a bit about them. Of course, I am a correspondent and strictly neutral, but somehow I can't forget that a century or two ago my ancestors lived in your old country. And, if you like, and you really want to have a dash for those guns, well, I'm going that way, and if your men follow me it isn't for me to go out of my way to make myself unpleasant."

"Is that what you want, sir?" Kemp asked eagerly.

"I think so. After all, it's only a question of a few hours for us. And if a dozen or so of you could get up to those gnus and blow them up with their ammunition and bring back some of our cartridges, well, I shan't stop you."

It was quiet in the trenches now, for the men had fed like wolves, and the company there were greatly thankful for the American's cigarettes. In the dim light their black and grimy faces were turned eagerly towards the big figure seated there on the empty cartridge box. It was so quiet, too, that every word he said carried all along the trench.

"Of course, we'll do it, sir," Kemp said. "And I am quite sure that every man will volunteer."

A sudden shout went up, and in an instant the thin line of khaki was on its feet. The colonel smiled approvingly, then he sharply commanded the men to sit down again. But there was no annoyance on his face; nothing in him but pride and sorrow in the knowledge that these were his boys.

"Yes, that's the spirit," he murmured. "Now, I believe that you two are old O.T.C.'s. You will regard yourselves for the moment as acting lieutenants. And that red haired man yonder who is so obviously listening to all I am saying had better become a sergeant for the moment. Come here, Smith."

With his jaunty smile and ready audacity, Ginger jumped to his feet and saluted smartly. The colonel prided himself on the fact that there was no man in his regiment whom he did not know by name. Ginger was no exception to the rule.

"I am proud of you, Smith," the colonel said. "I am proud of you all for the matter of that. Some day perhaps you will know what you have accomplished in the last twenty-four hours. You have managed somehow to hold up a whole German Army Corps, and you have saved the guns. And if you had retreated nobody could have possibly blamed you. Well, we're all in it together, and if we find ourselves tomorrow back with our brigade it will be nothing less than a miracle. That's all I've got to say. I suppose this gentleman won't mind my suggesting in the circumstances that I am taking some little risk."

"These two men of yours know me, my lord," Venables said.

Kemp confirmed the statement eagerly enough. Neither he nor Bentley was blind to the danger that lay before them; they knew well enough that the next few hours would probably see the end of the Musketeers. It was good and sweet to know that they and the rest of them had struck such a blow for the flag, to know that their work would be talked about in England, and that their names would not be forgotten by grateful countrymen. They had to die, but there was no reason why the end should come before they had given the enemy a further taste of their quality.

There was no one to lead them either. The colonel had other work to do, and already he was making his way cautiously towards the second line of trenches. They had to rely now on Venables' memory of the ground they had to cover, and on the little handful of men whom it would be Kemp's duty to select. As senior to Bentley, he was now in command of the hundred men, all that were left of that gallant company.

"Well, thank the Lord I'm goin' ter be one of 'em," Ginger struck in. "You might leave it ter me, sir, ter select the men. I knows 'em better'n you. An' they'll do exactly wot' I tells 'em. I wouldn't be out o' this for anything. And if we do come through all right, an' something tells me as we will—"

CHAPTER XIII - AFTER THE GUNS

It was an hour later that the little knot of men following Kemp and Bentley and Ginger, mightily conscious of his fresh importance, climbed noiselessly out of the trench and plunged into a field of beetroot where there was ample cover. It was not very dark, and when their eyes became accustomed to the gloom they could make out, beyond the field, a long upward sweep of stubble fringed away to the right by a big wood. A spur of this ran down the hillside, and it was here, so far as Kemp could make out, that the guns lay. In the deceptive light the spot did not seem very far away, though, according to what Venables said, it must have been a good two miles. Below the wood was a tangle of bracken, and it was here that the convoy bringing up ammunition to the Musketeers' trenches had been literally blown into fragments by the German gun-fire. Apparently the enemy had made no further attempt to possess themselves of the damaged wagon, probably being confident that the matter could wait, and that before morning there would not be a single English soldier within miles of the place.

"It's a good thing they don't know," Kemp muttered. "If they found out that our chaps yonder had run out of cartridges there wouldn't be one left in ten minutes. However, they don't know, and that's in our favour. Venables, do you mean to tell me that that hill is two miles away?"

Venables was absolutely sure of it. He pointed out that this was not his first campaign by a good many, and that he himself had served in the American army. It was he who had thrown out the suggestion that it would be just as well to have amongst the forlorn hope one man at any rate who could speak German fluently. Amongst a regiment of men largely recruited from London business men this was no difficult matter. He would probably come in useful later on.

For a time they crawled along on hands and knees, without a solitary word spoken. It was hot and weary work, especially to men who had hardly known what it was to close their eyes for three successive days and nights. It was still more dangerous work when they reached the open ground, for it was impossible to know where the German sentries were posted, and any moment might sound the note of alarm. It was only by spreading out on both sides and keeping along in the shelter of hedge and ditch that the lower spur of the wood was reached at length. Then Kemp suddenly drew back and held up his hand.

On the very edge of the wood two grey figures squatted in the bracken, rifle in hand, keen and alert, and obviously ready to sound the alarm at the first sign of the foe. It was an awkward moment, because it was impossible to proceed any farther before these men were disposed of. No doubt the sound of a shot could bring hordes of the enemy charging through the wood. For a few minutes Bentley and Kemp discussed the situation in whispers. What was to be done?

"It seems to me," Kemp said, "that this is where our friend who speaks German comes in. Hi, Malden. Here. I want you to crawl up to that hedge and fall over the other side. That will attract the attention of those chaps, and before they can put a bullet into you, you must groan for help in their own lingo. You had better be a German spy in khaki who has been wounded. Tie his head up with a handkerchief, Harold, and rub the handkerchief first on Ginger's coat sleeve. There's blood on it. Then you'll have to leave the rest to us."

The man called Malden grinned cheerfully. Three months before he had been a good-natured, rather obese, city solicitor, with a timid manner and a desire to live at peace with his neighbours. Now he was hard and lean, and only too eager to see the Germans writhing at his feet.

"That'll be all right, old man, at least I mean, sir," he said. "I used to be rather good at private theatricals. But I don't quite get the hang of it yet. How are you going to keep 'em quiet? Not that I am thinking about myself."

Kemp smiled encouragingly, for he was beginning to see his way. It was pretty evident, too, that these were the only two Germans in the spur of the wood, and that they had been placed there more as a matter of routine than anything else. But, all the same, they would have to be silenced; it was imperative that not a sound should escape them.

"Now, you go on," Kemp said, "and creep up as far as the fence. Hang there till you see one stand up, and then hoist your signals of distress. Ginger, you take three men and place yourselves two on each side of Malden, one each with a clip in his rifle, and the other two with fixed bayonets. As soon as those swine hang over the hedge, clap a rifle to the head of either of 'em, and whilst they are more or less paralysed let the other two men give 'em the bayonet without the slightest hesitation. It is not a pretty thing to do, but, considering that the lives of about 500 of us are at stake, don't have the least hesitation. Besides, you are not dealing with men, nothing more than brutes and savages."

All this in a hurried whisper, repeated again and again so that there should not be a misunderstanding when the critical moment arrived. Inch by inch, slowly and coolly as if he had been performing some exercise in his own suburban garden, Malden crept in, grinning to himself as he thought of the artistic bandage, grimy and bloodstained, that was tied about his forehead. There was not an atom of fear in the heart of the man who would have told anyone three months ago that he was the last man in the world to be trusted with a weapon. But he was hard and stern enough now, when he realised the responsibility before which not so long ago he would have faltered and trembled—the lives perhaps of 500 men, many of them friends of his, rested on his coolness and courage. On and on he went, this respectable British citizen, until at length he gained the fence and lifted his head over it. He gave one glance to assure himself that all was well on either side of him, and grinned as he saw the gleam of two rifle barrels and the glitter of a pair of bayonets.

He could hear the Germans muttering and groaning together. Apparently they felt perfectly secure of their position, for they made no effort to modulate their voices, and Malden could hear every word they said. Then he turned his head and saw that Kemp had risen to his feet. He lifted himself on the top of the hedge, and then appeared to collapse there with a moan of pain and a heartbreaking groan.

"I shall never do it," he said in German. "Also I shall never get there. Help! Help! I am—"

He broke off suddenly with a feeling that his little ruse had been quite successful. He heard the Germans jump to their feet as they made a rush towards him. Through his half-closed eyes he could see two swarthy faces bent over him, and two pairs of hands tugging at his limp body. Then one or two broken words came from his lips, words of explanation, as if he were more or less delirious, before he dropped like an empty sack.

He heard two hoarse exclamations, and as he struggled to his feet he saw the Germans standing there with the muzzle of a rifle pressed to the head of either. And after that two other forms came into the picture; there was a faint streak of light glancing upwards out of the ditch, and the sudden clash of two heavy bodies in the brushwood. The sentries had fallen, stabbed through the heart, and had collapsed with no more than a sigh.

"By Gad, you did that well, Malden," Kemp said. "And now, with any luck, we shall get hold of those guns."

CHAPTER XIV - BY TELEPHONE

Malden sat up suddenly and laughed. It was by no means a pleasant laugh, and Venables gripped him firmly by the arm.

"Here, none of that," he said. "You just keep yourself in hand. I know what's the matter with you."

Malden proceeded to check himself with an effort. There was a sort of speculation in his eye as he contemplated the grey corpses lying at his feet.

"I couldn't help it," he said. "Upon my word, I couldn't. It struck me all at once as being so funny. Ghastly and horrible, I admit, but funny all the same. Why, in the ordinary course of things I should be at home getting up my bulbs. I'm rather fond of reading sensational literature, but I never pictured myself doing this sort of thing. Oh, it's all right; all I want is a mouthful of food."

"Well, take a cigarette instead," Venables suggested. "I have seen these things before. I was all through the Balkan business, you know. Funny how hysteria grips men sometimes. But when it does get hold of them they fight like blazes."

But Malden was quiet enough now. The desire to laugh had left him; he was no longer a respectable business man, but a soldier with stern work in front of him. So far as they could make out, the spur of the wood was free of the enemy, and it was safe enough to move on in the direction of the guns. The main idea was to recover the lost ammunition for the men in the trenches, and then to render the 4.7's useless for future work. This would entail something more than the removal of breech blocks, and the scheme generally was to blow them up; not, however, until the ammunition had been saved, and even then by a time fuse which would enable Kemp and the rest of them to get back to their line before the foe had realised what was talking place.

All the same it was necessary to push on slowly and cautiously through the wood. It was Venables who impressed this firmly on his companions.

"Don't be too sure," he said. "You fellows haven't half grasped how thorough these Germans are. I dare say you will be astonished to hear that there are at least two underground telephone wires between the rear of your lines and the German front. This is just the sort of place where a telephone operator could lie snug for days. All he has got to do is to lie in a hole in the ground with some food, and he's just as safe as if he were in his own camp. You had better go forward as if every inch of ground contained a German. And if you do get into trouble, then I am your prisoner."

"You are taking no risks?" Kemp murmured.

"Well, I guess you've got to trust me," the American said. "I can't tell you everything, but I am no enemy of yours and don't you forget it. We're wasting time."

Without another word the American crept forward, followed by the rest, spread out wide enough to cover the whole of the wood. It was nervous work, pushing along there in the darkness far away from the English lines, with just enough light to distinguish the trunks of the trees. From somewhere in the distance came the boom of the heavy guns, and ever and again a flare high up in the black clouds picked out the wood clear cut as a cameo and made everything as light as a vivid flash of lightning would have done. And presently in one of these luminous intervals Bentley caught sight of something that caused him to gasp and grip Kemp by the arm.

"I believe we've done it," he whispered. "You keep your eyes wide open for the next flash. Up there to the left behind that big clump of trees. I could have sworn that I saw the gleam on the muzzle of a gun."

Bentley was right. A searchlight playing wide in the sky dropped its beams on the wood, picking it out half vividly much as if the moon was shining behind the clouds. The gleaming patch indicated by Bentley might have been half a mile away, but unquestionably what he saw were guns.

"Good for you," Kemp said. "The fun is about to begin. Well, as this is likely to be our last adventure, we will make the best of it. Half a minute. What's the matter with Venables? Isn't he signalling?"

The American, a little way in front, had risen as far as his knees, and with his upraised hands was waving the rest of the company back. They dropped in the undergrowth and lay close like partridges when there is a hawk overhead. A second or two later Venables was back amongst them.

"What did I tell you?" he asked. "I've had the narrowest escape of tumbling into a hole where a German is working his end of the field telephone. I should say he's got two instruments in there and is transferring messages. It's the neatest little dug-out you ever saw, covered all over with bushes, and it would puzzle a fox to find. I should have blundered right into the chap myself if I hadn't heard him speak. Then he was kind enough to strike a match to light his cigarette, and I had a full view of the desirable family mansion."

"Did you learn anything?" Kemp asked.

"Well," Venables said drily, "vulgar curiosity isn't quite the suit I'm playing just now. And I don't want to find myself an object of suspicion to the Germans. Now, what I suggest is that I show our friend Malden where the scientist is playing his little game and that he listens to what's going on. It's just possible that he will pick up a little information likely to be useful."

There was nothing wrong with the suggestion, and Kemp decided to avail himself of it. A moment later Malden was listening eagerly to a conversation that palpably was being transmitted from some other hiding place behind the English lines to a point somewhere near the German headquarters.

"Yes, I got that," came the hoarse whisper from underground. "Better repeat it again so that I shall make no mistake. So. How far do you say?"

Then followed a silence and a broken word or two from the signaller that Malden failed to understand. But gradually as he lay there he began to fit the pieces of the puzzle together, no very difficult matter to one who is really familiar with the use of the telephone. And as Malden lay there he gasped and thrilled with the joy of discovery. For even he, with his limited knowledge of the wily foe, was beginning to understand that he was picking up some priceless information. Then it became plain that the man down there in the dug-out had finished for the moment, for he replaced his receiver and proceeded to relight his pipe. Malden crept back to the others excitedly.

"Have you done any good?" Kemp asked.

"I rather think I have." Malden exclaimed. "I have just discovered that there is a strong picket of Uhlans out there at the back of the wood. I should think they are about as many as we are. They are in command of lieutenant somebody, and their game is to push forward at daybreak to see if we are still holding that village with the unpronounceable name."

"Ah," Kemp cried. "I begin to see what you are driving at. Well, we don't hold that bridge, and directly those chaps find that out we are absolutely done. So are the Royals for the matter of that. By jove, I've a good mind to try it! We can't be worse off than we are at present. Now, if we can surprise those chaps, we get hold of a score of good horses; and with those in our hands we can haul the guns and ammunition back to the trenches. Do you see what I mean? Now, supposing that we got hold of that Johnny in the dug-out and put Malden in his place. What do you think of that?"

CHAPTER XV - SAVED!

Malden demurred strongly. His German accent was good enough, but the whole plan might be ruined if some question were put to him that he was not in a position to answer promptly. It would be far better to leave the German signaller in blissful ignorance of the fact that he had been discovered, and push on at once, with a view to taking the Uhlans by surprise, especially as they were an isolated body and beyond the reach of help.

"Besides, I haven't finished," he said. "Those chaps know all about the guns, and they haven't worried about them because they regard them as their own absolute property. They have got the guns and the ammunition, and, what is more to the point, they are holding more than a score of our gunners too. Of course, it isn't for me to argue with you, but it seems a pity to risk the success of a coup like this for the possibility of picking up a bit more information. Still, it isn't for me to say."

There was a good deal of force in this suggestion, and Kemp acknowledged it without hesitation. They were at least as strong as the Uhlans, they were well armed and desperate, and the German horsemen would be taken by surprise. It would be a grand thing, too, if they could recover the guns and the gunners and get back to their trenches with the ammunition that they so sorely needed. And it was no time to wait, no time to think of discipline or what might be the effect of not lingering for orders. For they knew only too well that the overwhelming pressure of Germany's might was gradually forcing them back, and that the allies, for the time being, at least, were in full retreat. They knew only too well, too, that every hour gained, and every tiny check, however small, was so much gained for England and France. The time had come when they might be forced back, such of them as were left, under the guns of the Paris forts, but the thought did not dismay them, and now all the world knows that the disastrous retreat was in reality the beginning of a series of glorious victories that covered the old flag with new laurels. They knew also that every man there was ready to do his duty and ready to die in the defence of his country and the honour of a great people.

It was only in the last few days that these facts were being steadily borne in upon them, but the knowledge of them strung them up to fresh endeavour. Therefore to regain these guns now, and to hold those trenches for another day, might mean more than any of them dreamt. And, while nothing of this was said, it was in the back of the mind of every man there.

"We'll do it!" Kemp said. "Honestly, I believe we can do it. If we can catch those fellows napping, as we probably shall, we'll give the people of England something to talk about. Perhaps they will never know, but still we shall. Now, come on, lads; let's strike another blow for the glory of the good old Musketeers. Forward, my boys, forward!"

Here was something to be done: here was something to wipe out the bitterness of the last few days. They pushed forward, a strangely mixed crowd, drawn from the cricket field and the city and the slums, yet all bent on doing something to show the earnestness that was in them. Inch by inch they passed through the wood and thence to the open ground on the far side, where they could see a camp fire. The ground was unprotected in front, but on three sides of it barbed wire fences had been erected, and on the far side of this the horses were picketed. It was an ideal situation from the attackers' point of view, and Kemp and the others smiled grimly as they saw how the enemy had betrayed itself into their hands. It needed no more than a quick, irresistible dash and a volley or two, and the whole thing would be over.

"Let's be out and at 'em!" Bentley whispered.

"Steady on, steady on!" Kemp said. "Pity to run the risk of spoiling everything by undue haste. There's plenty of cover, and those chaps sitting round the fire will never spot us, for they couldn't possibly see as long as their blaze is going on. Now, get right up within five yards of them, and don't fire a single shot till I give you the word. Now then; forward, forward!"

It was a tense moment, and every man held his breath until in the silence he could hear the blood rushing through his head, could hear the tick of the watch on the wrist of the man next to him. They could catch the flickering sob of the camp fire now, and hear the Germans talking. A tall officer in his smart uniform approached the fire and took out a burning twig to light his cigar. It would have been an easy matter to pick him off, for he was a fine mark against the flare, and Ginger's fingers itched on his trigger as he half rose.

"Now, drop that," Bentley said sharply. "I understand your feelings, Ginger, but it can't be done."

"Wery sad," Ginger said resignedly. "This 'ere's one o' the drawbacks o' war. It's full o' disappointment. But there's another thing. If you cast yer eye over to the right yonder you'll see some chaps lyin' dahn there so wery close together as ter suggest the idea as wot they was affectionate twins. But if you arsk me, I'm bettin' as they're our own chaps, prisoners, an' if I'm not mistaken they're roped up together like convicts. It's a quid to a tanner as they're our gunners."

Ginger appeared to be right. Fortunately the same idea had occurred to Kemp at the same moment. He was glad now that he had not yielded to his first impulse and attacked the foe at 200 yards distance. If he had done so, the little knot of British prisoners would have suffered in their turn. But that danger had been fortunately averted, and the only thing to be afraid of now was the possibility of the rifle fire stampeding the horses. Still, there was barbed wire behind them, and they could only break away in the direction of the attacking force. Nearer and nearer Kemp and his little force crept, and as yet the Uhlans were absolutely ignorant of the coming danger. It was almost impossible to hold back any longer, and Kemp rose to his feet and gave the order to fire. It was as if so many lead soldiers had suddenly been swept away by the hand of a child who had tired of his martial game. The Uhlans went down around the camp fire, they rolled over sideways, until, in less time than it takes to tell, they were wiped out.

"Cease firing!" Kemp screamed. "Not another shot. Look to the horses: they are worth their weight in gold."

Just for a second it looked as if the horses would break from their pickets and tear themselves in their terror against the barbed wire. Then out of the attacking force one man darted forward and flung himself into the midst of the whinnying, lathering steeds. The touch of his hand and the sound of his voice seemed to soothe them as if he spoke a language they understood.

"That's the beauty o' 'avin' a bit of all sorts," Ginger cried. "'E's a 'orsedealer's runner, that bloke is. 'Ot stuff where the 'iar trunks is concerned. But, Lor' bless yer, they knows 'im as well as if 'e'd bin wif 'em all 'is life. It takes a lot o' queer things ter make the British army."

Ginger spoke truly enough, for the big Flemish horses were no longer fretting at their pickets. Then from behind them came a frantic British cheer, and a score or more of figures in khaki struggled to their feet. They were roped together, with wrists and ankles firmly bound; they were exhausted and starving; but the bright light of courage was in their eyes as they held out their hands to their rescuers.

"What about the guns?" one of them cried. "Don't tell us they've been done in!"

"Oh, the guns are all right," Kemp said cheerfully. "The question is, can we put our hands on the shells?"

CHAPTER XVI - THE LONELY FARM

The fine rapture of the moment was not dimmed by any thought of the peril that might—nay, would—follow on the morrow. It was enough to that little knot of Englishmen to know that they had set out on a breathless, desperate enterprise, and that the wild adventure had been crowned with success. And yet there was not one of them blind to the fact that it could only be for the time being. They knew that they had been overwhelmed by the great flood of the German invasion, and that the waters of that mighty river had swept by them on either side. There might be a possible chance to squeeze back, but every hour rendered retreat more and more difficult. Still, they were doing fine work, as their fathers had done on many a stricken field before them, and every moment gained was so much to their credit.

But they were not thinking of that, nor caring for the future. They cut the bonds of the gunners, who literally fell upon their necks and blessed them. A big sergeant sat on the grass and rubbed his swollen ankles vindictively.

"Oh, so you're some of the Musketeers?" he asked. "Where are we? We seem to have been on the run now for the last two days. And, if you ask me, we are all that's left of six batteries. I suppose they've got out guns all right? But where's your officer?"

"You can call me that," Kemp said. "We haven't got one left. A company of the Musketeers are back in a trench yonder, and about half the battalion is trying to cut its way through to the south. You needn't worry about your guns. They're not 200 yards away, at the bottom of the wood. Do you happen to know where your ammunition is? Because, if you do, we can give those fellows something to go on with tomorrow."

"Good iron!" the sergeant cried. "We were wondering where those guns had got to. Suppose they felt so sure of them that they left them in the wood. Well, we worked those guns all through the night and most of the morning till they were red hot. We worked 'em till we were the only battery left; then they came round from the left and cut us off altogether. It was no use going on. Some of our chaps fairly wept but what could we do? Then they took us prisoners and tied us up as you saw. They walked off with our ammunition wagons, and I believe they are somewhere on a farm over yonder. But we've got a man here who can tell us all about that. What's become of Uncle?"

A driver lying on the ground, pulling luxuriously at one of Venables' cigarettes, laughed aloud.

"I think he's in the ditch still," he said. "It's the farmer himself, sir. They tied the old chap up and dumped him down with us, and he's been doing nothing but swear ever since. Plucky old man, too. He knows they are going to try him to-morrow and shoot him for a spy, whether he's guilty or not. Here, I'll go and fetch him."

The driver came back a moment or two later with an old man, white-bearded and venerable, and clad in the blue blouse and baggy trousers of a working farmer. The sullen frown left his face, and he beamed as he caught sight of familiar khaki. He seemed to know instinctively that Kemp was the leader of the party, for he hastened to embrace him with forceful gratitude.

"Ah, the brave English," he said. "I speak some of your language. Years ago I stay with a countryman of mine in England. And now you come to set us free. Eh, the Germans? They come down on my farm; they steal everything, and ill-treat my wife and my daughter and her children; also they beat my old men on the farm, but they do not beat the young ones, because already they 'ave gone to fight. And then they beat me because I could not give them wine and chickens and veal. They say if I don't they shoot me. Then, because I go to a neighbour to help me and come back with what they need, they accuse me of being a spy, and they shoot me in the morning. Perhaps not."

"Not if we can help it," Kemp smiled. "Now, listen to me, Monsieur Jean, or whatever your name is."

"Jean is quite right, my captain," the Frenchman said.

"All right. We came here to recover our guns. And we have done that pretty effectually, as you can see for yourself."

"Ah, it was a fine sight, monsieur. It is only a pity that there were not a thousand of them, the pigs."

"Never mind about that for the moment, though we have every sympathy with your indignation. We're got the guns, but the sergeant here is of opinion that the ammunition wagons are up at your farm. It's long odds our cartridges are there, too. Now, do you think this is correct?"

"But indeed yes, my captain," the Frenchman said. "There are four ammunition wagons in one of my barns and they are all English. But in my farm are a number of German officers and their servants. They are boastful Uhlans. And at 10 o'clock to-night they sit down in my house, and they eat chicken and duck and veal, and they drink wine and swear at my family and my servants if they not get waited upon. Eh, what a joy if you brave English could come in just as they sit down and feed those pigs with lead and steel instead. It would be one great surprise. And my old men would bury them cheerfully."

Kemp nodded thoughtfully. A somewhat similar idea was beginning to simmer in his mind. If Uhlans were at the farm, it might be possible to surprise them and wipe them out altogether. This would mean the capture of still more horses, which later on might come in useful in a moment of retreat. There was another part of the scheme that need not be mentioned yet.

"What do you say?" Kemp said, turning to Bentley. "The odds are in our favour, and I daresay these chaps here have got a score they want to wipe out. Well, boys?"

Ginger licked his lips joyfully.

"There ain't no cause to arsk the question, sir," he said. "As for me, the mere thought o' wot ole 'Frenchy says about the wittles would buck me up ter fight the 'ole bloomin' German harmy. I feel as if I ain't 'ad a mawthful o' food since mother died. All right, sir, I'll dry up."

A few moments later the little band of adventurers were creeping along in the direction of the farm. Monsieur Jean stepped out sturdily in front of them until they passed over the brow of a little hill into a hollow below, where a low white house with lights gleaming in the windows loomed through the darkness. So far as Kemp could make out, no sentries had been posted, and doubtless the few men in attendance on the Uhlan officers were busily engaged inside waiting on their superiors. It was quite evident that the Germans were under the impression that none of the foe lurked within miles, for they had given themselves over to the enjoyment of the moment, as bursts of laughter and fragments of song from the interior of the house testified. The door was open, and inside, by the light of a lamp, Kemp could see the figure of an aged woman, who appeared to be utterly overcome with grief.

"My wife," the farmer explained in a whisper. "Doubtless she thinks I am dead. Those ruffians would probably tell her so. If I can engage her attention—"

Jean crept forward and whistled gently. The woman looked up and held out her hands. If she spoke now, all Kemp's plans might be blown to the winds. But fortunately she hastened out into the darkness, and before she could cry out the old man's hand was upon her lips, and he was whispering in her ear.

"We must get the others out of the house," he said. "Pretend that you want everybody in the kitchen for a moment. And then these brave men will do the rest. You understand?"

The old woman nodded, and a minute or two later came into the doorway and waved her hand.

"Come on," Kemp said. "Come on. At all events, we shall sup in luxury tonight."

CHAPTER XVII - BACK WITH THE GUNS

Twice did Kemp and Bentley walk round the house, keeping an alert look-out for possible sentries, but nothing of the kind could be seen. By this time the Germans, waited upon by a handful of their men, had made a start on their supper. They appeared to be in the best of spirits; perhaps they had indulged somewhat freely in the old farmer's wine before they sat down to table. They shouted to one another in boastful toasts and sang snatches of their arrogant patriotic songs. It sounded as if each had some ignoble exploit to speak of, but the din was comprehensible only to Malden, who smiled grimly as he listened. By this time the house was full of Musketeers. They poured in by the front door and the back, and Kemp and Bentley looking through the open door of the dining-room could see the lamplight glistening on brilliant uniforms, on gold lace and stars and decorations. There was another door at the far end of the room leading into the kitchen, where other Musketeers had been stationed.

A Uhlan officer, evidently of high rank, stood up at the end of the table with his glass in his hand and proposed a toast. He said something about England, and then, in good enough English, drank to the speedy destruction of French and his contemptible little army. There was a swaggering boast on his lips as Kemp stepped into the room and coolly surveyed the brilliant company.

"You can have your wish, sir," he said. "But, on the whole, you had best take it quietly."

The big officer dropped his glass and stared at Kemp in amazement. Then a revolver shot rang out and a bullet grazed Bentley as it buried itself in the wall. The Musketeers waited for no other signal. From both doors they burst into the room, firing as they came. It was all the work of a moment; there was no quarter given or asked, and presently when the smoke cleared away the Germans lay on the sanded floor beyond all power of further mischief. It was a sufficiently ghastly bit of business. But the Germans had done their best with their revolvers, and two or three of the Musketeers lay beyond the reach of mortal aid. But this was war, ghastly and grim, and there was no more to be done beyond removing the bodies of the dead Germans and throwing them hastily in a shallow grave.

"Stop," Kemp cried. "Strip them of their uniforms, get every uniform you can. I am not quite sure as yet, but we may want them presently. Where is Venables?"

"I don't know," Bentley said. "I expect he remained discreetly outside. This is hardly a job for an American journalist who is supposed to be with the German forces."

Kemp nodded approvingly. In the excitement of the moment he had forgotten the point. And there were many more important things to think of. The dead had to be buried first, and it was necessary to ascertain that the ammunition wagons were intact. At the end of half an hour all traces of the fray had been removed, and it had been established beyond doubt that the ammunition wagons contained not only shells for the guns but many cases of cartridges for the use of the Musketeers who still remained in the trenches. There were quite a number of horses, too, which Kemp had an idea he could use later on.

"And now," he said, "as there is no hurry, there is no reason why we shouldn't sit down and enjoy a good meal. More likely than not, it is the last we shall ever eat."

"The sort of feed they give a man the night before his execution," Malden grinned. "I suppose in time, if we live long enough, we shall get used to this sort of thing."

And indeed it did seem strange and weird that men who so short a time ago had been engaged in pacific pursuits, men who shrank with horror from strife or trouble or the suggestion of bloodshed, should be sitting laughing and joking callously here where only a few moments before a hideous slaughter had taken place, and where the soles of their boots where wet with the blood of the fallen Germans. Yet so it was; war had hardened these men as it had annealed the hearts of their fathers on the field of strife any time in the last eight hundred years. And the fact that they were just a handful in the heart and midst of a million foes, gave zest to the food that they placed in their mouths and the wine with which they washed it down. They sat there laughing and joking with the easy indifference to death and the half hysterical humour which to an English soldier is as the tempering of his steel.

"What do you want those uniforms for?" Bentley asked.

"Well, I've got an idea," Kemp murmured. "We'll get back to our trenches with our ammunition and hold on as grimly as we can till we are wiped out. This will give the rest of our battalion a chance to cut its way through. Then behind the trenches we could mask our recovered guns and give the Germans socks as long as ammunition lasts. This little dodge will probably make them think we are stronger than we really are, and it may keep them off for an hour or two longer. Now, if we can manage to hide those horses till tomorrow night, our company, or what's left of them, can get into those Uhlan uniforms and ride south with the object of pushing the German lines. You see what I mean. At any rate, it's a chance."

"It sounds like a forlorn hope," Bentley said.

"Of course it is. But there've been some pretty useful forlorn hopes engineered during this campaign, and I've no doubt there will be a good many more. It all depends upon how we carry it through. My idea is to put Malden into the uniform of that big swell who was in command here tonight. Evidently he was a man of considerable importance, but we'll find all that out presently when I have got time to go through his pocket-book. Malden shall lead us, and, as he speaks German so well, he ought to be able to carry us through. I know it all sounds like a chapter from some story, but there'll be heaps of chapters like that before this war is finished. Don't say anything more about it at present, and pass my plate for another slice of that veal. I could do with another glass of wine, too."

The meal was finished at length, and the ammunition wagons were drawn out and the horses fixed up. In the doorway stood the farmer and his wife with their grandchildren and servants calling down blessings on the head of the British.

"But what are you going to do?" Kemp asked the farmer. "You mustn't stay here, you know. You'll be shot if you do. You'll never be able to keep this business quiet."

The old man smiled proudly and yet sadly.

"I could not leave the old home, my captain," he said. "I would as soon those pigs took me and shot me. I have lived here for close on seventy years, and this is the second time I have seen those cursed

Germans with their heel on the neck of France. Last time I was younger, and I had a rifle in my hands. But behold I am not afraid. It is a clean piece of work you have made to-night, and there is not one of the Bosches alive to tell the tale. And if you think that my life is not safe in the hands of my wife and family, and these old servants of mine who have been with me all my life, then you are mistaken. And some day you push the Germans back and then you will return to find a welcome here. If not, monsieur, then farewell, for in that case we shall both of us be dead."

So far as he himself was concerned, Kemp thought grimly; the prophecy was likely to be fulfilled. But the thought troubled him not at all. His one aim was to be back in the trenches again with the guns safely masked behind. It was far into the night before the task was accomplished, and then with eyes heavy with sleep and limbs sore and weary, the men dropped exhausted in the mud. Then Kemp sat up suddenly and turned to Bentley.

"By the way," he asked, "where is Venables?"

But Venables was nowhere to be found.

CHAPTER XVIII - WOMEN'S WORK

The nights were growing longer and colder, and the leaves were falling from the trees, but so far nothing of a particularly cheerful nature had come through from the front, where the French and the contemptible little British army were struggling against odds far greater and more overwhelming than anyone in England realised. It was little that was permitted to pass the firing line in those early days, and the censorship of the Boer War was as nothing to that which was now in force. Everybody knew, of course, that Germany was ready at the very outset, but few people outside official circles properly appreciated what that really meant.

Only a few weeks before, the mere suggestion of trouble with Germany was scouted, except by a few who were looked upon as scaremongers and lunatics, for they were as so many voices calling in the wilderness. It was almost impossible to grasp that at this early stage of the proceedings Germany had poured over two millions of the flower of her manhood into Belgium and France. There were those, of course, who took a light-hearted view of the whole proceeding, and confidently prophesied that Germany would be a beaten foe by Christmas at the latest. These were soldiers on paper, armchair strategists who quoted comfortable documents from amateur critics who had proved to their own satisfaction over and over again that Germany could not last more than three months after the British Navy had made her command of the seas secure.

Well, the British Navy was mistress of the seas; the German Fleet had been driven in behind Heligoland, there probably to remain till the end of the war, with the exception of a few armoured cruisers which had already begun to fall victims to our fast armed cruisers; the waterways of the world were open to every nation except Germany and Austria; and for all practical purposes the world's commerce was proceeding as smoothly as usual. It is almost impossible to realise that millions of people all over the world, nations remote from the war, and not likely to be brought within its evil influence, were earning their daily bread and prospering as usual entirely owing to the magnificent work that Jellicoe and his men were doing.

But meanwhile, day by day, the allies were being steadily pushed back until it began to look as if the siege of Paris was only a question of time. England only heard occasionally of the great deeds which her heroes were doing; now and again the veil was lifted, and some brilliant exploit was revealed to the waiting country. One or two of the papers had commented amongst other things upon the fine work accomplished by the Musketeers, and gradually it became known that a part of the regiment had been cut off from the rest, without much hope of retreat.

There were anxious hearts in the Keep House, where Netty Bentley and Dorothy Kemp had settled down with Mrs. Bentley. One day passed after another without a sign, and it seemed as if Kemp and Bentley and the rest of them must have gone down before the rush of the German host. And then out of the darkness came a letter. It was written in a strange hand on foreign paper, and bore a Norwegian postmark. There was no beginning to it, and no end, the writer apparently being anxious to remain anonymous. But it was a consoling letter on the whole, and spoke of events which had happened up to the moment when Kemp and Bentley and the rest of them had made their raid upon the French farmhouse and got safely away to their own trenches with the guns. There was a promise to write further a little later on with more information, and meantime it was a great relief to find that when the letter had been despatched, only four days ago, all those in whom Netty and Dorothy were interested were safe.

"I cannot tell you," the letter ran, "who I am and what means I have used to communicate with you. But I want you to understand that every word is substantially true, and that I myself was present during the attack on the farmhouse, and that I saw the lost guns safely in the British trenches. I have every reason to believe that the scheme planned by Mr. Ronald Kemp will prove successful, and that with average luck the little company of Musketeers are by this time once more in touch with the British rearguard. I cannot speak too highly of the way in which the whole plan was carried out, and I speak with all the more confidence because I was one of them myself and had the honour of guiding the Musketeers to the spot where the guns and ammunition were concealed. As soon as possible I will write you further, but I want you to bear in mind that in communicating with you I am running a great deal of risk both to myself and to those who employ me. I am not an Englishman nor a Frenchman, nor am I a German who feels himself under an obligation to some of your friends.

"And now, there is one thing I am going to ask you to do. Directly you have read this letter and discussed it with Miss Bentley and her mother, I want you to destroy it and forget that you ever received it. I want you to promise me that you will not mention it to a single soul outside the Keep House. In conclusion, I give you my word that I am telling you no more than the truth; in fact, it would be impossible for anybody to read what I have written here and disbelieve a single word of it."

It was a sunny afternoon in the peaceful garden of the Keep House when the letter came and was read again and again round the tea-table. There was a good deal of it elaborated with a wealth of detail and sundry personal touches which served to bring out all the fine heroism of the work that Kemp and the rest of them had done. There was a long silence after the letter was finished with, and then Dorothy tore it into fragments, and put a match to it.

"It goes very much against the grain," she said. "I should like to have had the letter framed. Never in my life have I been so tempted to break a promise. But, whoever our good friend is, he must be obeyed."

"No question about that," Nettie said. "I wonder who he is? He can't be one of the Musketeers, for it would have been impossible for them to get a letter through. It is a great pity, too, that we cannot let the sender know how we appreciate his kindness. In fact, we can do nothing. Why can't we do something, Dorothy? I feel so horribly guilty going about my work by day, and spending my evenings in this beautiful old house, whilst all the time I feel that we ought to be doing something. What can we do?"

Dorothy turned a face that was somewhat restless and discontented towards the lawns and the flower beds, where the autumn flowers were blazing in the sunshine; the old house seemed to sleep peacefully, as if there was no such thing as war and suffering in the world.

"It is horrible!" she said. "Don't tell me that the women of England can do nothing except sit down day after day with a ball of wool and a couple of knitting needles in their hands. Of course, it's a good thing for us to make all these comforts for our men, but at the same time we must be taking the bread out of the mouths of the working women. And I for one am not going to sit down idly any longer."

CHAPTER XIX—SOMETHING ATTEMPTED

Dorothy rose to her feet, and walked up and down the lawn restlessly. Her eyes were shining with resolution.

"I am glad you mentioned it," she said, "because this idleness has been on my mind for some time. I am not one of those who believe that this war will soon be finished. I have been studying the papers, and it seems to me that we have not begun yet. What about the time when we have a couple of million men in the field? Who is going to look after the wounded? We are a most extraordinary nation; we never seem to anticipate anything. We muddle on, and muddle on, and when the big trouble comes we hold up our hands and say, 'Who would have thought it!' For the time being, at any rate, we have done quite enough in the way of extra comforts for the boys at the front. It's a job that wants to be properly organised and placed in the hands of women whose husbands are at the front, and of their children who are suffering from want of work. Don't tell me that hundreds of thousands of educated girls like ourselves have got to sit quietly down with their hands folded, whilst their brothers and sweethearts are dying for their country. Take my case, for instance. I have attended hundreds of ambulance classes, and I have all sorts of certificates, and yet so far I have apparently wasted my time. I am quite competent to undertake nursing work, and so are you. Before long, when the big fight begins in earnest, the wounded will be coming over here in streams, and so far there is little accommodation for them. Now, what I propose to do is this. I have thought the matter out carefully, and I believe we could accommodate about a hundred wounded here. Of course we cannot undertake very serious cases, but we could cope with those who want careful looking after. I believe we could manage with a dozen nurses, and I can easily raise those amongst my own friends. In fact, I have the volunteers already. Then there are two friends of ours, doctors who have retired from practice, but are both active and willing, and they would form our medical staff. Of course I should have to engage a matron, but that is merely a matter of money. Then in the big room down by the lake, which used to be a studio, I mean to establish a creche for children whose mothers are at work all day. This would find us plenty to do, and we should feel that we were really of some service to the state."

"It would cost a lot of money," Nettie said.

"It will cost five or six thousand pounds," Dorothy replied, "and quite as much to keep it up every year. But I think that can be managed. You see, I have money of my own, and before Ronald went away he made arrangements with his bankers by which I can draw on his account; in fact, he turned over his income to me, and, as you know, he is quite well off. I am perfectly sure that he would agree if he heard what I am saying now. Anyway, I am going to risk it. We will go up to London in the morning and call at the bank and put that right. Then we will find out the proper way to go to work and get one of my doctor friends here to plan out the house and give the necessary orders for the beds and all that sort of thing. Of course, we shall be amateurs to begin with, but I have do doubt we shall get into it in time. What do you think of the idea?"

"I think it's perfectly splendid!" Nettie cried. "You don't know how I have longed to do something really big. All this knitting business strikes me as being so futile."

For a long time they discussed the details eagerly, and by the morning most of the provisional arrangements were made. The Keep House was an ideal one for the purpose, as it stood in large grounds remote from the road and was very quiet. There was no difficulty about the money, either; there were ample funds for the purchase of the necessary outfit, and it was a pleasure and a joy to the two girls to carry out all their arrangements. They were fortunate in finding an old acquaintance of Kemp's in the War Office, for he took them by the hand, and put them in the right way of getting everything they required. It was he who obtained the sanction of the War Office to the scheme without which it would have fallen to the ground; he introduced to them a sympathetic member of the Medical Staff, who escorted them from place to place, and gave them the benefit of an invaluable experience gained during the Boer War; and he found the matron, a capable woman, the widow of a doctor, who had lost everything when hostilities broke out, and who was anxious not only to get her own living but to place her knowledge at the disposal of those who required it.

So gradually most of the rooms in the Keep House were stripped of their beautiful furniture, only a few apartments being reserved for the staff, and at the end of three weeks a hundred beds were established, and everything down to the last detail, was ready for the wounded.

It was with an air of pride and satisfaction that the girls surveyed their arrangements. They were all friends together, for every one of the nurses was personally known to the two girls; for the most part they were old friends of Dorothy's, girls who a few weeks before were thinking of nothing but tennis and golf and the prospects of summer holidays. But all that was altered now. The tennis racquets and the golf clubs had been laid aside and forgotten; the girls were as bright and cheerful as they had ever been; but the lightness and frivolity were gone, and a certain earnestness of purpose had taken their place, and there was not one of them who was not anxious to do her best.

"All we want now are patients," Dorothy said, as she surveyed the rows of neat beds in the cool wards. "But I suppose we shall have to wait for them. By the way, I suppose we are not going to make any distinctions? Some people I know who have a big place a mile or so down along the road are taking officers only, but I don't like the idea myself."

"I quite agree with you," Nettie said. "It seems to me that this war ought to destroy all social distinctions for the moment, for every man is doing his best for the country, and the country comes first of all. If you like, we might make the dining-room into an officers' ward, but really it does not in the least matter. I was talking to one of the doctors this morning, and he tells me that we may expect patients here at any time now. According to this morning's paper there has been a big battle somewhere not far from St. Quentin, and one or two of our regiments have been badly cut up. Amongst them, I see, were the Musketeers, who were saved at the time when our two boys were holding up the Germans in the trenches. I do hope, Dorothy, that we get some of them here. It would be a splendid thing to nurse men of Harold and Ronald's regiment."

"I have thought of that," Dorothy said. "One of the doctors is going to London this morning, and he might try to get some Musketeers sent here."

Two or three days later a telegram came from the War Office with an intimation that between 30 and 40 wounded men were on their way to the Keep House Hospital. Later on in the afternoon they began to arrive, pretty bad cases most of them, but none of them requiring surgical assistance. For the most part they could manage to get out of the motor ambulance, but there was one of them who had to be lifted into the ward, a cheerful little man with fiery-red hair who apologised profusely for the trouble he was causing.

"Do you know the name of that man?" Nettie asked a patient with his head bound up and his arm in a sling.

"'Course I do, miss," he said. "That's one o' our 'eroes. P'raps you might 'a' 'eard o' Ginger Smiff?"

CHAPTER XX - IN CLOVER

Ginger lay at full length in his bed gazing dreamily at the ceiling and trying to reconstruct his shattered universe and bring the world into proper focus. He had not the least notion where he was, and there was still enough of the casual left in him to render him utterly indifferent so far as that was concerned. At any rate, he was alive, and that was something to go on with. Jut for the moment when he was lifted out of the ambulance a whiff of consciousness had come to him, and he had realised that he was amongst friends. He had grasped the fact, too, that he was entirely out of his element, and that he was in contact with a class of people who had hitherto been outside his social outlook; hence his profuse apologies for the trouble he was causing.

He had been looking into a pair of friendly eyes, blue-grey eyes full of sweetness and sympathy; he had been listening to a voice, very sympathetic; and then gentle hands had lifted him from the Red Cross wagon, and he had been placed in a cool white bed. Then a man was looking down at him, a keen-faced man with a humorous smile and a pair of hands so gentle that Ginger could scarcely feel them. Away somewhere in the distance a voice was speaking, and Ginger rather gathered that he himself was the object of a discussion.

"I think he'll do now," the voice said. "The poor fellow has evidently been in great pain; in fact, he is now, only he is too exhausted to show any restlessness. What did you say? Yes, through the thigh and through the lungs. But he is going on quite all right. I think I'll just give him a touch of morphia to dull the pain, and then all he wants for some hours is complete rest. After that, regular food and careful nursing will represent his cure. I think that is all I can say for the present, Miss Kemp."

The name seemed to strike a familiar chord in Ginger's mind, and in his dreamy mood he wondered where he had heard it before. He did not know that for many hours now that he had been racked with pain, he did not even know whether he was conscious or not, and his brain was asking him questions that he could not answer. Then a hand touched his wrist. There was a prick, as if a needle had stabbed him, and the pain vanished in some heavenly mysterious way that left Ginger like a child who has fallen asleep in the shade on a summer afternoon. He slipped into a kind of heaven, the semi-celestial paradise that morphia brings, especially when it has been administered for the first time. And after that Ginger slept contentedly and sweetly for many hours.

The light was beginning to fail as he came back to himself, still in the same happy condition, so that he lay on his back gazing upwards, and gradually, very gradually, he began to realise the fact that his name was Ginger Smiff, and that he was a soldier of the King, who a week, or a month, back, or perhaps even yesterday, was fighting for his country away in France with his friends about him.

But where was he? And how had all this happened. His mind crept back inch by inch until out of the mist the picture began to grow less muddy and indistinct. Here was Ginger behind Harold Bentley and Ronald Kemp, together with a man called Allen and another called Garton, working their way out of a wood behind a battery of guns and ammunition wagons which had been rescued from a horde of Germans in the neighbourhood of a farmhouse, and, oddly, all of them were wearing the uniforms of German Uhlans; why this was, Ginger could not in the least understand.

Then into the vision came a trench, a battered trench, blown almost out of recognition, and inside it a hundred or so of men in khaki, who crowded round the guns with cheers and yells. And after this, hundreds and hundreds of Germans charging down into the trench, evidently expecting an easy prey, and on the top of this the roar of the guns and shells bursting into the ranks of the foe at almost point-blank range. This seemed to go on hour after hour until the Germans melted away into heaps of blue-grey refuse lying on the open fields, and somebody was saying that it was a narrow squeak, for there were not more than a dozen shells left. Then the vision changed again; the guns had been blown up and dismantled, and a handful of Musketeers in Uhlan uniform were bursting through a German patrol and dashing along a road where someone said that the British rearguard were only a mile or two away. Then it seemed to Ginger that something struck him between the shoulders and he rolled off the horse which he had been riding, and lay there on the hard road looking up at the frosty stars.

Followed a long blank, and then a confused vision of himself lying on a heap of straw in a charcoal burner's hut, with an old man bending over him and holding a bottle to his lips. The man was telling Ginger in broken English that the Musketeers had got clear away, and then he himself had seen them safely into the English lines. After this came a long dream of pain and some delusion as to a cart in which he had been placed and hidden under a thick covering of straw. Then in time he had heard the bugles again and old, familiar voices, and somebody was lifting him into a train. After that the rumble of engines, and the smell of salt water, and now this.

Consciousness was coming back, so that Ginger's eye gradually cleared and he could look around him. He could see a big room, in which were some 20 beds; he could see women moving about, nurses in hospital dress, and every now and then he heard a groan of pain from one of the adjacent beds. One of the nurses attracted his attention. She was tall and slim, with a pleasant smile upon her face; she had grey-blue eyes, and the fading light glistened on her fair hair. On the walls were pictures and panels of silk, here and there, with little ornaments on brackets.

"I'm in 'orspital, I am," Ginger told himself. "'Ope it ain't a German one; not that there's much the matter wif it if it is. But that angel over yonder ain't no German. An' if I ain't seen 'er before, call me a Dutchman. I've seen 'er playin' golf. 'Praps she'll come an' speak ter me presently."

Ginger turned over on one side and coughed. He was pleasantly surprised to find that the exertion gave him no pain. The last time his cough was troublesome it had racked him through and through with a physical anguish that brought out the perspiration all over him. But he was still under the spell of the powerful drug that deadened every physical sense, while it still left his brain clear and active.

A moment or two later the pretty nurse approached Ginger's bedside. She bent over him smiling.

"How are you feeling now?" she asked.

"Much as if I'd stepped straight into 'eaven," Ginger said. "I s'pose they got me all right; not as I remembers anythin' abaht it. 'Ow did I get 'ere, miss?"

"You came here by train," Dorothy said.

"Oh, somewhere in France, am I?"

"As a matter of fact, you are not far from London," Dorothy responded. "Near Harrow, to be correct."

Ginger lay back for a moment or two, trying to grasp the full extent of this miracle.

"Well, I'm dashed," he said. "The last thing I clearly remember is coming dahn in a road off an 'orse. I was the only one they got, and I giv' up meself as done for. I daresay as it'll all come back ter me later on."

CHAPTER XXI - GINGER'S ODYSSEY

Here was something altogether outside Ginger's outlook. He had, of course, expected that the time would come when he would either give up his life for his country or find himself grievously wounded, in which latter case he had been quite prepared to make the best of it and at best lie neglected on a heap of damp straw whilst better men than himself were monopolising the Army Service Corps. That he should have been picked up and waited upon hand and foot as if he had been a person of some importance struck him almost in the light of a joke.

"Strike me," he said, "they must 'ave taken me for a bloomin' orficer. It was that German uniform as done it. I was got up regardless of expense, somethin' between a comic opera major an' a circus rider. An' I expect the army service chaps took me for a German general at least. I wonder if yer 'appens ter know exactly wot I am, miss."

"One of the Musketeers, I think," Dorothy said.

"Well, I'm just that," Ginger replied. "A full-blown private, though when we got cut off from the rest of the battalion the colonel's come ter me an' tells me as I was a sergeant. I dare say I shall get my stripes in time."

"Oh, so you are the man who captured the German machine gun?" Dorothy asked.

"How did yer come ter know that?" Ginger demanded.

Dorothy bit her lip. It was impossible for her to tell Ginger whence her information came, or to discuss that mysterious letter from the front with the man lying there and regarding her with amazement in his eyes.

"'Twaren't anythin'," Ginger said. "Besides, somebody 'ad ter do it. An' if it 'adn't bin me, it ud 'ave bin somebody else. Lor' bless yer, miss, those things 'appen every day out yonder, and we don't think nothin' abaht 'em. Lots o' little things as would mean Victoria Crosses in an ordinary war go on just as regular as we 'as our breakfast, a good deal more regular than we got our breakfast the last fortnight."

Something like illumination had come to Dorothy. Her mind had gone back to the time before Harold and her brother left for France, and she recalled now the amusing story of Ginger and how he came to join the Musketeers.

"I'm sure I can't be mistaken," she said. "You look so different, and yet so familiar."

"I was goin' ter say the same thing abaht you, miss," Ginger replied. "But my mind is in such a muddle that I still don't rightly know whether I'm asleep or not. I'm afraid I shall wake presently an' find as it's all a dream. If it wasn't for that 'orspital dress o' your'n an' I was all right in my head, like, I wouldn't mind making a small bet as you was Miss Kemp, the sister of the man wot made me join the army an' saved me from bein' a loafer fer the rest o' my life. I suppose you don't 'appen ter 'ave a sister, miss?"

"I am Mr. Ronald Kemp's sister," Dorothy said. "And you are the a man I first heard sing 'Tipperary.' Surely you haven't forgotten the recruiting concert we held here?"

Ginger hunched himself up in bed and lay there a few minutes trying to get the whole thing clear in his mind. After all, the miracle had really happened. In some extraordinary way he had been conveyed to England, and by the most amazing good luck found himself amongst friends. And that they were friends in the best sense of the word Ginger did not doubt for a moment. He held out his hand eagerly.

"I shall get it presently," he said. "For three or four months now I've been living in a land of wonders and bloomin' miracles. But this is the absolute limit. It's a rightdown corker. It reminds me of a Drury Lane pantomime, a sort of 'Aladdin' or some of the other 'Arabian Nights.' To think as I should be brought over 'ere an' made such a fuss of by a lidy like you! 'Ow d'you manage it, miss? Did yer 'ave the tip ter look after me particularly, or was it a bit o' blind luck like 'avin' us dream abaht an outsider fer the Derby an' backin' 'im at a 'undred ter one? P'raps you got the tip from yer brother. A rare good friend ter me 'e was. 'E show'd me 'ow ter make a man 'o meself; yus, 'e giv me the charnce over an' over again, though I never 'ad brines enough ter tike it till this war broke aht. An' even then 'e more or less forced me ter do it."

"My brother doesn't even know that you are alive," Dorothy exclaimed. "We had a long letter from him a day or two ago, in which he told us a good deal about your exploits; in fact, he spoke of you in the highest possible way."

"Did 'e really, miss," Ginger said gratefully. "'E always were a kind'earted gentleman. An' aht yonder we was all brothers together. The gentleman who 'ad bin at public schools and Oxford Colleges didn't think no more abaht wot the Sunday pipers calls social distinctions. In the trenches we was just brothers together. There was Mr. Kemp and Mr. Bentley, likewise Mr. Garton and Mr. Allen, and me an' the rest o' my class all sittin' dahn eatin' our grub together as friendly as a litter 'o puppies in a kennel yard. An' only two or three months ago 'arf a dozen of us lot was loafin' abaht the golf clubs dahn Richmond way an' waitin' fer a job from the same gentlemen as is now fightin' side by side wif us with numbers on their shoulder straps and rifles in their 'ands."

"It sounds splendid," Dorothy said. "When you are a little better I should like to hear all about that wonderful retreat, and how your company recovered those guns and fought in the trenches while the rest of the battalion cut their way through to safety. I can't tell you how glad I am, Ginger, that Miss Bentley and myself have had this opportunity to show our gratitude to you for the splendid things you have done."

"That's a big word, isn't it, miss?" Ginger asked.

"What, gratitude? I don't think so. You don't seem to realise exactly what you have done. And it is little by comparison that we women can do. You must understand that this is my brother's house and that we have turned it into a hospital which is being looked after by Miss Bentley and myself and some of my friends. I asked the War Office to send as many Musketeers down here as possible, but when the poor fellows arrived this afternoon I had no idea that we were going to welcome anybody so celebrated as Private Ginger Smith. I know you won't mind my calling you by that name."

"I ain't celebrated," the gratified Ginger grinned. "I ain't no more than an ordinary Tommy doin' 'is little bit fer a shillin' a day. Not as the bob attracted me much. You don't mean ter say as they've bin talkin' abaht me in the pipers, do you? I ain't posin' as no 'ero."

"It is hardly for you to judge," Dorothy said. "At any rate, the public think you are, and I am of the same opinion. When you feel a little stronger and better I am going to get you to tell me the story of the Musketeers and how your company saved the rest of the regiment."

"You're actually goin' ter keep me 'ere fer a bit, miss?" Ginger asked. "Keep me 'ere and 'ave me waited upon by you lidies as if I was one 'o yourselves?"

"We are under the impression that you are," Dorothy said. "And you are going to stay here till you are well enough to go back to the front again."

Ginger lay back, trying to grasp the full meaning of this stupendous promise. He wanted to apologise, to explain how sorry he was to give all this trouble.

"All right, miss," he said helplessly. "I'll try an' tell you to-morrow wot I think, only words don't come easy just fer the minute. An' I'm more tired than wot I thought I was."

CHAPTER XXII - THE NEW REPUBLIC

A naturally strong constitution and a frame hardened and toughened by exposure stood in Ginger's favour, so that from the very first he began to mend. It was his own opinion that the end of a month would see him back in the trenches again, a thing that he longed for with his whole heart and soul. For Ginger had found that he had a vocation in life, and his own proper pride told him that he was no longer a human derelict thrown from pillar to post but a real live asset and respected as such by the state.

At the same time, he was extraordinarily grateful even for the smallest kindness. He could not grasp the reason why these ladies should pay him so much attention. Even if he had been in the same class as themselves, even if he had been brought up amongst them and shared their instincts and traditions, they could not have made more of him. From time to time since he had taken his shilling and enrolled himself as a soldier of the King, he had given occasional stray thoughts to what might happen to him if he were wounded. What the procedure would be in that case he had the vaguest possible notions. He was under the impression that he would be thrown into a tent or a hut somewhere, where he would be left to recover and perhaps occasionally see a doctor who would dress his wounds for him. In the course of his life Ginger had had one or two illnesses, and he had fought through these in some miserable garret or other, more or less looked after by some outcast only a little less wretched than himself. He had not grumbled, for this kind of thing had been his lot and seemed likely to be so for the rest of his natural life. He did not realise that there were thousands and thousands of his own class picked up out of the gutters by the recruiting sergeants and now in process of being moulded into useful citizens.

Therefore Ginger's gratitude knew no bounds. He told himself over and over again that if he had been what he called a bloomin' orficer he could not possibly be any better off. And he was also getting over a certain ferocious shyness which some people might have taken for blatant impudence. But that was the way of his class, though he did not know it himself.

As strength came back to him and he began to sit up in bed, he became more communicative, though as yet he had not told either Dorothy or Nettie the story of the heroic defence that had saved the Musketeers from destruction.

There were others of the Musketeers in the same room, but at first they had been too ill to think of anything. But as they got better and Ginger began to assert himself, there was a good deal of gossip to which two at any rate of the nurses listened with the deepest interest.

Dorothy and Nettie were happy in the work they were doing. They had the satisfaction of feeling that they were doing some real good. The knowledge that they were helping these modest heroes, instead of wasting their time attending lectures or knitting comforts, brought its own reward. They were busy from morning till night, and had little time to think or grieve. They were only two of the many millions of English women whose hearts were full of anxiety just then, and whose eyes were turned eagerly across the seas. But they had found the best panacea for trouble in good and honest work.

There were many men there whom they liked, for they were all grateful and only too eager to show how they appreciated the kindness shown them, but if there was a favourite amongst them it was Ginger beyond all doubt.

It was at the end of the second week that Ginger found himself sitting out in the sun in a bath-chair smoking a cigarette as if, in his own words, he had bought the bloomin' place.

It was a mild, warm morning, bright and sunny, and Ginger was feeling the joy of life coursing through his veins. Nettie established herself in a chair by his side, and Dorothy was not far off, in close attendance on a few more convalescents, all of whom had been in the trenches with Ginger and the two men who occupied so much of the girls' thoughts.

"This is jest great," Ginger said. "If anybody'd told me six mouths ago as I should be sittin' 'ere to-day in this beautiful garden with you two ladies waitin' upon me, I should 'ave laughed. 'Ere we are as large as life an' twice as natural, me wot was the nothin' more than a loafer made as much fuss of as if I'd done something to be proud of."

"And so you have," Nettie smiled. "So you all have. At any rate, we are proud to be here with you. Anybody would be for the matter of that."

"Do you 'ear that, you chaps?" Ginger said turning to his companions. "Why don't you get up an' make a bow to the lidy? There's those three on the seat, miss, grinnin' like a lot o' monkeys an' leavin' me to do all the talkin'."

"Nobody could do it better, Ginger," one of the men on the seat said. "You go on an' we'll listen."

"All right, Joe," Ginger said. "An' 'Arry an' George'll contradict me if I say wot ain't true. Now jest look at those three chaps, miss. They're three o' my recruits. Four months ago they was sellin' pipers in the West End. Three miserable weeds o' chaps as you could 'ave blown away almost. But it was only because they didn't get enough to eat, an' slept most o' the winter out o' doors. An' jest you look at 'em now, though they are wounded and a bit run down. Joe yonder once lived for three days in an outlyin' trench with 'arf a dozen biscuits an' a bottle o' water. An' because there was a man with 'im who was wounded 'e pretended as 'e'd got 'is full rations, an' for the 'ole o' those three odd days Joe never 'ad a mawthful o' nothin'. An' 'e never said a word abaht it ter nobody, an' it was only by accident we found it out."

"Don't you believe a word of it, miss," Joe said blushingly. "Besides, even if it was true, there ain't nothin' in it. I'm used ter that sort o' thing. Many's the time I've gone wifout food for three days when things was slack."

"I think I know whom to believe," Nettie said gently.

"An' then there's George," Ginger went on. "George is the man wot climbed out 'o the trenches one wet night an' brought in three of our wounded from within a few yards 'o a German trench. Brought 'em on 'is back one after another, 'e did. An' that's 'ow 'e got wounded. An' 'e said nothin' abaht it neither. An' 'Arry, I don't jest know wot 'Arry did for the moment. Wot was it, ole man?"

"Blowed if I remember," 'Arry responded.

"Oh, yes, yer do," the man called George exclaimed. "We were short o' food that day, for the Germans 'ad rushed a part of our trenches an' we dare not move till the reserves came up. So 'Arry 'e volunteers ter do wot 'e could, an' 'e sets out in broad daylight with the bullets a-whizzin' around 'im, an' 'e comes back presently with enough to go on with till dark. An' nobody says nuffin' because all these things are in a day's work, if you lidies know wot I mean."

"It all sounds splendid," Dorothy said, "It makes me wish I was a man myself."

"An' I'm jolly glad you're not," Ginger said. "We should not be 'avin' the 'appy times we are if you were. There was a time not so very long ago when I thought lidies was good fer nothin' except ter run abaht in motor cars an' play golf an' go to theatres an' that sort o' thing."

"I am afraid we used to share the same opinion," Dorothy said. "But don't forget that you promised to tell us how your company saved the Musketeers."

CHAPTER XXIII - IN THE VERNACULAR

"There ain't anybody could do it better," George said.

Subdued applause came from the other two.

"Well, I'll do my best," Ginger said. "You must understand, lidies, as we was more or less cut off from the rest of the battalion. Our company was in the advance trenches, an' it was fortunate for us as the Germans in front didn't know jest 'ow weak we was. An' one night the colonel 'e comes to us, an' 'e tells us exactly 'ow it was. When 'e'd finished speakin' we know'd as we was done for. Wot we 'ad to do was to fight to the last man an' give the rest of the battalion a chance to cut their way through an' join the division. We'd used up all our food pretty well, an' there weren't no ammunition left, so we was goin' to rely upon the bayonet. It was all the worse for us, 'cos we was enfiladed on the right by a machine gun which looked like wipin' us aht altogether. Well, we managed by a bit o' good luck to get rid o' that."

"'Ere, stop!" George cried. "None o' that, Ginger. I ain't much good at tellin' a story myself, but I knows when the other chap's tellin' it wrong. An' you promised ter tell these lidies all abaht it. Won't you make 'im tell the truth, miss? God knows wot might 'ave 'appened to us if we 'adn't got rid o' that machine gun."

"It ain't for me to speak o' that," Ginger said hotly. "If you feels as you wants to do a bit o' gassin', I'll trouble you fer another cigarette whilst you take up the tale."

"It's got ter be done, miss," George said as Ginger subsided more or less sulkily into his chair. "Those chaps 'ad worked up that gun to the very edge o' the trench, an' we couldn't 'ave stayed there ten minutes longer. It was too dangerous to call for volunteers, but Ginger 'ere 'e jest 'opped along the top o' the trench into a field o' beetroot where the machine gun was placed. Then 'e crawls along on 'is 'ands an' knees right up under the muzzle o' the gun and upsets it. Then 'e goes for the gunner, and quicker'n I'm tellin' you does 'em in, an' 'e's back again with the gun all in less than five minutes. An' if Ginger says that ain't true, all I can say is 'e's a liar."

"Anybody could 'a' done it," Ginger growled. "It was as easy as fallin' off the top of a 'ouse. You see, I was quite 'idden under that beetroot, an' all I 'ad to do when I'd worked myself up under the gun was to jest grab for it an' upset the whole bag o' tricks. You never see three blokes so astonished in yer life. Before they could do anything I was on top o' them, an' you can guess the rest. An' now p'raps I can get on with my story without any more vulgar interruptions."

"I only wanted to 'ave it right," George protested. "As the story's got to be told, there's no reason to leave all the best parts of it out. There was some bloomin' fine things done that night. But when we come to talk it over afterwards amongst ourselves, we give our vote to Ginger an' that little business with the machine gun."

"You're wrong there, ole man," Ginger said modestly. "To my mind, the best bit o' work was with that German sentry. I mean when we was makin' our way into the wood where the guns was 'idden. You see, it was like this miss. We come to a place where we 'ad to cross a fence and get into a wood. It wouldn't 'ave bin difficult in the ordinary way, but there 'appened to be a couple o' sentries there, and we couldn't get another yard till they was out o' the way. O' course, we could 'a shot 'em easily enough, for they was almost at the muzzles of our rifles. But that would never 'ave done. As it 'appens, there was no Germans in earshot, except those two, but we wasn't expected to know that, an' we didn't want the 'ole o' the German army down upon us. So we jest stopped an' 'ad a bit o' a confab, an' Mr. Kemp—that's your brother, miss—'e thought o' a little plan. You see, there was not more than twenty of us altogether, an' we crept out o' the trenches lookin' for our captured ammunition wagon an' the field guns that came in so useful later on, and those German sentries absolutely blocked the way so far as we was concerned. Did I tell you as we was a kind o' forlorn 'ope? There was only about a score o' us altogether. Well, we 'ad to do in them sentries, and Mr. Kemp 'e asks if there is anybody amongst us as can patter the German lingo. An' up gets a chap named Garton, wot's a merchant in the city in peace time, an' says 'e can speak German a treat. Mr. Garton, 'e's rather a fat chap, a jolly-lookin' man, a sort as you'd never think could kill a fly in the ordinary way. But 'e was quite ready, because, you see, 'e could speak the language, 'avin' spent some years in Germany when 'e was a boy. The gime was fer 'im to crawl up the fence an' pretend as 'e was a' wounded German lookin' fer 'is friends. 'E was to arsk them to 'elp 'im over the fence, an 'e 'ad a chap on either side o' 'im ready to do in them sentries as soon as ever they put out their 'ands to 'elp their wounded comrade, as they thought 'e was. We all 'eld our breff for a minute, but it come off all right, an' a minute or two later we was in the wood on the track o' the guns.

"Oh, we found them, too, an' the ammunition, also our cartridges, and we found something better'n that. By a bit o' sheer good luck we blundered right into a lot o' prisoners wot turned out to be our own gunners, and then up comes an ole Frenchy 'oo told us as 'is farm'ouse was full o' German officers, Uhlans they was, with a few troopers waitin' on them. 'E was a proper ole chap was that farmer, wot 'ad fought in the Franco-Prussian War, 'an' 'e gave us a hinvite ter go along o' 'im and drop in jest as those chaps was sittin' dahn ter supper. Well, miss, I don't mind tellin' you as the suggestion of a good feed on roast chicken and duck sort o' appealed to us, considering as we was livin' on abaht two biscuits a day an' 'arf a pint o' water. So far as we could gather, there wasn't any Germans within three miles. So we turns up at the farmhouse, jest as that little lot were openin' their wine and carvin' the ducks, and you never see such a 'Ho wot a surprise in your life' as we marched into that kitchen through two doors. They was plucky enough, I will say that for them, but we took 'em quite unawares, an' in less time than it takes to tell we 'ad 'em out in the farmyard, an' buried 'em, after which we ate their supper an' drank their wine.

"Well, I'm gettin' near to the end o' my story now. Long before daylight we was back in the trenches with those guns of ours, an' jolly useful they came in. All the next day we mowed the Germans down with 'em till we 'adn't got any shells left, and then we togged ourselves out in the Uhlans' uniforms an' mounted the horses we 'ad taken from them, an' made our way to the rear. We knew pretty well where we should run into the British again, an' for 'arf a mile or more we rode through the German lines without bein' challenged. You see, they took us for some o' themselves. Then something happened, I don't know quite wot it was, but I suppose they smelt a rat, an' the next thing I remember was a volley from their rifles; but it was too late. Most of us were through by that time. I may be wrong, but I don't think they got anybody but me, an' I managed to stick on to my 'orse for a few 'undred yards before I collapsed. Afterwards, I believe, an old peasant picked me up, an' I don't recollect anything more till I come to myself 'ere, an' you, miss, was lookin' after us as if I'd been yer own brother. An' that's 'ow we managed to save the Musketeers from being wiped out. An' I'm afraid it isn't much of a story after all, is it, miss?"

Dorothy made no reply for a moment or two. It was the sheer simplicity of Ginger's story and the modesty of it that appealed to her more than anything else.

CHAPTER XXIV - NEWS FROM THE FRONT

The days were going on. Already the hospital at the Keep House had lost some of its wounded and others had taken their place. Ginger and his own friends still remained, though they were getting strong now, and looking forward to rejoining their comrades in the trenches. For some little time now the story of the retreat of the Musketeers and how they had been saved by a handful of their own regiment had been public property, and Ginger and the rest of them were in a fair way to be made much of; but they resolutely declined to regard their accomplishment as anything out of the common, and though more than one resolute journalist presented himself at the Keep House, Ginger resolutely declined to see him or open his mouth on the subject.

"It ain't nothin' ter make a fuss abaht," he said. "Now, what is it that little man in the straw 'at and white spats wants me to do? 'Ave I got ter make a speech and tell 'im all abaht it? It ain't anybody's business but our own. Wot do you think, chaps?"

"You'd better see 'im and arsk 'im if 'e'd like ter come back wiv us," George smiled. "'E evidently tikes yer fer a celebrity. But I shouldn't wonder if 'e's come along with an invitation for the lot of us to do a turn at the 'alls. 'Ow Ginger an' 'is pals 'eld up the German Army, and wot Bill Kaiser 'ad ter say abaht it. Tell 'im if that's 'is gime we've already booked engiements to appear in the leadin' music 'alls at a thousand quid a week, includin' beer."

But Ginger was in no mood just then to see the humour of the situation. He wanted to know why people came bothering him in this way. He was perfectly happy and comfortable, and all he wanted to do was to get well so that he could be in the firing line once more. Nettie listened absently to this suggestion on the part of George and the rest, for the post had just come in bringing a batch of letters for Dorothy and herself, amongst them being two from her brother and Ronald Kemp, and she was naturally anxious to see what they had to say. For these were the first letters which had come through since the boys had cut their way back to the regiment, and so far the girls had had to be content with field post cards.

There was a good deal on the subject of Ginger in Harold's letter to Dorothy.

"I have only just heard," he said, "about your hospital scheme. I have talked it over with Ronald, and we both think it absolutely splendid. So far as I can see we shall lack nothing in the way of comforts this winter, and you are much better employed nursing the soldiers than in knitting socks, which of course ought to be organised labour in the hands of women who are accustomed to that kind of thing. But I need not go into that. The hospital scheme is the thing, and you two girls are doing as much good as if you were out here fighting. Since I began to write this letter one of our subalterns who has been home on short leave has turned up, and he tells me that he has been staying in your neighbourhood and that your patients mostly consist of Musketeers. In that case, I expect you have a man called Ginger Smith amongst them. If so, you'll recollect him. He was the man who did so well at that recruiting meeting we had. You will remember that Ronnie enlisted him out of the ranks of the Richmond caddies. It was one of the best day's work he ever did, for Ginger is a real good chap and a born soldier. He is always cheerful and always happy, and he has a big hold over his mates. In fact, I don't see how we could possibly have saved the battalion and cut our way through without him. Let me tell you there were some pretty big things done in those days; in fact, it would take me a week to tell you all about it. It's no use asking Ginger, he'll only make fun of the whole thing, and pretend that he did nothing. But if you get hold of some of the other chaps you won't find them so reticent, especially if Ginger doesn't happen to be within hearing. Of course, he will never get a commission or anything of that kind, because he's not that type of man, as you never can get him to take anything seriously. But probably some day, when he tones down a bit, he will make a good sergeant major, or perhaps a quartermaster. I want you to keep a special eye upon Ginger, and send him back as soon as possible."

There were other letters besides this, one of them in an official envelope that caused Dorothy to gasp when she read it. It came from the secretary of a very exalted personage, and intimated that the great Person in question and his Consort would like to pay a short visit to the Keep House hospital and say a few words to the wounded. This was in the earlier days of the war when private hospitals were more or less of a novelty, so that the venture that Dorothy and Nettie were running was still something rather out of the common.

"What shall we do about it?" Nettie asked.

"I don't see there is anything to do about it," Dorothy replied. "This suggestion is in the nature of a command, and as our distinguished guests have fixed their own time, the day after tomorrow, all we can do is to write to the Palace and say that we shall be honoured by the visit."

Two days later the Royal party presented themselves at the Keep House. Much to the surprise of the girls, they came in a motor just like any Great Man and Great Lady, the Personage in khaki and the Lady as simply dressed as if she were just doing a morning's shopping. With them were two staff officers, distinguished generals in their day, and beyond this there was nothing to attract the least attention. After the first moment the girls were entirely at their ease, for the Royal visitors shook hands with them in the most simple, unaffected way and congratulated them upon the fine work they were doing. Then they proceeded to go over the house and into the ward where the wounded were prepared for their coming.

The Great Man seemed to know exactly what to say and do; he had heard all about Ginger's exploit, and he and the Great Lady sat down by the wounded hero's bedside and chatted to him in a way that, as Ginger said afterwards, made him feel that he had known them all his life. But he was obstinately shy on the subject of his own exploit, and could not be brought to say anything about it. It was only by judicious promptings from the neighbouring beds that the distinguished questioner elicited the story of the machine gun and of how Ginger's conduct on that occasion had saved the whole of the company. For the best part of an hour the Royal party stayed there, and everybody was sorry when they took their leave, which they did after congratulating the girls upon the perfection of their arrangements.

"I suppose we can still speak to you, Ginger, can't we?" George said when at length the room was quiet again. "When is it as you're goin' to put in a weekend at the Palace?"

"'Ere, not so much of it," Ginger said. "Anybody'd think to hear you chaps talk as I'd never spoken to Royalty before. It's the first time as I ever shook 'ands with the King and I don't suppose I ever shall again. But I ain't givin' myself frills, because 'e did the same wiv all of us. An' I don't mind tellin' you as

I've caddied for Royalty down at Richmond more than once. But I wasn't called anything but caddie in those days, an' I never expected as a King would tike me by the hand an' call me sargeant and say I was a credit to me country. This 'as bin a big day fer us, an' we ain't goin' ter forget it. We can laugh at it, but it's something I'll be proud of to my dyin' day. Wot yer grinnin' at? You know jolly well you're as proud as I am. An' now wot's all this talk about goin' to the football match this afternoon?"

CHAPTER XXV - PLAIN WORDS

It happened to be Saturday afternoon, and a few miles away two of the leading clubs in the first division of the League were meeting to decide which of them should go into the next round of the Association cup. There was not a man in the Keep House who was not anxious to be present, and perhaps half a dozen of them were well enough to go. They were as anxious to see the match as if they had been a lot of boys, and they had been talking about it wistfully for the last few days.

At first it had not occurred to either Dorothy or Nettie that it was in their power to give Ginger and some of the other convalescents a real treat. Then the girls suddenly discovered that a chance had come to do so.

"I don't see why they shouldn't go," Dorothy said. "This war puts everything else out of one's head. I had quite forgotten that I am a bit of an enthusiast over football myself. Two or three years ago Ronald used to play for a league club, and when the match was near London I generally went. I found out this morning how keen some of our men are to see the game, and telephoned for half a dozen stand tickets and they have just come. We will take six of them in two of the cars, so you had better go and tell Ginger all about it. There is no occasion to leave here before two o'clock."

Nettie walked into the ward where the men were having their dinner and introduced the subject of the League match.

"I am going with Miss Kemp," she said.

Ginger's eyes gleamed and he caught his breath.

"Wish I was goin' along," he said. "There's George and 'Arry an' one or two more as would give a bit to go an' cheer on the Rangers. But wot's the good o' thinkin' abaht that?"

"We won't think about it," Nettie smiled; "We'll go. I've been discussing the matter with the doctor, and he has given his permission for us to take six of you. The car will be at the door in about a quarter of an hour."

"What d'you think o' that," Ginger said when Nettie had departed. "Nothin' don't seem ter be too much trouble where we're concerned. They ain't just lidies, they're angels as ain't 'appy unless they're doin' something for us chaps. An' we're goin' in style, too, don't forget it. We're goin' in our car like regular toffs, an' we shall sit on the grandstand away from all the common lot. Who wouldn't be a soldier?"

On the whole it was an afternoon to be remembered. As Ginger had prophesied they occupied seats in the centre of the grandstand, conspicuous in their blue uniforms; they were the only wounded present, for it was still in the comparatively early days of the war and so far the broken British had been seen little or nothing of in their own country, so they came in for a good deal of embarrassing attention which tried Ginger sorely.

"It's a pity as we didn't disguise ourselves," he growled. "In these blessed blue togs I feel as if I was a monkey on a stick. Sort o' cheap swank, eh?"

But Ginger and his companions forgot all that presently in the excitement of the play. For three-quarters of an hour, until the interval, they followed the game breathlessly, and then Ginger began to take an interest in the crowd.

"They're a queer lot, ain't they," he said. "There must be fifteen thousand here altogether, an' not a tenth o' them in uniform. Blimme, wot're they thinkin' abaht? I could form the best part of an Army Corps out o' the chaps loafin' abaht 'ere with cigarettes in the corners o' their mawths whilst we're doin' our bit over yonder. It's a bit o' a shock ter me, that's wot it is. I thought the bloomin' ole country'd woke up, but it seems to me that it ain't. These chaps 'ere don't seem to realise wot we're up against. I ain't got much use fer the gab, but if some body don't 'old me down I'll 'ave ter get up presently and address the meetin'."

A keen-eyed man next to Ginger turned to him eagerly.

"Would you like to do it?" he asked. "I understand that during the interval the member for the division is going to make an appeal for recruits from the stand. That's him coming along now. In my opinion, if one of you chaps got up and said a few words, it would do more good than an address from any number of members of Parliament."

Ginger growled something and subsided into silence as the little procession advanced to the front of the stand, preceded by a band of pipers. They took up their place just in front of Ginger and his companions, and the member of Parliament began to speak. He meant well enough, and he spoke earnestly enough, but there was not the right ring about it. He was trite and commonplace, full of platitudes, and when he had finished and invited recruits to step forward there was no response and hardly a cheer from the grandstand. Then the speaker smiled feebly and invited further comment.

"Get up and say a bit, Ginger," George said.

Ginger hung back for a moment, growling to himself, and then he rose to his feet; he swept the ring of young active men with a contemptuous eye; he was full of bitterness against those young fellows who seemed to have only one single thought, and that for the game, in exclusion to everything else.

"I'd like to say a few words," he began. "I ain't no speaker like the bloke—I mean the gentleman—as has just sat down; I'm just a Tommy I am, one o' the Muskekteers wot did that little bit for the flag when we was fallin' back before six 'undred thousand Germans. Try an' think o' that. Six 'undred thousand of them. More than double the size o' the Regular British Army when it's on a war footin'. An' when you chaps 'ave just bitten that bit off an' swallowed it, try an' realise as the six 'undred thousand Germans I'm talkin' abaht is only a tenth part o' wot the Germans 'ave got in the field. You sits quietly at 'ome 'ere, an' you pats yerself on the back becorse ye've got three 'undred thousand men out yonder as' you goes abaht shoutin' Rule Britannia as if the whole bloomin' thing was over. And don't you get imagin' as one British soldier's as good as ten Germans, 'cos they ain't. I ain't sayin' nothing abaht their manners and their customs, which is disgustin', but they can fight an' don't you forget it. Wot's goin' to become of us if all you chaps stays at 'ome watchin' football matches an' spendin' yer evenins in picture palaces. That ain't the way to beat the Germans, you can take it from me. An' now listen—"

Very simply, and with a rugged eloquence that appealed to the hearts of the crowd, Ginger told the story of the Musketeers, keeping back his own part and mentioned no names. But presently some one in the crowd seemed to guess who the speaker was, and as the name ran from lip to lip there was a wild outburst of cheering, far louder than anything that had followed during the time of play. There was no forensic agility about Ginger's effort, but it came straight from the lips of a man who had suffered himself and who knew what war meant. He dropped into his seat presently, hot and breathless, and for some reason a little ashamed of himself. But his words had not been wasted, for when the recruiting sergeant in front of that stand asked for a practical response to Ginger's appeal there was a rush to come forward, and somebody announced that this had been so far the most successful campaign on any football field in London.

"Anybody could 'ave done that," Ginger said. "The chap as spoke first didn't understand. Wot's 'e know abaht war? 'E's never seen any of it. I 'ope you didn't mind, miss?"

"It was splendid," Dorothy said. "We shall have to send you round the country doing this sort of thing."

CHAPTER XXVI - THE OLD SPIRIT

The philosophy of Ginger is, generally speaking, the philosophy of the British Army, and it is this spirit that helped largely to break down the conspiracy which has been preparing on the other side of the Rhine for the last forty years. Our army in Flanders may not be entirely composed of Gingers; it may largely lack the saving sense of humour, but the dogged spirit and indomitable will are there, and will be until the great peace is signed in Berlin.

The British public has never realised, and probably never will realise, the deadly peril of the first few weeks of the campaign in the west. We were a nation caught absolutely unprepared, and much the same thing can be said with regard to the French—an amazing thing concerning the warnings they have had—but there were a few people in Europe last August who fully appreciated the situation. In the early days at Liege it began to appear as if the gallant little Belgians would be able to hold up the German hosts long enough to give England and France an opportunity of saving the situation. The Germans perished by the thousand, but they were nothing daunted and once Liege was passed they overran Belgium like a plague of locusts. General French's army of less than a hundred thousand men was forced back from Mons on August 23, and for a few days the retreat threatened to degenerate into a disorderly rout. From some cause which will probably never become known, the French supports and reinforcements failed to materialise, and the struggle degenerated into a soldiers' battle the like of which has never been seen since the historic field of Inkermann. A fortnight later, on September 6, the battered and bruised British army halted to the east of Paris, prepared to take part in the siege of the French capital. Just for a moment it looked as if the fall of Paris was certain. The Germans, under von Kluck, were actually in sight of the forts, and they boasted that within a week they would be inside.

The wonder is that any British army was left at all. For up to a brief breathing spell when the British army moved from its position on the Aisne to fresh quarters farther west, it had been fighting desperately day by day and hour by hour for the best part of two months.

To begin with, there had been the onslaught at Mons where the comparatively small British force, not numbering more than two army corps altogether found itself attacked by a hundred and sixty thousand of the foe magnificently armed and equipped in every branch of the service, and flushed besides with what they regarded as sure and certain victory. In addition to this, General French with Generals Smith-Dorrien and Haig found themselves outflanked on the left by another army corps. This discovery was followed by four days of stubborn retreat the like of which perhaps the world has never seen. It was as if all hell had been let loose, as if every German soldier had been not only a fighting unit but also supported with a heavy gun of some sort. Worn out and harassed and half dead with fatigue, the gallant British force slept when they could, when the roar of the guns and the bursting shells allowed them. They were so many Wellingtons praying as that great soldier prayed at Waterloo for Blucher or night. Day by day the massed German lines four deep were thrust on headlong and with an utter disregard for life by their own officers, only to be mown down again and again by rifle and machine gun fire until the retreating British were worn out by sheer slaughter.

But this stubborn defence was not wasted. For in it men and officers fought side by side as if they had been brothers. For the time being all distinctions were thrown on one side, and each fought with one single object, the honour of the flag.

But it was impossible that the fight should continue at this high pressure, and even the oncoming Germans had had nearly enough. What we lost in that terrible conflict we know by this time; what it cost the Germans will probably never be disclosed. Not for the first time they had been taught that attack in mass formation can be over-costly in the face of machine guns and modern rifle fire. Outside Liege they had left over sixty thousand of the flower of the German army, and of the famous Bradenburg, or Iron, division only a handful of men was left. So it came about that even against these fearful odds the British army fought them to a standstill at the end of four days, and the Germans could do little or nothing for the moment, though they were as four to one. It was this precious breathing space that enabled French's men to pull themselves together and continue the retreat, which had now become merely strategic, at the cost of a comparatively small number of rearguard actions.

It was well for us that the two army corps under General French and his lieutenants were composed of men who had learnt the art of battle in the field. For the most part they were troops who had followed the flag to Pretoria or had won their laurels in Indian Frontier campaigns. They were, as a matter of fact, the only soldiers so far who had ever seen the game played in earnest. They were disposed to resent this continuous retreat to the gates of Paris, for tired as they were, they were still eager to be up and doing and to push the Germans back to their original line. No one recognised this spirit better than General French himself. He knew what he had to deal with; he had had many of these men under him before; he went amongst them as they lay tired and weary by the roadside and promised that their time should come later on; he mingled freely with his troops, and he was so considerate of them that he would not even allow them to rise to the salute. And so until September 6 it was a case of stubbornly retiring on Paris; the same ruthless slaughter went on until French finally called a halt, and on the night of September 6 the British army had passed in sight of Paris and halted to the southeast of the capital, in what looked perilously like a final stand.

It was a black and bitter time for the leaders of the British army. They alone knew what the peril was, but it would have been all the same to Tommy had he been taken into the counsel of his leaders. He had no thought of defeat or surrender; he had cut his way through the best part of a German army corps, and though whole regiments had been practically wiped out, the fine old spirit was still undamped.

Yet certain staff officers admitted that they could see no way out of the darkness, and that all they could hope for was a good position for a last stand and a final opportunity for making the Germans pay as dearly as possible for the capture of Paris.

But even this was not the worst. On the night of this historic September 6 Sir John French and the leaders under him lay down to sleep, only to be awakened an hour later by a dispatch rider from the lines, who brought news that a German force to the north had joined hands with a new army corps of Bavarians which had appeared like a dream from somewhere to the east of the lines. If this dread news were true, the British were cut off entirely from the French army, and there could only be one end. Before morning the fresh avalanche would be unloosened and the Kaiser's dream of walking over the British army would be realised. What were the British leaders to do?

CHAPTER XXVII - LIGHT IN THE DARKNESS

This was the problem that faced the supreme commander of the British Expeditionary Force and his lieutenants, Smith-Dorrien and Haig. What they resolved upon we may know when the history of the great fight comes to be written by those in a position to know. So far as we can tell there was no fighting the next day, though the British were in hourly expectation of it, but eyewitnesses say that during the morning there was a strange slackness and want of cohesion in the German attack, and suddenly the news spread that von Kluck had turned his front facing east and was in full retreat from Paris. This was the welcome information that one after another of the aviators brought to Headquarters. Then gradually it leaked out that Joffre had masked a whole army to the east of Paris, with which, incredible as it may seem, von Kluck and his army were almost in touch before they were even aware of its existence. It was almost beyond credence that the German spy system should have broken down so badly just when its information would have been of the utmost value. And thus almost in the twinkling of an eye, the peril which had menaced the existence of the British army resolved itself into the promise of annihilation for the forces of von Kluck. Had he remained in ignorance of his danger for a few hours longer a good deal of recent history would have been very different.

But there was no getting away from the fact that the enemy was in full retreat all along the line, and that for the moment at any rate the menace to France and Paris was lifted. Here was French's chance, and he took it without the slightest hesitation. He had promised his men a fight under conditions fairly favourable to them, and now he struck with all his might. It looked as if the retreat from Mons was about to be followed by a big advance along the same lines. At the same moment the French army at Paris was moving up against von Kluck's rearguard—moved up not in the ordinary way by forced marches, but much as the average man finds his way to a railway station. It was an army moving in taxi-cabs and motor-cars, and moving so swiftly that within five days the Germans were pushed back from the gates of Paris across the strong lines of the Marne, right up to the Aisne, and from that day the reconquered plains of France have seen nothing of them.

German strategy had suffered much to gratify the pride of the madman who is responsible for plunging a whole world into a sea of blood. One of the most useful allies our armies in the west ever had was Kaiser Wilhelm himself.

The western army of von Kluck that swept across France and pushed on Paris until Uhlans that fell were buried within Paris city limits, was never intended by the Kaiser to take Paris. This is why it lingered and why there was that amazing slackening in the attack that General French noticed in the morning of

September 7. It was the army of the Crown Prince that was intended to march triumphantly through the streets of Paris and accept the surrender of the citizens. Von Kluck was to wipe out and pulverise the French and English in front of him, and then to deploy to the left and join the Crown Prince's army at a point somewhere between Rheims and Paris. As soon as this was done the rest of the programme would only be a matter of time.

And this is just where pride had its fall. It has always been assumed, for some reason or other, that every German leader, from the Kaiser downwards, is a heaven-born strategist. But military genius is no exclusive privilege of crowned heads and their offspring, and it has been made clear that the Kaiser's heir is indebted for none to his birth; he stands revealed as a feather-headed youth with no military capacity whatever, and since the first weeks of the war he has never been heard of.

But be that as it may, there was no joining up between von Kluck and the army of the Crown Prince. It does not follow that, from the German point of view, von Kluck made a mistake at all. Probably he worked everything out to the letter, probably he was outside the gates of Paris at the very moment appointed by the Supreme Command. But something went wrong with the Crown Prince's army, owing, possibly, to the fact that the arrogant German takes no account of what the enemy is doing, preferring to ignore him as if he had no existence.

It is pretty certain too that the German General Staff entirely underrated the power of the British army; at any rate, that is the theory entertained in France of von Kluck's madness in ignoring or being ignorant of the fact that he was leaving a really strong army on his flank.

General French realised the position. He struck at von Kluck with all his force, and at once the whole position was changed. A few hours before the British appeared to be in deadly peril, and Paris at the mercy of the foe. Now the British backed up by the army of Paris, thrust rapidly forward, smashing the foe as they went, and simultaneously the entire French line, right away from Basle as far as Paris, using the Vosges as a pivot, moved up the whole of its reserves and commenced a general attack. This new thrust fell heavily upon the front of the Crown Prince's army and threatened to roll up his left flank. There was no help for it now. Von Kluck fell back with a hastiness that almost amounted to panic, and in three days his army was practically wiped out at any rate for offensive purposes. In the face of this disaster it was impossible for the Crown Prince to make any impressive show, and so in his turn he fell back with his supporting army to the line of the Aisne.

The 7th September saw the beginning of the siege of Germany. It will be a long siege yet; months will probably pass before the Kaiser's hosts are flung back bruised and bleeding across the Rhine, and many months more before the Russian forces have set their faces steadily in the direction of Berlin; but, be the time long or short, the moment that French and his gallant little army turned on von Kluck and sent him reeling back across the Aisne was the moment in which the downfall of Germany began.

On September 12, only five days later, the British force had recovered all the lost ground as far as Rheims; and there they waited and rested for the best part of a fortnight while the French were asserting themselves and pushing back the Crown Prince's army to the rear of Verdun. Within a week or two the long line from Flanders to the Swiss Frontier, some four hundred miles together, was locked securely against the Germans, and has been locked ever since. The Germans settled down more or less permanently to defensive tactics and the British army was free for good work elsewhere. It was on October 4 or 5 that Sir John French's army quietly faded out of France, and settled down in Flanders.

It was about this same time that Ginger and his friends said good-bye to the Keep House and went back to what was left of their regiment. The British force had now begun to move secretly up to the north, having exchanged trenches with the French higher up the line in the neighbourhood of La Bassee. On the whole they were not sorry to move, for this was their first relief from almost continuous fighting for the best part of two months. It was a masterly move, carried out so perfectly under the direction of Major-General Robertson that the Germans had no idea of what was taking place until the first of their prisoners began to fall into our hands. A Bavarian captain picked up wounded near La Bassee could hardly believe his eyes.

"I cannot understand it," he said. "We were under the impression that we were fighting French Territorials. Not a soul of us but what thought the British were quite thirty miles away. It is a miracle."

But so far the British had done their work, and when things slackened halfway along the line it began to dawn upon the German General Staff that the Great Adventure had failed. The Kaiser and his associates had started out on August 4 with a cut-and-dried time-table that was the result of something like forty years' scheming and planning. Year in and year out it had been cut and polished and studied till its authors could see no flaw in it anywhere. To accomplish it, strategic railways had been built not only in Germany but with German capital in Belgium as well. At various points depots had been established for the mobilisation of troops and rapid movement of immense stores both of food and artillery. When Germany launched her thunderbolt on August 4 it seemed to her leaders that nothing had been forgotten.

They knew perfectly well that France was not ready, that Great Britain had been lulled into a sense of false security, and that Russia was wholly unsuspicious. It did not look a very difficult matter, therefore, to keep to the time-table. One after the other the frontier fortresses were to be overrun, and within the month Paris would be at the feet of the foe. After that a speedy peace with the French would be concluded, and then a rapid series of crushing blows on the eastern frontier would serve to convince Russia of the hopelessness of invasion.

It was a splendid scheme, on paper, but it entirely failed to make provision for what the other fellow might do. It failed to take into account the entry of Britain into the war; it failed to anticipate that wonderful mobilisation of the British navy which drove the German fleet back to the Kiel Canal where, with the exception of a swaggering flourish or two, always ending in disaster, it has remained ever since; it failed to take into account the misunderstanding which kept von Kluck's and the Crown Prince's armies apart; it failed to forecast the movements of the great force that Joffre had gathered together behind Paris; and, worse than all, it failed to take into account the amazing stubbornness and stupendous fighting qualities of the British army. Never in the history of the nation has the British soldier given such an account of himself as he did during the retreat from Mons and the subsequent advance that threw the foe headlong back across the Marne.

In that moment the Great Adventure was broken.

Just for the moment the British work was done. But the qualities of French's men had been duly appreciated by our allies; their patience and stubbornness was an asset beyond price, and it was to them that Joffre looked to hold back the great War Cloud that threatened to burst in the north. For by this time von Kluck had recovered from the lightning thrust that had pushed him and his supporters back to the Aisne. He had made up his losses and filled up his gaps, and by the middle of October was a power to be reckoned with. It was apparent that the Germans had given up thought of forcing their way to Paris by way of Rheims and Verdun, but there was still a wide path open to them north of La Bassee, and it was 'up to' the Kaiser to show his people that the fall of Paris was a secondary consideration for the moment, and that the first one was an irresistible advance through Belgium via Dunkirk to Calais. The German public, therefore, were fed with amazing tales of an invasion of England from the north French coast, and the date when the Prussians would march through London was published in the Berlin papers.

The danger was a real one, moreover, for between La Bassee and the sea, for a distance of over fifty miles, the road lay actually open to Calais. There was nothing between the German hosts and the great invasion but the comparatively small force of the gallant Belgians. It was only the fact that Antwerp had not fallen that restrained the German onslaught. So far as the foe could see, the road was an open and an easy one. And to add to the difficulties of the allies, on October 8 Antwerp fell so suddenly and unexpectedly that a division of British troops commanded by General Rawlinson, and sent to aid the Belgians in defending the outer forts, could not arrive until the Germans were in a position to build in their huge siege guns and thus render the defence of the forts a military impossibility. All that General Rawlinson could do was to join up with what was left of the Belgian army and retreat with them along the coast beyond Zeebrugge and Ostend. It was here that the Belgians took up their final position on the Yser, which they have defended ever since with a gallantry and tenacity beyond all praise. Then General Rawlinson joined forces with them on their right, and cautiously felt his way along the left as far as Ypres.

And here it was that Ginger and the rest came once more in contact with their old companions. They came up in the pouring rain into the wet and muddy trenches, knee deep or more in water, and there they were destined to remain for many weary months, making history as remarkable in its way as the history they made on the banks of the Marne. It was as if they had encamped in the tributary of some small river. A sea of mud was everywhere, a blank and gloomy outlook, but drab as it was, nothing could repress the spirits of the British soldier.

"I suppose this is wot you call 'ome sweet 'ome?" Ginger said as he and his companions waded into the filth and surveyed their comrades wet and muddy and grimy beyond description. "Bit of a change, boys, ain't it? I'd like to know 'ow long this gime's likely to go on."

A little while later Kemp and Bentley appeared.

"So you're all back again," Bentley said. "Well, we can do with you still. So far as I can understand, we shall not be allowed to go to sleep here. They seem to think that the Germans are going to try and force their way through along this route to Paris, taking Calais by the way. You look as if you'd had a good time over there in England."

"Good time ain't no word for it," Ginger said. "We was treated as if we'd been so many princes. You don't know how good those young lidies was to us. But we're not sorry to get back again, an' that's a fact."

"We can do with every man," Kemp said. "It isn't always as dull as this, as you will find before long."

The danger was even greater than the troops in the trenches anticipated, for this time the Germans were not hurrying matters. They had learnt a lesson from the wild dash on Paris, and had gained a wholesome respect for the striking power of the British army. But they had the men ready, which in those early days could not have been said of either the English or French, and it was only a matter of collecting them together, sufficiently supported with the requisite artillery and, cavalry, though so far the latter arm of the German service had not played a brilliant part in the campaign.

It was the French who gave their Allies the first intimation of the great coming strife and incidentally conveyed to Paris and London certain news that sent a chill down the spine of the authorities.

About the middle of October the French official communique reported that dense masses of cavalry had appeared on the Tourcoing-Armentieres road, screening an important new force of the enemy. The news was ominous, though so far it had not been confirmed by the French and British airmen. But there was no question as to its truth, and before long Sir John French realised that he was up against a force quite six times his own strength. Then the foe began to put pressure on the British trenches, keeping up the attack night and day until gradually the British were forced to take new ground. For two nights and the best part of three days the Musketeers held on as doggedly to that muddy ditch as if they loved every inch of it; they fought on, short of ammunition and practically without food, till very reluctantly the order was given to retire, and what was left of the regiment found themselves not far from Ypres in the ruins of a farmhouse.

It was dry here at any rate, with straw to lie on, and for the first time for many hours the men tasted food. But that they could remain there they did not believe for a moment. At dark they were rushed again, but through the night they clung tenaciously to their cover, aided by half a dozen machine guns which Bentley had brought up at a great risk to himself; by means of these they forced the Germans back, and when the raw daylight came they were still in possession of the farmhouse.

Every man had distinguished himself in some way or other; every man had done his best, and the casualties had been very few. Not once had the Germans got inside the outer walls, and hundreds of their dead lay on the field.

"Blimme, but those Bavarians are 'ot stuff," Ginger said, as he threw himself down exhausted on a heap of straw. "I used to 'ave an idea as one Englishman was worth ten Germans, but I've got to change me mind. I suppose it's no use 'opin' to get a bit o' breakfast. It seems abaht a week since I 'ad any food. An' you never know when you're well off. I was fairly fed up with that trench of ours, but we did manage to get our grub fairly regular there."

"You be thankful as you're alive, Ginger," George said. "Don't always be thinkin' abaht your inside."

"I don't see as there's any 'arm in thinkin' abaht it," Ginger said. "An' thinkin' don't keep you from 'avin' your breakfast. Anybody got a fag?"

But apparently not a man amongst them had so much as a cigarette. They were cut off from the rest there, and as far as they knew were in touch with no other regiment. At any moment the attack might break out again and, tired and worn out as they were, they would have to fight for their lives without the slightest chance of support from outside. They were ravenously hungry, too, and unless they had food of some kind, would be almost unable to meet a further attack.

Something as near kin to despair as a British soldier ever permits himself to feel was beginning to settle down upon them when from outside came the sound of feet and the old barn was filled with reinforcements. They had forced their way through the German trench on the right, taking many prisoners, and now they had swung round the ruins with a battery or two of machine guns, for the Musketeers had fallen back to a point of vantage and this the reinforcements had been told to hold at all costs. A cheer greeted their appearance.

"They're our old friends the 55th Fusiliers," Ginger cried. "The same chaps as fought alongside us that night when we turned back from Mons. I wonder if they've brought anything with 'em."

"How are you lads off for food?" a subaltern asked.

"Search us, sir," Ginger said. "We've almost forgotten wot it's like. We ain't seen any for three days."

But there was no further trouble as far as food was concerned. The communications were opened up again, and down there on the straw the Musketeers ate to their hearts' content. There was enough and to spare even for the sullen little group of prisoners who, with a couple of scowling officers, lay in a corner of the barn. And then some one more richly endowed than the rest produced a case which he proceeded to tear open and disclosed a box of cigarettes. In a moment all thought of hardship and fatigue was forgotten. Ginger and the rest of them sat there as if there was no such thing as a German within a hundred miles. For all this was in a day's work, mere incidents hardly worth comment.

A moment or two later a dilapidated figure emerged from the little knot of German prisoners and approached half a dozen Musketeers who were lying smoking on the straw. He bore a familiar air to Bentley and Kemp, but they failed to recognise him until he spoke.

"Would you mind giving me a cigarette?" he said. "And it wouldn't be a bad thing if you passed a few over to those chaps in the corner. You see they regard me as one of themselves, and though that officer with the cut on his head declined any suggestion that I should come here cadging tobacco on his behalf, he made no objection. The others can smoke your tobacco if they like, but they were pretty sure that you chaps wouldn't give them any."

"They're wrong there," Kemp replied. "Because they don't play the game that's no reason why we shouldn't. It's a funny little world, and I am pretty sure I have seen that sullen-looking German before. Go and ask him if his name isn't Echmann, and if he didn't meet a man named Kemp in the semi-final of the gentlemen's singles at Bournemouth tennis tournament last year. I'm quite sure it's the same man. But tell me, Venables, how the dickens did you manage to get here?"

"I am supposed to be attached to the German force on behalf of my paper," Venables replied, for he it was. "I hope those chaps can't hear me; most of them speak English as well as I do. If you'll send one of your men over with some cigarettes they won't be so suspicious. They can't very well object to my talking to you, seeing that I'm a neutral and nothing more dangerous than a war correspondent."

"Rather a dangerous game you're playing," Bentley suggested.

"Well, perhaps it is. But they can't prevent me having my private views, all the same. As a matter of fact, I allowed myself to be taken prisoner. But please don't ask me any questions, because I'm afraid I can't answer them. I want you if you can to get me a few words with your brigadier and forget afterwards that you've ever met me before."

"All right," Bentley said. "Just one moment. Are the Germans in any great force here?"

"They are," Venables replied. "There can't be less than six hundred thousand of them altogether."

CHAPTER XXX - A MYSTERY

Bentley and Kemp listened gravely. There was something staggering in the information that Venables had given them. It seemed almost incredible that Germany could have amassed all those troops on so narrow a front without the Allies being aware of the fact. And if what Venables said was true, what was the maximum of the foe's forces in France? And how would it be possible to prevent a headlong dash north of Ypres straight along the road to Calais? At most the British could only muster a hundred thousand men, supplemented by the weary Belgians and a few regiments of French territorials. If this was substantially correct, Calais was doomed. Stubborn and resolute as the English were, they could never hold back such a force, equipped as it was with an overwhelming amount of artillery. As the two friends looked at one another each read the thought that was passing through the other's mind.

"If what you say is correct," Bentley remarked, "that Mons business is going to be a mere picnic in comparison with what we are up against now."

"I don't quite agree with you," Venables replied. "I believe you fellows will be able to do it. I flatter myself I know a good deal about English military history and I was all through the Boer War, on both sides of the fighting line. You are bound to admit that the Boers were splendid fighters, and they taught you a lesson there which a good many strategists in Europe seem to have forgotten. I was at Modder River where the Boers, not more than ten thousand strong, held General Methuen's men many times stronger than themselves for nearly ten months, simply because they could shoot. It was almost impossible in the Boer campaign to force strong positions at the point of the bayonet, when they were held by resolute men. And that is why I feel pretty sure that your handful of British will be able to hold the Germans now that the line is locked as far as the sea. It will cost you more than half your force, but all the same it will be done, and once more Kaiser Wilhelm will be disappointed. I happen to know that he looks upon the thing as a dead certainty, though he pays you the compliment of believing that it will take him a fortnight; at the end of which time he is coming here with all his big bugs to goose step his forces into Calais. I happen to know this because a few days ago the Kaiser told me so himself."

"He told you?" Kemp exclaimed.

"Why, certainly," Venables said coolly. "He invited half a dozen of us to lunch with him. To hear him talk anybody would think it was all over except the shouting. And he firmly believes it, too. Oh, the man is mad beyond the shadow of a doubt. He spoke of the Russians as if they didn't exist. But we will go into all this later on if we get a chance. The point is that I want to see your brigadier at once, because there are certain things that he must convey to Headquarters. And I shall be glad afterwards if you two will kindly forget that you have ever heard the name of Venables before."

"Don't you think in the meantime you had better go back to those chaps over yonder?" Bentley suggested. "I mean, hadn't we better let them know that we regard you more or less as a prisoner? Then, when the rest of them have gone back under escort, you can remain here till we find the colonel."

This suggestion seemed to commend itself to Venables and a little later, after the German prisoners had gone, he was brought back, and Bentley went and searched for the colonel.

Lord Hailsham listened with knitted brows to what Bentley had to say. Clearly he was puzzled.

"Is the fellow a German spy or what?" he asked.

"As a matter of fact he is not a German at all," Bentley explained. "As a question of nationality he's a pure American and beyond doubt a representative of an American newspaper. You know, sir, that Germany can't do too much for America just now, and they are making no end of a fuss of the New York correspondents. Venables says that he was lunching with the Kaiser a day or two ago and that there are six hundred thousand men opposite us."

The colonel looked exceedingly grave.

"I knew it was bad," he said; "but I didn't know it was as bad as all that. Now, you've been talking to this American. How does he strike you? Do you think he is a German spy, or do you suppose that he is anxious to give us all the information in his power? Do you happen to know anything about him? Somehow his name seems to be familiar to me."

"It would be, sir," Bentley replied. "It isn't for me to say whether Venables is playing some deep game or not, but if it had not been for him we should have never got away in that retreat. It was Venables who appeared out of nowhere and told us where those lost guns of ours were hidden. You will remember he took us to the spot where the guns were concealed and helped us to recover them and the ammunition. I am talking of the time when we bayoneted all those chaps in the farmhouse and got back with the guns to our trenches. In fact, Venables saved the whole situation."

"And what happened to him afterwards?" the colonel asked.

"He vanished, sir; went back to the German lines, I think. Oh, I forgot to tell you that he is a friend of Kemp's. He was a guest of his before the war, and I believe he and Kemp played a good deal of golf together. But if you'll excuse me, sir, it isn't for me to say anything about it. Venables is very anxious to see the brigadier, though he won't say a word as to the reason why. Won't you see him, sir?"

"Of course I will," the colonel replied. "I'll come at once. Lead the way."

Colonel Lord Hailsham failed to learn anything fresh. Venables was perfectly polite, but apparently there was only one thing he wanted, and that was to see the brigadier without delay. A moment or two later he vanished, and then for the first time the handful of Musketeers were in a position to take stock of their position and see exactly how they stood.

For the moment, at any rate, they were safe behind stone walls and all right so long as the German artillery was not trained upon them. In front of them lay sixty or seventy yards of flat open ground, and beyond that a gentle slope upon which stood a heavy stone building which at some time or other had formed part of an old castle. In front of this was a German trench circling round the ruin, and in advance of this ran a small stream or rather an elbow of one of the canals; if the Germans brought up machine guns there the position of the Musketeers in their barn would not be tenable for many minutes. Together with their reinforcements they were about five hundred strong, but this number would not be nearly sufficient to hold the position in case of a determined attack.

It was getting late in the afternoon now and the Germans had slackened fire. Whether they would continue to hold themselves back or whether they would wait till dark before they moved farther was a question that the commander of the Musketeers would have given a good deal to be able to answer. His impulse was to make an immediate and vigorous onslaught on the German trench and capture the ruins of the castle, a plan which, at any rate for the moment, would have got rid of an awkward bend in the British Front.

But was it worth the risk? Lord Hailsham asked himself this question over and over again. What was the strength of the Germans holding the trench? And were there strong reserves lying in waiting on the other side of the old castle under the brow of the hill? And how were they off for machine guns? Darkness found the colonel still in two moods.

CHAPTER XXXI - TO THE RESCUE

The more the colonel of the Musketeers debated the matter, the more anxious he was to get something done. He knew only too well that he could expect nothing in the way of further reinforcements, and it would be useless to ask for further machine guns. Moreover, in case of an attack, the Musketeers might be overwhelmed before they could fall back on their supports. If, on the other hand, they could force the Germans out of that snug little position and take possession of the ruin, protected as it was on the far side by the elbow of the canal, it would be possible to hold it against all comers. It was only a small matter by comparison, but one of those small matters that, successfully attained, cover a regiment with glory and frequently have an important bearing on the big engagement.

It was about eight in the evening when the colonel called his officers about him and disclosed his scheme.

"We must push those chaps back," he said. "We are far too close to them to be pleasant. You see, they are in a position to bring up strong reserves from the other side of the hill without our being able to see them, and if they attack us in the night in anything like force they might cut us to pieces. On the other hand, it is quite useless for us to attack them until we know how strong they are. Now, I want a few of you to volunteer to creep forward and if possible get into the trench opposite. Those fellows haven't had time yet to get up their barbed wire entanglements, and with a bit of luck we might be able to spring a little surprise upon them."

"Might I be allowed to make a remark?" Kemp asked, when the suggestion was being generally discussed. "You see, sir, we all realise the danger and we are all anxious to do something. A little time ago an old Belgian peasant blundered in as if he had dropped from the skies. None of the sentries seemed to know a bit about where he came from, or how he managed to get here without being spotted. So a Frenchman who happens to be with us asked him a few questions, and the old man showed us how he managed it. You see, sir, in a very dry time they can flood the low-lying land here, and it appears that a few yards away there is a covered culvert running from right under our feet past the spot where the German trenches are and round to the canal where there is a floodgate, of which the Germans know nothing. If we could get to the floodgate, we could blow it up, and by to-morrow morning there would be thirty or forty yards of deep water between here and the German trenches. But we don't want that just yet, and still less do the Germans. That culvert is quite dry now, and there is a trap leading into it only a few yards away. I suggest that a dozen or two of us should crawl along the culvert as far as the German trenches, and perhaps a little beyond them, and come up one of the surface drains; we can easily manage it, as the old man I speak of promised to show us the way. Then we shall be able to look down into the trench and see how strong the Germans are. There is no danger in it at all."

"It sounds all right," the colonel said. "At any rate, it can do no harm to have a try. Take a score of men and see what you can do. And if you happen to have any good luck, give us a call and we will follow you."

Immediately the scheme was mooted there was no lack of volunteers. It all sounded easy enough, but when the top of the culvert was removed there was nothing inviting about the black hole that was disclosed. It was only possible to move in single file on hands and knees along the stuffy tube where the air was not too fresh. In front went the pioneer, who made little or nothing of it, for doubtless it had been his business many times to go down there to see that the waterway was clear. The air was foul and stifling, but it was possible to breathe, and so they crept on yard after yard on a journey that seemed to have no end, though it was only the matter of a bowshot altogether. At the end of what seemed to have been an hour the old Belgian rose from his knees and lighted a match. Just where he was standing the roof of the culvert lifted sufficiently for anybody to stand upright, and very cautiously he proceeded to try to lift what appeared to be a wooden trap covered in overhead with earth and grass. But this was more than the old man's strength was capable of, and Ginger, who was close behind, offered his services.

"'Ere, let me 'ave a go," he said. "I ain't afraid of doin' my bit in the daylight, but this 'ere mole business brings the sweat out on me something crool. I don't mind bein' shot, but I abjects to bein' stifled."

The old man made some inarticulate sound and a gesture with his hands, which Kemp, who was following close behind, rightly interpreted as an indication that caution was needed. It would never do to force that wooden trap open in the careless way that Ginger had suggested, for they had to consider the chance of finding themselves confronted by German sentries.

"Not quite so fast, Ginger," Kemp suggested. "It would be a pity to spoil the whole thing now. Just a bit at a time, my lad. And no noise, if you can help it."

Very gradually, the wooden cover began to give way, until at length it was pushed aside and a sweet cool breath of air came down, infinitely refreshing to lungs that were beginning to pump heavily in that stagnant atmosphere. Then the little knot of men listened eagerly for any sign of the foe. The old Belgian smiled and nodded and said something in indifferent French that it was not easy to understand. By dint of asking him several questions it became plain that they were beyond the German trenches on the far slope of the hill, and this was the reason probably why there was no sign of a sentry to be seen. One by one, as quiet as mice, they crept out into the open and crawled up the slope till they came to the parapet of the trench. They were behind the Germans, who were expecting no danger from that quarter. Here and there lights were visible, strong clear lights below the line of the trench, glowing so strongly that for a moment the little knot of Musketeers were fairly puzzled. They crept on inch by inch with absolute caution until the leaders could look down into the trench itself. In the foreground lay Ginger together with his friends, closely followed by Kemp and Bentley, and the rest.

It was a strange thing that lay before them, the like of which they had never looked on before. So far a British soldier had never seen a trench like this one. It was lined with concrete and protected on the side nearest to the British lines by a perfect network of wire entanglements, and at intervals along it electric lights gleamed from an insulated cable. The floor was covered with boards, under which the water could be heard trickling. Here and there were ingenious little dug-outs, presumably intended for officers, each fitted with its own light, and each boasting a camp bedstead with a table and chair. In one of these four subalterns were playing bridge, and Kemp could see the hand of dummy laid on the table, so far as he could judge, the man whose back was to him had just gone no trumps on a splendid hand. The whole thing was so simple and homelike and so far remote from all struggle and strife that Kemp could hardly restrain a smile.

But they were not there to see what the German would make of his hand, they were here on stern business, nothing less than the capture of the trench. From where Kemp lay he could command the whole length of it, and he thrilled when he realised that it did not contain more than fifty Germans altogether.

"We've got them in the hollow of our hands," he said. "We can do it on our heads if we rush it."

CHAPTER XXXII - "SAVOY HOTEL"

Just for a moment Bentley and Kemp and the rest of them had forgotten the fact that they were so many units in the great struggle. For here they had blundered upon an adventure after the heart of them all. There was a touch of sport in it, with just enough risk to render the incident exciting. Despite all they had gone through, and all they knew that lay before them, it was impossible to quench in them the spirit of British light-heartedness and contempt for danger which has always been the mainspring of British pugnacity. For here was a gigantic spree, an unexpected lark that gladdened the heart of them all and relieved the monotony of the deadly trench work. It is this amazing light-heartedness which has made the British Empire what it is, though historians would have us believe that the driving power behind it all is something deeper and still more sacred.

But that is not the spirit in which the British Tommy has approached his work in the field. Whatever he may feel deep down in his heart, he never shows his feelings; he is ready to die for his country, but he must do it in his own way and after his own fashion, with a jest on his lips and a cigarette in his mouth. Probably it was much the same in the old days of the bowmen at Agincourt and Cressy and Poitiers.

And that is how the Musketeers felt as they lay there on the edge of the trench looking down into the luxurious quarters which the Germans had built for themselves. It would have been an easy matter to slide over the shoulder of the trench and take those men prisoners before they could realise what had happened. At any rate, that would have been Ginger's way, and the way of most of them who lurked behind him. But there were cool heads guiding the expedition, and there was much to be done before they took possession of what Ginger compared in his mind to the lounge of the Savoy Hotel. He had been there on more than one occasion, selling his papers or calling taxis on a wet night, and it seemed to him that here was a chance to share the luxuries of such a place himself.

"Did ye ever see anything like it?" he whispered to his next-door neighbour. "Fancy them sausage eaters livin' in a plice like this! Look at that chap over there with the big pipe in his mouth; it's odd to me if I ain't seen 'im before somewhere. They tells me as lots of these chaps 'ere lived in London before the war. Come to think of it, I've carried clubs for several Germans in my time, great fat chaps as treats you like dogs an' never thinks o' givin' you a tip. Yus, I knew as that chap's fice was familiar. 'E used to come down to Richmond on Saturday an' Sunday with another bloke about the sime size. I forget 'is nime for a moment, but 'e weren't popular. 'E'd got a golf bag about as big as a 'ouse an' when you 'adn't 'ad nothin' to eat for a couple o' days before it was as bad as draggin' a big gun abaht. But wot are we wastin' time like this for? Why don't they give us the word to drop in an' join the supper party?"

But the lieutenant in command was in no hurry to move. He knew there was a good deal to be done yet. It would have been no difficult matter to rush the trench and take the handful of Germans by surprise, but there was always the chance that there were others of the foe hidden in those masses of old ruin, and it was necessary to explore them before anything else was done. A minute or two later a little knot of Englishmen worked their way slowly and cautiously back in the direction of the ruin, leaving Ginger and half a dozen of the rest to keep watch on the edge of the trench in case there was anything in the nature of an alarm. There was another thing to be guarded against, too. If the foe on the far side of the canal threw up any of their starlights it was long odds that the presence of the British would be discovered. One by one they crept round the ruin and entered it cautiously. Apparently no one was there, and nothing was discovered with the exception of a few machine guns which had been stored there in preparation for an attack. Evidently the attack was to take place soon, for the level ground beyond the arm of the canal was connected with the castle by two or three pontoons which had been laid down quite recently. Before anything else could be done, these would have to be cut away and sent adrift down the sluggish stream. Without any tools at hand for the purpose this was a slow business, but it was accomplished at length, and then the little force turned back in the direction of the German trench. They held on the edge of it for a moment or two before the lieutenant in command gave the word, and then they dropped down amongst the astonished Germans as if they had fallen from the sky. There was practically no fight; the foe was taken at too great a disadvantage for that. At the first volley they came swarming out of their dug-outs and along the line of trench, and threw up their hands. One or two managed to scramble over the parapet and disappear in the darkness in the direction of the canal, but there was no escape that way, and they were rounded up before it was possible to give the alarm.

"You had better come quietly," the lieutenant in command said as he looked into the snug dug-out where the four German officers had been enjoying their game of bridge.

There was no help for it, so they surrendered at discretion. The fat German who had been pointed out by Ginger stared about him in undisguised amazement.

"How did you get here?" he asked in excellent English.

"We walked," Ginger said. "We came in by the back door by way of Constantinople. I suppose you don't remember me, old man. It don't seem very long ago since you an' me was playin' golf together at Richmond. At least, you was supposed to play, and I used to lug that old iron monger's shop o' yours about. D'you recollect it?"

"Ach," the German said. "You are the caddie we used to call Ginger. Those was happy days, and I wish they was back again. There are three or four of us here who used to live in London, and I wish we were there once more."

"Don't you worry about that, old man," Ginger said. "You will be back again soon enough. I suppose, like the rest of them, you left the missus and kids behind you. But you ain't goin' back to that little plice of your'n in Park Line, an' you ain't goin' to ride about in that big car o' your'n any more. Not as I ain't sayin' as you're pretty snug in these 'ere quarters. Fancy you chaps livin' in all this luxury while we freeborn Britons 'as got to fight up to our waists in water! It was wery good o' you to tike all this trouble on our account, an' now we're in this 'ere fust class 'otel we'll stick to it. Nothin' like a change of air an' scenery."

By this time most of the Germans had been rounded up and word had been sent to the British trench to the effect that the night's adventure had been crowned with success. The rest of the battalion came swarming across the open ground to take possession of their new quarters, which had been gained without the loss of a single life so far. There was everything here that was needful, including an ample supply of cigars and cigarettes and wine.

"I think we shall be comfortable here," Kemp smiled. "And once we have settled down we shall take a good deal of moving. I've always heard the Germans were pretty thorough, but this knocks spots off anything we have found so far. We shall be quite happy here for a bit."

They did not know it yet, but many weary days were to pass before the Musketeers found themselves on the other side of that canal, and much was to happen before then.

CHAPTER XXXIII - A STAGGERING TASK

The mysterious Venables had spoken no more than the truth when he had declared that the Germans had massed six hundred thousand men in the neighbourhood of La Bassee and Ypres. Probably General French had some shrewd idea of this fact; certainly he did not underrate the magnitude of the task that lay before him. He knew, too, that for the moment, at any rate, he could expect little or nothing in the way of reinforcements from England, so that in the coming strife he would have to make the best of the little force that had stood him in such good stead during the last two months. The big outflanking movement was still going on, a movement by which the French were compelled to retire the left of their line, abandoning Lille and concentrating on La Bassee, which town itself was already practically in German hands. But it might be possible to hold the heights behind La Bassee a little longer, and here the French had made a stand and dug themselves in.

All this time the gap between La Bassee and the sea was open to the enemy, and the allies were hard put to it to keep them back here. It was managed for a few days by dragging out the Belgian line until it began to wear dangerously thin like a piece of over-stretched elastic. Here, too, were French Territorials, mostly men over forty, doing their best and fighting to the breaking point.

And this breaking point was very near when in the middle of October the pioneer regiments of the British main force detrained near St. Omar. It was a great task that lay before them. Theoretically, it was their duty to throw lack the advanced German forces along a given line and at the same time keep not only in touch with the French at La Bassee, but establish communications with the Belgians on the east and Rawlinson's division in the west. This operation, almost impossible in the face of overwhelming odds, was assigned to General Smith-Dorrien, in command of the second Army Corps, who lost no time in forcing action before La Bassee. But from the very first any chance of a successful attempt at the offensive was impossible. By the end of the following week the British army was fighting a desultory scrambling engagement focussed on Ypres, while at that time the Belgian army, partly re-organised and rested, was engaged in holding the Yser at a point on the line against the sea. Over and over again here the bridge-head of the Yser had been lost and won, and lost and won again until it became necessary to adopt a desperate experiment which practically meant the sacrifice of the last few yards of Belgian soil. The dykes were cut and the country flooded, and for the first time the road to Calais was secure. Nature had done what man had failed to do.

Each day, until somewhere about the last week of October, things were getting more and more critical. At this time the main force under Sir John French extended for some twenty-odd miles from before La Bassee to a point north of Ypres, and each day it became more and more difficult to hold the Germans back. Both French and English were so exhausted that they could not keep up a successful driving movement. But, on the other hand, the line was established. And, moreover, it was a direct and straight line, terribly insecure perhaps, but reaching out far enough to touch that of the French and Belgians on either side. And all this time more and more Germans were being rushed across Belgium, with the one object of smashing through that line and carrying everything before them in their headlong push for Calais.

And still French carried on, still the English held on with teeth and nails, waiting and waiting for the reinforcements which never seemed to come. And then one day when hope was abandoned and nothing but an ignominious retreat threatened along the whole line, there came over the ridge towards the trenches a solitary figure cloaked and turbaned, and looking strangely out of place on the western field. And beyond him came the turbans of the Sikhs and their cavalry, and up from the trenches went a mighty cheer in which the pent-up emotion of weeks gave itself expression. It was a sorely needed relief, but great as it was, it was no more than a drop in the great ocean of General French's requirements.

So far the first British Army Corps had not come into action. While the second and third Army Corps had been struggling through the big advance, the first Corps under General Haig was still making its way to the appointed place from its original position north of Rheims. It was ready now, and its presence obliged Sir John French to ask himself a question which might possibly have a vital influence on the autumn campaign. This was whether or not he should use the first Army Corps to reinforce the second and third, and thereby consolidate the ground already won.

As a matter of fact, the second and third army were really carrying out that which all military authorities had declared to be impossible. What would Sir John French do? The decision lay entirely in his hands, and for the moment he decided to let the second and third corps go on doing the impossible. He sent the first corps to the lines about Ypres, and there they settled down to a dogged fight which went a long way to produce the result which meant—though it was not apparent for the moment—that all the might and strength of the German armies was not sufficient to cut its way through that thin line down to the coast which the Kaiser coveted so much, and on the possession of which he had built some of his fondest hopes. Day by day and hour by hour the Kaiser flung his masses on the British lines—flung them forward in close formation and with utter recklessness of human life which will stamp him for ever as the most callous-hearted general who ever regarded his fellow-countrymen as mere pawns on the chess-board of his ambition.

Day by day the attack was renewed, first on one part of the line and then on another. Here ground was gained and here ground was lost, but nothing seemed to make any impression on the British trenches, and then the Kaiser came down in person to see the great thing done.

Superhuman efforts were about to be made. Each hour brought worse news to General Haig, culminating in information brought in the raw dawn of an early December day by an aviator who came down in the British lines with the wings of his plane riddled with shrapnel, and reported that he had seen three fresh German corps advancing against General Haig's front. He had seen the roads and rail ways thick with men; he had seen fresh batteries working into position and close behind them huge masses of men advancing to the fray in review order and singing their patriotic songs under the eyes of the Kaiser himself. A little later on the news was confirmed, and fresh intelligence arrived to the effect that one of these mass attacks of German infantry had broken through the first division near Ypres, and that the French support was retiring. It was on this day that the Royal Scotch Fusiliers were cut off root and branch. It was on this day, too, that the Germans, in a fresh artillery position were actually shelling General Haig's headquarters, and a shell had burst in the house itself. It was well that General Haig was outside at the time, for practically every staff officer on the spot was killed or wounded.

This was the position then on the first of November, and there was no man there from General French downwards would have dared to prophesy what the morrow would bring forth. And General French's task was only beginning.

CHAPTER XXXIV - THE DEADLY GRIP

The first Army Corps was in deadly peril. It was impossible for French to send any reinforcements, or do anything except encourage them by his personal example. All that day he exposed himself to peril as freely as if he had been the humblest recruit in any ordinary line regiment. He used his motor freely that day, and rushed up to the line of the first division; as a matter of fact, it was no great journey that lay before him, for the line had retired for a distance of more than four miles. He could see quite plainly from where he stood that his men were locked in a deadly grip with the German infantry, who were attacking everywhere in enormous forces, and practically unled. In the literal sense of the word it was a soldier's fight on both sides. The English were struggling valiantly in every direction, hitting a head or bayoneting a body wherever it presented itself. And there was not an atom of method in all this either. Apparently there was no attempt at leadership in this scrimmage where every man was doing his utmost and officers and men, infantry and cavalry, were fighting side by side, and officers' servants were loading spare rifles and handing them on until they were too hot to fire any longer.

The Musketeers were in the thick of it. There were moments when their trenches were rushed and they fought at short arm-grips, hurling the foe back with machine gun and bayonet, for even here, guarded though they were by the flood, they were not safe. Heedless of the danger, a German infantry regiment had plunged into the water up to their armpits, and were making their way across. It was a hideous and unnecessary slaughter but still they came on in dense masses, utterly indifferent to the fire that mowed them down, until the Musketeers were weary of throwing them back from the trenches.

About this time it became generally known that General French himself was behind on foot and in the very thick of it. He gave his orders as calmly as if on parade. Even in the midst of this deadly peril he began to see that victory was possible. Presently he gathered up a part of the broken first division and hurled it on the flank of a terrific German attack which seemed to be proceeding on the assumption that the victory was won and that the English were entirely beaten. A wounded officer fell headlong into the Musketeers' trenches with an order that they were to form up at once and follow.

All this time the old, amazing cheerfulness prevailed. There was not a man there who regarded that battle as anything but the finest sport in the world, a great and glorious game designed especially for his benefit, and there was not a man there who dreamt of defeat. Death might come—probably would, but no one thought of that for the moment; indeed, the chief regret of the Musketeers was that they were about to leave the tiny strip of Flanders which they had come to look upon more or less in the light of a home.

"I wonder wot the gime is," Ginger murmured to his next door neighbour. "At any rate, it looks as if it was good-bye to our 'appy 'ome. I expect the General Staff's got jealous of us, an' wants this trench to themselves. Perhaps the general is goin' to breed rabbits 'ere."

"Didn't you 'ear wot the officer said?" the other man asked. "It sounded as if we'd caught the Germans badly on the flank, and if we can keep 'em on the run now we'll be back on the original line. Come on, Ginger, ole man; don't stop talkin' 'ere all day, unless p'raps you wants ter take the German army on to your own cheek."

Still grumbling, after the way of his own kind, Ginger followed. And then it seemed as it the miracle had really happened. The German flank had broken before a furious attack of not half its strength, and the men that French had rallied were pushing the foe back headlong towards Gheluvelt. For the moment, at any rate, it looked as if the greatest attack in the history of warfare had failed. For there was no holding the British now; they swept on with an irresistible dash, fighting their way back to the original lines, and long before dark they were again in the old positions.

From a purely technical point of view, the British had merely held their own; in reality they had won that long battle which meant that in future the Allies would dominate the course of the campaign in the West. But it was a victory won at a terrible price. One regiment went into that fight twelve hundred strong, on the evening of that fateful day they mustered seventy. Of another regiment three hundred answered to the roll call instead of fifteen, and practically every one of the other twelve hundred men had fallen on that never-to-be-forgotten October 31.

It was much the same with the cavalry. One of our most famous brigades rode into that action nearly five thousand strong. When they emerged they had been decimated, but they had something to boast of. For during that long and trying day they had succeeded in holding off the whole of a German Army Corps of over forty thousand men. The mind staggers before the prospect of such a triumph as this, and yet it has been done. The impossible has been achieved and the price to pay had not been perhaps too much.

When the night of the 31st fell the assault on Ypres, long planned and contrived by the German General Staff, had failed. For days and nights the contemptible little British army, numbering a hundred and twenty thousand men, had succeeded not only in holding at bay but actually in driving off something like five times its number, armed and equipped as no body of troops had ever been equipped in the history of warfare.

But even then the German Emperor was not satisfied. During those fateful two or three days he must have seen at least two hundred thousand of the flower of his army mowed down by the British rifle and artillery fire. He had the galling experience of seeing the men he regarded as invincible wiped out of existence without gaining so much as a single yard. He must have known in his heart of hearts that of all the wild dreams that had ever crept into that mad brain of his, the vision of Calais was the wildest. But the Butcher of Europe had not shot his bolt yet.

Absolutely blind to the loss of life, and callous to the suffering imposed on those who followed him so faithfully with sublime belief in the justice of their cause, he made one more effort on the following day.

The British had yet to learn what it was to face the full force of the weight of his own Prussian Guard. He did not know that in the meantime the French had brought up reinforcements; all he could see was himself proclaiming the annexation of Belgium in the historic Cloth Hall of Ypres. It is said that he himself led the attack and urged his massed forces on to what proved to be the greatest slaughter in the campaign. The Prussian Guard came back to it again and again in sweeping waves, climbing over their own dead, but all in vain. When night fell three-quarters of the Prussian Guard lay dead in the woods, in ranks piled eight or ten deep one upon the top of the other, in a holocaust that baffles all description. That night the Germans fell back suddenly, and the battle of Ypres was finished. But at what a cost will never be known, not even when history comes to be written.

CHAPTER XXXV - A CHEERFUL TOMMY

It is only by slow degrees that the true story of Ypres and the stupendous result of the fight there is coming home to the world. For a long time the fog of war lay over the battlefield and the curtain has been lifted only inch by inch, despite the fact that not more than four hours separate the scene of the combat from London itself. These are the days when intelligence travels fast, yet weeks and months passed before the significance of that great struggle began to get home to the British people. They knew, of course, that fighting was going on, but they did not realise for a moment that a mere handful of men were engaged in what was really a life and death struggle on behalf of the Empire.

And yet there can be no question that the magnificent stand made at Ypres by French and his gallant men is entitled to rank with the decisive battles of the world, with Marathon and Cressy and Waterloo, with Moscow and Austerlitz. It broke for ever the German dream of the possession of the North Coast of France and the delirious idea of an onslaught upon England by way of Calais. It spoilt the pleasant scheme which was to include Northern France within the German Dominion and attach Belgium and her seaboard to Germany. It cost Prussia three hundred and seventy-five thousand of her finest troops. And it enabled Russia to concentrate and become a serious menace to the eastern frontier, so that a division of forces was necessary. In a word, it broke up the great conspiracy and showed the Kaiser and his friends plainly enough that the dream of half a century was no more than a mere nightmare. They might boast and brag and swagger as much as they liked, they could proudly point to the fact that they held Belgium and a large slice of France and that their own territory was intact, but at the same time they knew that the end was coming, and from that moment idle vapourings ceased and Germany began to talk as if an honourable peace was all that she could hope for.

For the time being, therefore, there was quiet on the western frontier. The winter had set in now. November had arrived with its fogs and rain, and the trenches were waist deep in water. The roads were becoming impossible for the transmission of heavy artillery, and the Allies were settling down to a dogged resistance behind their lines. Very little could happen now until the spring, by which time France would be ready and England's new army in a position to take the field. Russia would be able to move freely too, and the eyes of the world were beginning to turn towards Italy.

The Musketeers were back again in their trench, which was now safe from surprise for a long time to come. They were worn and battered, and of their original number not a couple of hundred remained. But luck had been with Bentley and Kemp and the rest of their little group, and all the familiar faces to be seen. It was only for a day or two, however, that they remained where they were, for orders came for them to go down to the base.

"Why can't they leave us alone?" Ginger grumbled. "We are 'appy enough 'ere. We discovered this plice an' took possession of it in the nime of the British Government. It's just as snug and comfortable as if we were at 'ome. Now I suppose they wants to turn us out to make room for a lot o' recruities wots never seen a shot fired."

"I think you're wrong there, Ginger," Bentley said. "From what I can understand we are going down to the base for a month's rest. We've been at it now for over three months, and we've been in the thick of it all the time."

"There's some people as can't be done without," Ginger said. "Where would the British army be if it wasn't for the Musketeers? Wot's the good of us goin' down to the base? Fat lot of good we shall do there. We come 'ere to fight, not to make bread or to show 'em 'ow to cook."

"Ole Ginger ain't never satisfied," George remarked, "'e don't know when 'e's well off. We're goin' to Paris, that's wot they're goin' to do wif us. They're goin' to shove us in a fust class 'otel an' tike us round all the theatres. I dunno as I'm sorry as we shall be aht of it for a bit."

Ginger wasn't sorry either, though it was his way to grumble at the new order of things, for to tell the truth what was left of the Musketeers were thoroughly worn out. They had had no sleep for over a fortnight, except what they could snatch in odd moments; they were hungry and tired, ragged and stiff with mud, and for the most part verminous. But they had become attached to their trench with all its solid comforts, and they were proud of it. It was the envy of the brigade and of such visitors as came their way with orders or ammunition.

"I wouldn't mind so much," Ginger said, "if we could get the brigadier to promise us as we should come back 'ere again. It mikes my 'eart fairly ache to think as this little grey 'ome in the west of our'n. Wot them German coves was so kind as to make for us, should be 'anded over to a lot o' rookies as don't know a good thing when they see it. Wot do you think, sir? Are we comin' back?"

Ginger turned and addressed his remark to the lieutenant in command of his platoon. The officer in question was doing his best to remove a fortnight's beard with the aid of a commandeered safety razor and a bit of broken looking-glass. There were other men lying about in the trenches engaged in scraping the mud from their uniforms. They were a sorry-looking lot, ragged and rough, but every man was in the pink of condition and ready to fight for his life. It was amazing how cheerful they were, and how little they made of their hardships. There was not a single man amongst them who would not have resented the suggestion that he was the least bit of a hero. This same sporting air prevailed with them all. They had been through the doors of death and into the very gates of hell, but had not Englishmen been doing the same thing for hundreds of years? And would not unborn generations do the same thing again?

War, and the doings of war, were the last things they thought of. For the moment all strife was behind them, and the future mattered nothing. What they had done in the past they could do again, and that was the beginning and the end of it. They were just a cheery, happy, inconsequent band of brothers who had been fighting side by side for a common end; where the newspaper boy and the young Oxford man had respected each other and were only too ready to hold out a helping hand to a comrade in time of distress and suffering. Despite his growl Ginger was as happy as the rest in the prospect of going down to the base and getting out of all this mud and misery, at any rate for the time being.

"I shall, be glad of it," George said. "If I don't get a change soon this old uniform of mine will fall to pieces. You chaps may not think it, but I've always been accustomed to me bath regular, and I ain't 'ad a wash for weeks. Anybody got a cigarette? I ain't smoked for days."

CHAPTER XXVI - AT THE BASE

The Musketeers went back from the firing line with less than two hundred of their original strength. They had, of course, been supplemented by draughts from time to time, but this was not the same thing to those who had been through the campaign since the middle of August. These were all known to one another, and were banded together by ties that were almost sacred. It mattered little or nothing whence these original men came, whether they had been picked up in the gutter or were the finest product of the English public schools. For all those distinctions had been sunk now, and the Musketeers were as a band of brothers.

They had come out of the trenches, battered and scarred, ragged and unshaven, but every man was as fine as a star, and as hard as a bar of steel. They were going back to the rest which they needed a great deal more than they were aware, for it was only when the tension relaxed that they realised what the nervous strain of the last three months had been. There were men amongst them who could not sleep, or who started up in the middle of the night crying that the foe were upon them, and that the trenches were in danger. There were men who could not write a letter, men who could not still the quivering of their nerves or steady their hands without something to rest upon. It was only when danger was near that they could forget all this and string themselves up for the fight again. They had marched towards the base hardly conscious of their limbs, and there were some amongst them who declared that for weeks past there had been no sensation in their lower limbs whatever. It was only when they cut away their ragged breeches and puttees, reduced to a mere strip, that they begun to realise that they were walking upright.

It was not very far behind the firing line that they went. They were still almost within reach of the German heavy guns, and it was no unusual sight to see a German Aviatik or a Taube flying menacingly overhead. But here, at any rate, were huts, tents, and clean bedding, to say nothing of fresh uniforms and underclothing, and the baths that they so sorely needed. As they went along the sense of responsibility lightened, and they swung presently into their quarters as lighthearted as a lot of schoolboys. For the next few days, at any rate, they would have very little to do but rest and smoke and enjoy themselves. There was a break in the incessant rainfall just then, and it was possible to sit out in the sunshine and enjoy an air which at any other time would have been cold and raw. But by comparison it was as if the Musketeers had stepped out of winter into the full beauty of the spring.

They were looking forward keenly now to anything in the way of enjoyment; they did not expect much, but their hopes were raised when they caught sight of a big tent, where there was seating accommodation for many hundreds, and outside which was a notice to the effect that a concert party performed nightly for the benefit of the troops.

"There ought to be some good local talent 'ere," said Ginger. "I did 'ear as some of the big stars was comin' over from England. 'Oo's that chap in the soft 'at over there? Blimme, if it ain't Seymour 'Icks!" And Ginger, clothed afresh from head to foot, warm and comfortable and well fed, with his pockets full of cigarettes, set out to make enquiries. He came back presently from the lines of another regiment down from the front, full of excitement.

"It's all right, you chaps," he said. "It wasn't a mere accident as brought that chap over 'ere. Seems to me we've come just at the right time. 'Arf the big bugs on the music 'all stige is over 'ere. There's a 'ole lot o' them in the farm'ouse yonder. If we'd 'ave been 'ere last night we should 'ave 'ad a concert as they can't get in the West End not all at once even if they pays a guinea to sit in the stalls."

And Ginger proceeded to reel off a list of names that fairly staggered all his listeners.

"Wot's the good o' trying to fill us up with that?" one of the listeners scoffed. "You carn't kid me as all them swells, drawing their two or three 'undred ponds a week, is goin' to get leave to come over 'ere an' sing to a lot o' bloomin' Tommies in a tent. You go off an' tell that story to somebody else, Ginger. I'm too old for it."

"It's the truest thing I ever said in my life," Ginger said. "There's a regular party of them. They come over 'ere to cheer up the wounded. They've been at it for days. An' they was persuaded to come along 'ere an' give us chaps a charnce. There's a concert on to-night as the King 'imself couldn't better, not even if 'e was entertainin' 'is pals at Buckingham Palace. There ain't nothin' to pay neither. If you don't believe it, you go into the tent an' walk as far as the platform, an' you will see the nimes of the 'ole star caste I'm talkin' abaht. Why, I've paid a shillin' many a time on a bank 'oliday night to 'ear even one o' them."

One or two men kicking a football about took Ginger at his word. They professed to believe that he was still taking advantage of their innocence, but they hesitated no longer when Ginger produced the last sixpence in his possession and offered to bet that coin with anybody that what he stated was nothing but the absolute truth.

Presently the others came back and confirmed what Ginger had said. They had seen the programme, and in the big tent later on in the evening a packed audience witnessed a performance that was practically unique in the history of the British Empire. And never before had any company of entertainers met with so enthusiastic a reception. Their kindness was thoroughly appreciated, and every entertainer was at his or her best. It was all over at length, and the Musketeers went back to their quarters to talk over the amazing evening long after lights were out.

"We shan't know ourselves if this sort o' thing goes on," Ginger said. "Not as we can expect another show like this. Didn't I 'ear something said about those chaps in the next line wanting to tike us on at football?"

"I did 'ear something abaht it," George said. "They calls themselves the 'Ard Nuts.' A chap in G lines told me this mornin' as they'd bin 'ere abaht three weeks gettin' ready to go up to the front, and 'e said as they'd taken on pretty well every battalion so far an' beaten 'em out o' sight. They've got a lieutenant as used to play for Oxford University, an' 'e gives 'is men five quid amongst 'em for every match they wins."

"Oh, 'e does, does 'e," Ginger replied. "You told Mr. Selwyn that, George?"

Ginger mentioned a lieutenant in the Musketeers who, two years before, had figured, as an amateur, of course, in the final tie of the Association Cup. Whilst the Musketeers were still training in England the lieutenant had been very keen on forming a football team, and the Musketeers had done exceedingly well against all clubs who had come against them. The Musketeers were holiday-making now in the best sense of the word. They wanted to forget as far as possible all they had been through during the last two months, and this football idea seemed to be as good a way as any other of achieving the desired result.

George was a football enthusiast, too, and might have gone far in the game if only in his degenerate days he had brought himself to undergo the rigours of training.

"That's all right," he said. "I've got a little gime on if the lieutenant will back me up. We'll teach them 'Ard Nuts a lesson that they won't forget in a 'urry."

CHAPTER XXXVII - THE MUSKETEERS AT PLAY

This kind of thing was beyond the grasp of a foreign mind. It was certainly a thing no German could understand. Though the Teuton has invaded this country to his advantage and our detriment for the last fifty years, he has never grasped, and probably never will grasp, the true inwardness of the British spirit. He knows, of course, that England finally overthrew Napoleon at Waterloo and freed Europe from the same menace that the Kaiser would impose upon her now, but he could not grasp the true inwardness of Wellington's expression that Waterloo was won on the playing fields of Eton.

The commercial German, with his nose ever pressed close to the mercantile grindstone, cannot understand that the British Empire has been founded and maintained by the sporting spirit. That is why there can only be one end to the present conflict. With the German it is war all the time, it is one constant struggle, with no relaxation at all; and that is what is going to beat him. That the British Tommy should turn his back, even for it moment, on the foe and indulge in one of his favourite pastimes, causes the German to sneer and speak spitefully of a race that is utterly incapable of taking anything seriously for many days together. But it is this very lightheartedness and optimistic spirit that render England impervious to defeat.

But no such thoughts as these occupied the simple minds of Ginger and his friends as they discussed the scheme whereby they were to reduce the proud record of the Hard Nuts. They were thinking about football now and nothing else, and they would go back to the fighting line presently all the better for it.

"We ain't particularly strong an' that's a fact," George said. "A couple o' months ago we would 'ave taken those chaps on wiv a very good charnce, but we must 'ave lost at least seven or eight of our best men since then. An' those chaps don't 'arf fancy themselves. I was talkin' to one o' them this afternoon, their centre forward 'e is, a chap wot used to work down at Woolich, an' 'e told me as we could get a few substitutes if we liked. 'E said as there was about fifteen thousand men in this camp an' we could make 'em up from wherever we liked. An' 'e wanted to know if Mr. Selwyn was good enough to back us for a fiver. An' o' course I said as 'e was. I couldn't do nothin' else."

"You might 'ave arsked 'im first, George," Ginger said. "'E's a proper young sport, but I don't suppose 'e will thank you to chuck 'is quids abaht in that fashion."

"Yes, 'e will when 'e knows wot's in the back of my mind," George said confidently. "An' don't you forget we can pick our men from wherever we like. There ain't above five of us as are any good, but I've got my eye upon one or two more, an' I don't care where they comes from so long as they wipes the floor wiv them 'ere 'Ard Nuts."

"Where're you goin' to get 'em from?" Ginger asked.

"Well, I've thought o' that too," George replied. "It ain't no difficult a matter as your think when you comes to realise as there are fifteen thousand men in this camp. Did ye ever 'ear tell of the 5th Royals?"

"No, I never did," Ginger said.

"Well, these 'ere 5th Royals was recruited after the beginnin' o' the war by a chap called Reynolds 'oo used to be goal-keeper for Blackburn Rovers. 'E only played football for amusement, because you see 'e was rather a big man up there in the cotton tride, an' when 'e couldn't play no more 'e become President o' the Club an' is on the Council o' the league. You must 'ave 'eard of 'im, Ginger."

"Nime sounds familiar," Ginger admitted. "But go on, George. I'm beginnin' to get a bit interested."

"You'll be a jolly sight more interested before I'm finished," George replied. "Well, this 'ere Reynolds wot's a very decent chap an' wot the newspapers call universally popular, thinks as it wouldn't be a bad thing if 'e tried to raise a battalion amongst coves wot's interested in football. You see, e's a Territorial officer 'imself, an' 'e 'ad a natural ambition to command a battalion of 'is own. So 'e just sets to work, an' in less than a week 'e'd got all the men 'e wanted. Now, you know something abaht football, an' you might be glad to 'ear of certain coves wot's joined the 5th Royals."

Whereupon George proceeded to reel off half a dozen names which are known all over the world where football is played. Ginger and the rest listened with a grin on their faces, for they began to see what their comrade was driving at.

"D'you mean to say," one of them asked, "as them 'Ard Nuts don't know wot you've just told us?"

"They don't," George grinned. "I was arskin' a few questions just now, an' they're all as innocent as a lot o' kid's. You' see the Royals ain't worryin' much abaht football now; their one idea is to get to the front as soon as possible; but they are as 'ard as niles an' fit to play for their country. They ain't like us who 'as come dahn to this 'ealth resort for the sike of our nerves, an' that's why they very properly ain't troubling much abaht football. But they wouldn't mind a gime, an' I'm quite sure, from wot one of 'em told me, as they'd be only too pleased to 'elp us to tike down the 'Ard Nuts an' pocket 'arf a quid at the sime time. An' for their own sikes they won't say anything abaht it. You leave it to me to see Mr. Selwyn in the mornin' an' put it right."

But apparently the little scheme for getting the best of the Hard Nuts had been discussed in the hearing of the lieutenant, for it was he who approached George in the morning.

"Well, George," he said. "Are we going to have any football while we are down here? I'll get up a list of fixtures for you if you like. We shall only be the ghost of the team we used to be, but we can do our best. Besides, we must do something while we are down here. It will never do for a regiment that has got a reputation like ours to slack it as some of them appear to be doing."

"There's nothin' we'd like better, sor," George said. "We'd very much like to 'ave a go at these 'ere 'Ard Nuts."

"So I understand," the lieutenant smiled drily. "What have you been up to, George? I saw Colonel Reynolds of the 5th Royals last night, and he told me that one of my men had been on to one of his with a view to getting up a team with the laudable object of lowering the pride of the aforesaid Nuts. Can I see your handwriting in this, George?"

"I ain't goin' to deny it, sir," George replied. "I'm fair sick o' the swank o' those chaps. They wants to tike us on, an' they was good enough to say as they don't mind us gettin' 'elp from anywhere. Their captain 'e gives them a five pahnd note for every match they win, an' one o' their chaps 'e arsks me if you, sir, would back us wiv a five pahnd note."

"It would be throwing money away, George."

"Not if you works it my way," George responded. "They said as they didn't mind substitutes, so I thought as we might borrow 'arf a dozen from the 5th Royals. Well, we could make up a 'ole International line, to say nothin' of a man wot'd keep goal for England. An' the best o' the 'ole joke is as them 'Ard Nuts don't even know as there's such a thing as the 5th Royals in existence. Bacon, as used to play for Ashton Villa, told me so this mornin'. Don't say as you're goin' to spoil the little gime, sir? It'll be somethin' to laugh at for months."

CHAPTER XXXVIII - TOMMY'S LITTLE WAY

For some not very apparent reason the forthcoming football match between the Musketeers and the battalion who had christened themselves the Hard Nuts was occupying a good deal of attention in the base camp. It seems almost impossible for people far remote from the scene of that awful strife to understand how a body of men with so stern a task before them could forget the perils and privations of their position and concentrate their attention upon a mere game. But this is a rule that works both ways, and there are thousands of Englishmen at home to-day who have not yet grasped, or perhaps do not want to grasp, the true inwardness of the position. If men of military age can follow sport at home and devote themselves almost exclusively to such a pastime as racing when their country is in danger, every allowance should be made for the man who has taken his share in the fighting line and is only too willing and ready to go back to it again.

The Musketeers had done their share, and more; they were glad enough of the rest and change; they had not asked for it, but now it had come their way they meant to enjoy it to the utmost.

Probably the man called George had taken many people into his secret, for there was a great deal of whispering and laughing, and when the time came there would be a goodly company to witness the downfall of the Hard Nuts—a certainty in the opinion of George and those in the know.

All arrangements had been handed over to Lieutenant Selwyn and a major of the Hard Nuts, a sportsman to his finger tips, who, though too old himself for such a strenuous game as football, was the leader of all games so far as his battalion was concerned. It was upon him that Selwyn called to make the final arrangements.

"Of course, I quite understand," he said. "As you are at present, your people are not strong enough to tackle us single-handed, and you are at perfect liberty to get a few substitutes from the other battalions here."

"I understood that," Selwyn said. "And we have practically made up our team."

"I hope you have found something good," the major said. "I should like to see something like a game."

"Oh, I think we can promise you that," Selwyn replied drily. "There's a regiment over behind the hills yonder that is very keen on football, and they have lent us one or two quite good men. You may have heard of the 5th Royals."

Obviously the major hadn't, for he shook his head. The lieutenant smiled with the air of a man who is pleased with himself. The plot was going on nicely.

"I suppose you don't want to back your men!" the leader asked. "I am good for a small wager."

"I think I would rather not," Selwyn observed. "I promised our lot a treat if they won, which means that I shall have to give it them in any case. But I won't back them if you don't mind. You'll know why later on."

Still the major suspected nothing.

"Have you any idea what football is like out here?" he asked. "For instance, have you seen the ground we play on? It will be a bit of a shock for you when you do."

It was. It was a football field by courtesy only. Months back it had been prepared for defence, at the moment when it looked as if nothing in the world could prevent the German march to Calais. There was not a blade of grass upon it, and here and there were little pits and hollows which had been formed by shells from the German heavy guns. All round were half-made trenches, and almost in the centre of the ground a big house had stood at some time. In the background were woods, partly destroyed and with roads out through them for the passage of transport wagons. The brown faced major indicated the prospect with a wave of his hand.

"There it is, and we must make the best of it," he said. "It's like making bricks without straw. I don't suppose you know this part of the country, but I do. You would hardly believe it, but twelve months ago I was over here pheasant shooting. I'm on the Stock Exchange, and the man who owns this property used to do a good deal of business through me. The poor chap's dead now; he was killed at Bruges at the beginning of the war. He had cotton mills here. Within a few yards of where we are standing was a beautiful old house, built at least three centuries ago. It was surrounded by Italian gardens and a moat, where we used to catch fish. Those woods yonder were woods in the proper sense of the word, full of pheasants and snipe. I can't bring myself to believe that this was only twelve months ago, but so it was. I don't think we've got anything more to talk about know, have we?"

"I don't think so," Selwyn said. "At two o'clock on Friday afternoon then."

It seemed strange to Selwyn that so keen a sportsman as the major had heard nothing of the reputation of the battalion known as the 5th Royals; but the latter had only just come up from the sea, and the Hard Nuts had been recruited for the most part along the Thames waterways between Wapping and the Medway. With one or two rare exceptions, they had not seen anything of first-class football, for they were too far away from London to touch Woolwich or Tottenham or Chelsea and their own local clubs were confined to such combinations as the Medway League and the South Eastern Group. Therefore, George had cunningly reckoned on the probability that practically none of the Hard Nuts had ever seen the substitutes whom he had gathered together on any football field.

George grinned broadly when the lieutenant told him the gist of his conversation with Major Brawnwood.

"It'll be a fine joke," he said. "They'll come to us, and we shall play with them as if they was a lot o' little lambs. It'll be a treat to see their fices when they come up against our first line. Why, that night as we took those trenches of ours won't be nithin' to it. If our chaps wot's in the know'll only keep their mouths shut, they'll 'ave the treat o' their lives."

"I think it will be a bit of a surprise," the lieutenant said. "But there's one thing I want to impress upon you, George. There isn't to be any betting. Knowing what we do, it would be something very much like a swindle."

George looked a little askance at the suggestion, for he and some of his friends had anticipated some small addition to their income from the discomfiture of the Hard Nuts. But the lieutenant was perfectly firm on the point, and George was bound to agree that he was right. There was nothing more to be said or done now except for the Musketeers to wait with what patience they could for the following Friday afternoon, and hope that no boasting Musketeer who was in the know would so far forget himself as to betray the secret preparations which had been made for the downfall of the battalion who were beginning to regard themselves as the football champions of the British army. It was Ginger who warned his friends against this kind of thing, and threatened them with what would happen if they forgot themselves and went too far.

"We ought not to 'ave said anything to anybody," he observed, "It's a rum thing to me as those chaps ain't found anything out abaht the Royals. It's a rum thing, too, as they ain't thought o' playin' a match themselves. I'm glad as they're in camp such a long way off. I was in their lines this afternoon, talkin' matters over with them champions o' theirs, an' they're as keen on the joke as we are. I wouldn't miss the fun not even to be back in the trenches again."

CHAPTER XXXIX - THE END OF THE GAME

The afternoon of Friday was fairly fine, with a keen wind blowing across the ground that gave no advantages to either side. All round the ropes soldiers from a dozen regiments were gathered, including a large number of Indian troops, who were just as keen as the rest of the spectators, and by no means the least critical amongst them, for most of them had played the game at home. It was quite evident from the first that the sympathy of the crowd was on the side of the Musketeers, who were held to have done a very sporting thing in challenging their opponents, who had carried everything before them up to now. But when the two sides came to a line up, and Major Brawnwood stepped out into the field to kick off for his side, a keen-faced London territorial whistled softly as he ran his eye over the Musketeer forwards, and turned eagerly to a sporting comrade.

"Look 'ere, Bill," he said, "you're a bit of a sportsman in your way, an' you're generally keen on a gamble. I think I'd like to back these 'ere Musketeers. They're a scratch lot, an' I'll want a shade of odds. You lay me half a crown to a shilln', an' as a favour I'll tike yer."

"It ain't like you to chuck your money away, ole man," the other responded. "An' I don't suppose you've come aht as one of those bloomin' philanthropists. I should say the odds are 20 to 1, but you've seen more football than I 'ave, bein' a regular follower of Chelsea, an' I shouldn't be surprised to find aht as you know something."

"But is it a bet, Bill?" the other asked.

"No, it ain't," his friend snapped. "I've known you now for 15 years, an' you never risked a penny yet on anything as wasn't a dead snap, so you'll kindly excuse me, mate. There's Ned on the other side o' you. He's a bit more softer'n wot I am. You try an' touch 'im for 'arf a dollar."

The would-be sportsman gave up his effort with a sign. Indeed, he had spotted something, but much to his grief he could see no way to make anything out of it. All he could do, therefore, was to keep his knowledge to himself and enjoy the coming surprise to the Hard Nuts.

What the baffled spectator had seen was a tall figure in goal, a figure that he recognised at a glance as a football player who had represented his country in at least half a dozen international matches. Then he began to recollect that there was such a thing as a footballers' battalion, and that a great many prominent players had joined it. And then he recollected that the name of the same battalion was the Royals.

His discriminating eye could see nothing in the back division except Lieutenant Selwyn, who, as everybody knew, had played for his university, and Kemp, who shared the same honours. But it was the five forwards who occupied the discriminating sportsman's attention to the exclusion of the rest. There was not one amongst them who had not an international reputation; they had figured at the Palace and other historic grounds; indeed, it was amazing to the baffled capitalist that they were not recognised by scores of people round the ground.

The ball was kicked off and taken with a rush down to the Musketeers' end, where in the first minute a goal seemed to be inevitable. But the big man between the posts fielded the ball with the greatest coolness and drove it far down the ground. A moment or two later it was back again, for it took the Musketeers' forwards a few minutes to find their feet. But when they did so the centre forward threaded his way through three or four opponents, and then slung the ball right away to the left wing, where an elusive little man with a red head trapped it cleverly and flashed down along the line to the corner flag, where he coolly tricked two opponents and sent it beautifully right in front of goal. Like a flash the centre forward was through, and meeting the ball as it fell, shot it with terrific force into the corner of the net, giving the goalkeeper no chance whatever. It was as pretty and neat a bit of football as any ever seen at home, and deservedly applauded. The man who wanted to make the bet sighed deeply. It almost seemed to him that he had a grievance against Providence. His next door neighbour turned to him and demanded to know what it all meant.

"You're a nice chap," he said, "tryin' to tike advantage of a pal like this. This is class football, this is; and the British army ain't seen nothin' like it before. An' seein' as there is no chance of workin' yer little games on me you might as well tell me the joke."

"I only spotted it when they come up on the field," the other man said. "Stright, I did. An' then when I saw that chap in goal I begins to tumble. 'E's an international, 'e is, an' so's all the forward line."

The speaker reeled off five names that made the other gasp.

"But wot're they doin' 're?" he asked.

"Why, they belongs to the 5th Royals, wot only come up a day or two ago. Don't you see as it's a put-up job to tike down the number o' the 'Ard Nuts? Nobody don't know as the Royals is up 'ere yet, an' they ain't been advertisin' themselves, because you see they thought they was goin' on to the trenches. I expect the lieutenant wot's playin' for the Musketeers found out all abaht it an' worked the whole joke."

From that moment the Musketeers and their friends lost no grip of the game. They were all over their opponents, simply playing with them, and by the time the interval came were not less than seven goals up. It was obvious, too, that they could easily have added to that total if they liked.

It was a strange scene that the spectators looked upon, 22 men struggling there as if their whole existence depended upon it, as if the greatest struggle in the history of the world had not come about, and as if the firing line was not within an easy march. Even as the struggle went on the sullen booming of a gun came from the distance, and once a shell dropped just over the farthest ring of the spectators, and burst harmlessly in a wood. It had just about as much effect as the discharge of a popgun or a boy's cracker on the fifth of November. There was not a single man looking on who had eyes or ears for anything else but the fine game which those famous forwards were playing. And then, when the game was drawing to a close, there was a sudden fusillade quite close at hand, and one or two of the spectators, looking up, saw that a German aeroplane was hovering overhead.

"Now, I call that rotten bad taste," Ginger said. "An' somebody ought to write to the Kaiser abaht it. Wot they want comin' 'ere for when we're enjoyin' ourselves?"

The aeroplane swayed from side to side, and a cheer went up from the crowd as one of the wings was seen to collapse and the aviator came with a rush to the ground, just saving himself from injury as he alighted near the Musketeers' goal post. The prevailing feeling for the moment was one of exasperation that the game should be interrupted in such an unsportsmanlike way. Then the whistle sounded, and there was a rush from all parts of the ground in the direction of the aviator and his pilot. They had sustained no injury, but the plane was wrecked, and scores of willing hands dragged it out of the way. Thrilling as the incident was, it did not detract for a moment from the business of the afternoon. Lieutenant Selwyn came forward and regarded the aviator with a glance in which recognition was not wanting.

"Hello, Kaharn," he said. "I didn't expect to see you like this. And I didn't think you took any interest in football. Major, shall we go on with the game?"

A yell of appreciation came from all parts of the ground. For this was the spirit in which the Englishmen fought and played.

CHAPTER XL - THE RED COTTAGE

There were, of course, many other sports and pastimes down there at the base besides the historic encounter between the Musketeers and the Hard Nuts, which had become a joke of which the troops never seemed to tire. For instance, there was a gymkhana organised by the Indians, which in its way was a revelation to the British Tommies, who, except for the handful of seasoned troops that had seen service in our great Eastern Dependencies, had never seen anything like it before. They had a wholesome respect for the Ghurka and the Sikh, whom they knew to be magnificent fighters, but this was the first time they saw what our coloured soldiers could do in the way of horsemanship and feats of strength and skill.

There was plenty of time for all this now, for the winter had set in, the cold, wet winter which resolved itself into a game of patience and endurance on both sides. There would be nothing much doing before the spring, a fact in which the German leaders sullenly acquiesced. It was a case of sitting tight in the trenches and watching one another carefully for months. There might be outbreaks here and there, half-hearted attacks, but beyond all doubt the amazing defences of Ypres had reduced the Germans to a standstill for the time being. There were plenty of reserves now, so it was possible to give the heroes of the campaign the spells of rest that they so sorely needed. Three or four times during the next few weeks the Musketeers were back in the trenches, but only for a few days at a time, and then it became possible to give certain units the opportunity of a few days' leave.

It was getting near Christmas, and Bentley and Kemp had begun to wonder if they might be among the fortunate ones when they found themselves with half a dozen of their comrades before the colonel one morning, without the remotest idea why they had been sent for.

"I suppose you men know," the colonel said, "that it has been possible to send certain of you home from time to time. Would any of you like to go?"

There was only one answer to a question like this.

"Well, I have picked certain men out," the colonel went on. "We certainly have had a cruel time during the last three or four months, and it is no boast to say that no regiment in the British army has done better than the Musketeers. It is almost impossible that anything big can happen now before the spring, and it is not a difficult matter to spare you for a few days. You had better arrange to go down to the coast with our next draft on Saturday, and you can tell the captain I said that you can have ten days, which ought to carry you over Christmas. This is a bit longer than most people get, but I may say that I am particularly pleased with your section, and I am only sorry that I cannot send that man Smith and one or two more as well. But he had his holiday during the time he was away wounded, if you understand what I mean. And I think that will do."

Here was a bit of luck greater than Kemp and Bentley had dared to hope for. It would not be one of the old fashioned Christmases, but it would be a fine thing to be back home again, and they rejoiced openly in the prospect. There was only one man amongst them who did not appear to be enthusiastic or to care about going. He even offered to give his place up to somebody else. Then Kemp detained him and asked the reason why.

"You don't want to go home?" he said. "You don't want to see your people again, Gordon?"

The man called Gordon shook his head.

"I haven't any people," he said. "I haven't a relation in the world that I know of. When I was quite a small boy I went out to Canada with my father and I stayed there till he died. He never mentioned any relations; he always struck me as a sour, disappointed man, though he was a good father enough to me. He sent me to England to be educated. Soon after I went back to Canada my father died, and I found myself very well off. I thought I should be happy in England, but somehow I haven't got the knack of making friends. And when this war broke out I hailed it as a sort of godsend to me. I wanted something to do, and I found it. I know now that I was always meant to be a soldier, and I don't seem to care for anything else. I think if you were me you would rather stay here than go back."

"But you are coming all the same," Kemp said. "We've always got on very well together, and you ought to have had a commission long ago. It will be your own fault if you don't find friends in Bentley and myself. We are looking forward to a quiet time at home, at my home, that is, for Bentley and his mother live with my sister and myself. My sister and Bentley's sister are running a hospital there, and I have no doubt they can make room for us all. Now, listen to me, Gordon; I am not going to take any refusal. We both like you very much; in fact, we have discussed you a good many times, and we have come to the conclusion that you are much too good a fellow to be knocking about the world all by yourself. I shall be greatly disappointed if you don't come with us. You are one of the lonely soldiers they are making such a fuss about in the papers."

Gordon's rather melancholy face lighted up with a gleam of amusement.

"I am that," he said. "I was ass enough to write a letter to one of the London papers advertising the fact and inviting correspondence. That was a month ago."

"And you had many replies, of course?" Bentley asked.

Gordon burst into a hearty laugh.

"I should think I had," he said. "I had no idea there was so much spontaneous kindness in the world. I must have had at least three hundred replies. They came from all sorts and conditions of people, and I have got invitations to stay in houses from ducal castles downwards. I had enough cigarettes and provisions to keep any platoon living on the fat of the land for a month. I had to tip the man who brought up my letters. Inadvertently I have raised an impression that I am a poor Tommy; hence all those parcels, which I didn't want. But, mind you, it touched me very much all the same. It did me good, because I was getting hard and cynical, which I may say is by no means my nature. And that is why I am going to avail myself of your hospitality. I will come with you with pleasure. The word Christmas conveys nothing to me, for my Christmases have always been spent in lodgings, or alone in a farm miles away from civilisation. I should like for once to sit down on Christmas Day amongst friendly faces."

"That's all right," Kemp said. "We regard the matter as settled. See you again on Saturday."

With that Kemp and Bentley went off to their quarters feeling like two schoolboys just before the holidays. The way to their lines led them through the angle of a wood where stood a small red cottage inhabited by a widow peasant woman who had stayed there all through the trouble, and who appeared to gain a precarious livelihood by selling such produce as was left to her by the troops and supplying them with coffee. She appeared to be utterly indifferent to everything that was going on around her, and for the rest her spare time was devoted to her only child, an infant in arms, of whom she seemed to be devotedly fond. In her way, mother Mary, as the men called her, was a favourite. She was standing at the cottage door, as Kemp and Bentley passed, and she wished them good afternoon.

CHAPTER XLI - INSIDE THE COTTAGE

She was a little woman of about middle age, picturesque, essentially French and quiet in her manner. But it was not Mother Mary that attracted Bentley's attention just at that moment, for down a little path leading to the side of the cottage appeared a figure that was familiar both to Kemp and Bentley, a figure they had not seen for some time.

"Why it's Venables!" Kemp cried. "What on earth are you doing here, and where do you come from?"

The American offered his cigarette case.

"As a matter of fact," he said, "I was looking for you fellows. I want to have a little conversation with you."

"You had better come over to our hut," Kemp said. "I don't suppose anybody will be there at this time in the afternoon. Besides, the cavalry have got some sort of a show on this afternoon, and everybody will be there. But you haven't told me how you got here, and where you came from. To tell you the truth, Venables, you are a bit of a mystery to us, and I'm not quite sure if I ought not to ask you to report yourself to the authorities and explain your movements. Mind you, I'm not suggesting that there's anything wrong with you; and I'm not forgetting that the Musketeers owe you more than one good turn; but you must admit that a chap who seems able to hop backwards and forwards and who is equally friendly with both sides, is bound to be more or less an object of suspicion."

"I wouldn't worry about that if I were you," Venables said. "You are at perfect liberty to take me to Headquarters if you like, but if you do you will only be told to mind your own business. Still, I have been intimate with one of you at home; you have been very kind and hospitable to me, and I owe you something like an explanation. Only you must promise me that it goes no farther. I know you're not quite sure whether I'm an American or not, but I can assure you that I am, and I can easily prove it if necessary. But I am something more than a journalist. When the war broke out the Germans couldn't do enough for the Americans, and when I applied for permission to represent my paper in the firing line I was welcomed with open arms in Berlin. But those people didn't know what I'm going to tell you now. They didn't know that for five or six years I have been an agent in your Secret Service and that it is my work to find out all about the German conspiracy to capture America. You don't know, of course, that for years past Germany has been sending something like a million emigrants to the States every year, and though your Foreign Office is not suspicious, they are not blind to the fact. And this is where I came in. Of course, those Germans are supposed to become American citizens, but once a German always a German, and you can see where their sympathies would be. This has been going on for years, and when I point out to you that most of those emigrants are military-trained you can see where the danger lies.

At this moment there must be millions of trained Germans in America, a country that has no navy, comparatively speaking, and practically no army. The German idea was to capture America, which would have been no difficult matter if the present campaign hadn't broken down. But there's nothing to worry about now, because the American Government is alive to the danger, and their understanding with the British Government is more complete than you imagine. But this isn't what I want to talk about. I am supposed to be heart and soul in the German cause, and those fellows have no idea of my real sentiments. They are under the impression that I have been taken prisoner once or twice and that my native cunning has saved me on each occasion. But that is not the fact; I have allowed myself to be taken prisoner, I have gone out of my way to bring it about. And that's why I was able to do you so good a turn in the big retreat."

"I believe he's telling the truth," Bentley said.

"Search me," Venables responded. "Of course I'm telling you the truth. Don't forget what happened when I asked to see your brigadier on a certain eventful occasion. I had no difficulty in satisfying him of my bona fides."

"It's a jolly dangerous game," Kemp said.

Venables looked serious just for a moment.

"You're right there," he said. "It is a dangerous game. But I love excitement and adventure, and after all thousands are doing the same thing. If ever I get found out they will shove me up against a wall and shoot me. But a man can only die once, and there's an end of it. And this brings me to my point. I have had a good deal of experience in this sort of thing lately, and I can assure you that the foreign spy who takes his life in his hands and makes a profession of it is nothing like as dangerous as the dirty traitor who poses as an honest patriot and sells his country for money. There are thousands of these about; in fact, they are the curse of every nation. And they are not always men either. As a rule, they are the very last people to be suspected."

"Are you on the track of one now?" Bentley asked.

"I am," Venables said. "And a precious cunning one, too. Let me tell you, you chaps are mere children compared to the Germans at this game. Now, for some little time past, practically everything of importance that happens here has got through to the foe. No regiment is moved up without it being known to the German lines. And it's my business to discover how the information leaks out. For days and nights I have watched to see if anything in the shape of a spy came through, and nothing suspicious did I see. I was forced at last to conclude that it was done by telephone. Long before the war began, sections of telephone wires were laid underground all over northern France and their position carefully noted on charts. During the last week or two I must have spotted and cut at least a dozen of these myself. They are in houses and woods and barns and underground drains and all that kind of thing. I think I have located the one I am after now. I wouldn't mind betting you fifty dollars that the instrument at this end of the telephone is in yonder little red cottage."

"Impossible," Kemp cried. "The woman there is the widow of a French soldier. I am sure she is a patriot if ever there was one. The poor woman hangs on here because she has nowhere else to go. She makes some sort of a living by selling odds and ends to the troops, and her coffee is the best in the neighbourhood. She and her baby live alone there in the cottage."

Venables eyes twinkled shrewdly.

"Oh, she's got a baby, has she?" he asked. "A dear little thing that lies quietly in its cradle on the cottage floor, all day, eh! Very sad and pathetic, isn't it? And I suppose the unsuspecting Tommy thinks a lot of the woman, and calls her mother and all the rest of it. If you don't mind I'd like to walk down as far as the cottage and have a look round. I am a friend of yours, of course, and you have been telling me all about the delicious coffee. You understand."

"All right," Bentley said. "But you are after the wrong fox this time. But come along."

In the door of the cottage stood the woman herself with a pitcher of freshly made coffee in her hand. She was pleased to see the English gentlemen she said, for they had always been her good friends. Would she make them some coffee? Of course she would if they would only wait for five minutes till she came back; and keep an eye upon her baby, the dear little one asleep in her cot. Directly she had gone Venables advanced into the cottage and lifted the sleeping child in his arms.

"What do you think of this?" he asked.

"By Jove!" Kemp cried; "a telephone receiver!"

CHAPTER XLII - THE HIDDEN BATTERY

A sudden change seemed to have come over Venables. He was no longer the light-hearted, easy-going war correspondent, cheerfully taking his life in his hands and devoted to the interests of his paper, but a keen and eager individual with important work in hand.

"One of you stand in the doorway," he said, "and try and look as if you are just hanging about there till the woman comes back. This is the thing that I have been looking for for a long time. I suppose I have located at least a half a dozen of these during the last week, but I knew that there was one that had evaded me, and behold, here it is. You can see for yourselves how cleverly it has been arranged. The wire comes up under the floor boards, and you will notice how cunningly the instrument has been concealed in the false bottom of this old oak cradle. The other receiver, unless I am greatly mistaken, is in a wood not far behind the place where your trenches were. And from there again it will go underground back to one of the German batteries. Now what we have to do is to locate that German battery."

"I think I know the one you mean," Kemp said. "It is a battery that has given us a great deal of trouble, and, try as they would, our airmen could not find it. You don't mean to tell me that this ignorant peasant woman knows enough to be able to communicate with those guns?"

"I'm not so sure she's an ignorant woman," Venables said. "I should say she is French, beyond all doubt, and she appears to be no more than a peasant. Now do you happen to know how long she has been here?"

"I haven't the slightest idea," Bentley said. "'From what I can understand she has lived in this cottage for years. She is rather a favourite with the men here, who regard her as being exceedingly plucky to stick to her cottage when everybody else has gone. She is in danger here."

"Not she," Venables laughed. "She has no occasion to be frightened of you chaps, and she need not fear the Germans. The only thing she has to worry about is a chance shell. But she is probably being paid handsomely for this work, and can afford to take the risk. Now, I don't know, of course, but I wouldn't mind making a small bet that this woman has come into the neighbourhood during the last year or two. You can make enquiries if you like; that is, if any of the original inhabitants are still about. My idea is that she is a regular German spy, and that she was placed in this cottage a few years ago for this very purpose. There are hundreds of such creatures in Northern France. But when you come to think of it, the whole scheme is not very difficult. Whoever dreamt two years ago that to-day Germany would be holding the whole of Belgium, and a part of Northern France? And who would suspect a workman who was seen digging a trench across a field or two? People would suppose that he was putting in a drain. Then all he has to do is to hide those wires in small pipes and have manholes at certain places, just as you see on the ordinary sewage system. I tell you, Germany worked this matter out to the last detail. You chaps are mere children by comparison."

"We'll admit all that," Kemp said. "You see, we haven't spent all the last forty years thinking about it. The question is, what are you going to do?"

"For the moment I am going to wait and watch," Venables said. "The woman herself is a mere blind. She gives the whole thing an air of reality. But it is not she who sends the messages. We'll just conceal ourselves in the wood yonder and wait. And before long I'll astonish you."

With that Venables left the cottage, followed by the other two, and proceeded to some undergrowth in the wood from which it was possible to keep a close eye on the cottage. A few moments later the woman came back, apparently quite unsuspicious, and entered the house. At the end of a quarter of an hour the figure of a man in khaki came down the road and hailed the cottage in excellent English. Then the woman came to the door and the man with the British uniform went inside.

"Did you spot his regiment?" Venables asked.

"I did," Kemp said. "He is apparently one of the Grenadier Guards. You don't mean to say—"

"No, I don't," Venables replied: "You can disabuse your mind of the idea that one of your own men is in this business, and I will make you a present of the fact that that man's English is as good as yours or mine. But all the same he is a German, as you will see presently."

"But the audacity of it!" Bentley exclaimed. "The thing sounds incredible."

"That's just why it's possible," Venables said coolly. "There was a man in a Highland regiment yesterday in one of the canteens asking for hot water. I happened to spot him, and I had him followed. He was a Bavarian in a line regiment, and he recognised at once that the game was up. He was a brave chap, too, and he died like a man. But we needn't trouble about that just now. Our friend in the Grenadier Guards' uniform at the present moment is sending certain information to the front. Now when he comes out of the cottage I want you fellows to follow him. It is too risky for me to go, because he may have seen me in the German lines. I think you will find that he will make his way into the wood, where his comrade is listening at the other end of the telephone. But here he comes. You'll have to be cautious, and I will come on behind as near as I dare."

For the best part of an hour Kemp and Bentley dogged the footsteps of the spy along the road and across the fields, until he entered the wood about a mile or so behind the trenches where the Musketeers had fought for so long. There was plenty of thick cover here, and it was possible to get close up behind the German and watch his movements from a distance of a few yards. But the man was taking no risks. For some time he looked cautiously around him, and then he proceeded to remove a heap of dead brushwood that hid a hole in the ground. From where they were standing Kemp and Bentley looked directly down into the cavity. Below them was a circular hole lined with concrete, a snug enough retreat for the man who sat there with the telephone receiver in his hand. A moment. or two later he put down the instrument and crawled out of the hole. He stretched himself with the air of a man who is cramped and tired.

"I have been waiting for you for a long time," he said in excellent English. "I am glad you have come, for I could make nothing of your last message. I think something has gone wrong with the transmitter."

This was true enough, for Venables had seen to that. It had been part of his scheme.

"All right," the other man said. "I'll stay here while you go back and put it right. Is there any news?"

"I think so," the other said. "I understand that the British are falling back just here with the view to straightening out their line. If that is the case we shall have to bring up our battery another half-mile or so."

The men changed places, and the one who had been working the telephone turned his face in the direction of the British lines. He had not gone 10 yards before Kemp and Bentley were upon him.

He threw up his hands and shrugged his shoulders. A quarter of an hour later the two spies, disarmed and helpless, were being marched to the base. Once they were in safe hands Venables appeared again.

"That was very smart," he said. "I know those two chaps well. They were in America two years ago."

CHAPTER XLIII - HOMEWARD BOUND

"What are you going to do now?" Bentley asked.

"Oh, the rest is easy," Venables said. "Now that I know exactly where we stand, I am going to take the place of the man who is working the telephone, and send information that I want to convey to the battery. I'm not quite sure, but I think this battery is hidden in an old sandpit and our game of course is to get them out. If they believe that we are abandoning those front trenches, it will be useless for them to stay where they are, and once they begin to move we can smash them all up."

It was an hour or two later before Venables was ready to put his plan in execution. With his knowledge of German and the exact position it was not difficult for him to transmit to the German battery exactly what he wished them to believe. At the same time he could work the telephone back to the base into the woman's cottage which had now been taken over by the British authorities, and warn them that he had been successful in deceiving the officer in charge of the German battery. All he wanted now was an observation on the part of the British airmen, so that every movement of the battery could be watched and the guns destroyed by British fire. There was no hitch, and about an hour later the German guns that had been such a thorn in the side of the British for the past week or two began to crawl out of their shelter, disguised as hay carts, and made their way forward to another sheltered spot which had been carefully prepared with a view to an advance.

Scarcely had they emerged into the open when a British aeroplane shot up from the lines and hovered like a hawk over the battery. Then certain signals were made, and almost before the Germans knew what had happened the English field guns opened fire upon them. From the very first shot the fire was deadly. The initial shell dropped into the centre of them, followed by another, and another, until the German guns were scattered and broken, and not a single man in charge of them was left. It was only one of the small incidents of war, but it was exceedingly exciting while it lasted, especially to Kemp and Bentley, who stood at the edge of the wood watching the whole thing with breathless interest. It was all over and finished within less time than it takes to tell, and there were not more than a dozen people down at the base who knew anything about it. But it was something for Bentley and Kemp to look back upon when they started on their holiday. Venables pointed out that there must be no discussion of the subject amongst the Musketeers.

"Somebody had to know about this business," he said, "and by good luck it happened to be you two. I don't suppose there are half a dozen people at the base who will know what has become of that old woman. There are only one or two people who are aware how it happened that that German battery came out into the open. Even the aviator who spotted them does not know that he was sent up on purpose to find the battery which was already there before he started. He is hugging himself with the delusion that he has done an exceedingly smart piece of work. You see, men who do what I do have to work entirely in the dark, and if any of the people here got to know what my occupation is, more than half my utility would be gone. Besides, there are so many spies hanging about that it would be sure to come to their ears, and the next time I showed my face inside the German lines I should be greeted with a bullet. So you see my life is more or less in the hands of you two, and I'd rather trust you than any Englishmen I know. So please be good enough to forget that you have ever seen me, and that you know anything about this telephone business."

"You can rely entirely upon us," Bentley said. "And thank you for a most exciting afternoon. It was fine to see the way we smashed up that German battery; it was a sight that I would not have missed for anything. But what are you going to do now? Won't you come and have some supper with us? As we're leaving for home to-morrow, we've got rather a special spread."

Venables shook his head regretfully.

"I'm sorry I can't do it," he said. "Just for the moment I have finished my work, and I have a very delicate task in front of me. By this time to-morrow I shall be back again in the German lines, and goodness knows when we shall meet again."

He shook hands, and disappeared in the direction of the village. The others watched him out of sight.

"That's a queer chap," Bentley said. "And it's a queer sort of life he's leading."

"I rather envy him," Kemp replied. "You can't say his is not a strenuous existence. I should think that Venables would be able to write a most interesting book on his adventures. There's something fine in a man taking his life in his hands like that. He doesn't appear to have a nerve in his body. I hope he will come out all right. It's a queer sort of world, old chap, and there are queer ways of getting a living. When I first met Venables and played golf with him I never dreamt that he was leading a life such as novelists write about."

It was a fine, still evening, and a lively party gathered in Kemp and Bentley's hut to partake of a farewell supper. They were a select gathering in a way, but Ginger and George and the rest of them were there, frankly envious of the good fortune of their comrades.

"Not but wot I've 'ad my time," Ginger said. "The week or two I spent at 'ome was like a dream to me. I've read in pipers an' books all about them lucky chaps wot's picked up in the streets an' taken to 'ospitals, where they've been waited upon as if they'd been a lot o' bally dooks, an' then sent down to plices like Margate and Southend to get well, but I never believed it was true; I thought it was all a sort o' gime, made up by them chaps wot write for the pipers. But some o' you chaps knows as wot it's true, because you've been through it yourselves. You knows wot it is to be waited on 'and and foot by real lidies, an' tiken to foitball matches in a motor car. It seems like a regular dream to me, but it's a dream I don't want ter forget an' wot I'll remember to my dying day. But George an' Joe, they knows all abaht that. An' before we says good-bye to our mates to-night I'd like to drink the 'ealth of Miss Kemp an' Miss Bentley an' the other lidies wot went out o' their way to make life pleasant for us poor blokes."

"Regular orator, ain't 'e?" asked George.

"It's only becorse me 'eart's full," Ginger said. "When I think of them angels, an' wot they did for me, I can't be grateful enough. It's all very well to say as we're all pals 'ere, but there's a difference, an' a gentleman's a gentleman all the world over, even though 'e does wear a number on 'is shoulder and gets ordered abaht by a sargeant wot at one time was perhaps a groom in 'is own stable. But it's all in the day's work, an' all for the glory of the old flag. An' there ain't nobody who appreciates the difference more'n us blokes round 'ere who used to caddy for them. So if you don't mind, gentlemen, perhaps you'll give our kindest regards to the lidies. God bless 'em, and tell 'em as we're still 'ere playin' the gime, an' we ain't forgot all their kindness to us. There may be others 'ere as'll get wounded, an' if they do, all the 'arm I wish 'em is that when they gets 'ome they'll find theirselves in the Keep 'Ouse 'Ospital bein' looked after by Miss Kemp an' Miss Bentley an' all the rest o' the lidies there."

"There, that'll do, Ginger," Kemp said. "We'll tell the ladies what you say, and no one knows better than we do that you mean it. And now let's join hands and sing 'Auld Lang Syne' before they come round for lights out."

CHAPTER XLIV - THE NEW LONDON

The favoured Musketeers made their way slowly down to the coast in cattle trucks and wagons attached to returning munition trains. As they went along they picked up others here and there, until by the time Havre was reached they numbered something like fifteen hundred altogether. It mattered nothing that the weather was abominable and that the journey proceeded in a perfect downpour of rain; they were used to all this; the trenches had hardened them against weather of all sorts, and, besides, they were going home. That word would have meant a good deal to many of them in ordinary conditions; now it had a peculiar significance all its own. And there was not one of them who did not feel that he was earning his holiday.

There were some amongst them, of course, who were fighters by instinct, men who had served with the colours in all parts of the world, professional soldiers to whom all countries are more or less alike so long as they draw their pay and have sufficient to eat and drink. But there were many others, Territorials and volunteers, who a few brief months ago had never dreamt of the coming strife. They had come out of all walks in life; the country gentleman from his old family home, with its almost sacred ties, leaving his dogs and his sport and all that goes to make up most that is pleasant in life; and his tenants and the sons of his tenants, his game-keeper and the labourers from his estate; and others who had earned their bread by hard, monotonous labour in workshops and factories.

To all of them this adventure had fallen out of the skies. They were not soldiers by compulsion either. The call had come to them, and they had heard it and there had been no occasion to blow the bugle twice. They were the best and brightest that England could produce, men who had not waited for the wave of patriotism to sweep them forward, but keen, bright spirits who had come along in front of it. They were people to whom England would ever owe the deepest debt of gratitude. For they were the pioneers, the leaders who showed the way so that in the course of time three million others followed, and they had not to be fetched.

And now they were going back again for a brief space, back to the mansion and the cottage, back to the open country and the close clustering houses in the great northern towns, every man of them a hero just as if he were carrying the Victoria Cross on his breast. Yet there was not one of them who had a word to say about his own particular exploits.

Kemp and Bentley stood on the deck of the Dog Star and watched the shores of France receding in the distance. It was as if they had left all troubles and dangers behind. The deck was crowded with all sorts and conditions of men, from commanding officers downwards, all looking forward to their Christmas holiday. There was no distinction between them there; officers and men were mixed up together, comparing notes and exchanging experiences and all in the best of spirits.

"There isn't much the matter with the old country, after all," Bentley said, "I must confess that I had my doubts at one time. I can't recollect much about the Boer war, but it never seemed to me that we had much to be proud of there. There were too many 'regrettable incidents,' and too many unnecessary surrenders. I may be wrong, but that's my reading of the history of the war."

A lean, long captain in a line regiment sitting on a camp stool close by turned in the speaker's direction. He appeared to be a man over old for service, for his hair was grey and there were deep lines about his face. But his eyes were keen, and there was a row of ribbons across his left breast. He realised that the men by his side were gentlemen, and without further hesitation he plunged into conversation with them.

"I was in the Boer war myself," he said. "I was there from the start till peace was declared, and I came through without a single scratch. I was at Ladysmith and Pardeburg; indeed, I missed very few of the big engagements. In my opinion we never took that war seriously enough, not even when Roberts and Kitchener went out. England knew from the first that it was a dead certainty. But we did find some good men there and we are benefiting from the experience now. Don't forget that a large proportion of the men out at the front at the present moment fought under French in the Boer war. And there isn't a man who hasn't the greatest confidence in him. They know what a born leader he is, and how careful he is of their welfare. In my humble opinion the Boer war was an awakening to Great Britain. On the battle fields of South Africa we found the spirit which we had lost, or mislaid, if you like the expression better. You mustn't forget that this is our first big experience since the Crimea; don't forget that our first army is the only one in the world that has ever been under fire, with the exception perhaps of the Balkan States, which by comparison is another matter. You know what we've done; that is, if you have been out long enough to see."

"We've been out since the beginning of September," Kemp said. "We are Musketeers."

"Then I congratulate you," the other man said. "You know all about it."

"We have been in all the big engagements," Bentley observed. "I don't think we've missed anything."

"Then I won't enlarge upon the topic," the man who had been through the Boer war said. "We don't boast about it, but we know what we've done. We steadied the French down, and bore the brunt of it until their chaps found their feet. They are all right now, and they will cover themselves with credit, but at first, when they were new to the game, and when the Germans came down in such overwhelming force, it was touch and go for a few days, just like it was on more than one occasion in South Africa. You see, it's absurd to talk about veteran troops unless the men have been under fire. They must be supported by a man who has been through the mill, and that is where our chaps came in so useful when von Kluck was in front of Paris. I never thought I should fight again, but I volunteered directly the war broke out and left my place in the north to go and fight."

"Did they give you a commission?" Bentley asked.

"They couldn't very well help it," the other man laughed. "For a fortnight I was in a Territorial regiment as a Tommy. I slept on bare boards the whole time and shared their food. I thought I was too old to get a commission, but they found me out and sent me to a depot to help train recruits. There must be thousands like me who have gone through the same thing."

CHAPTER XLV - HOME, SWEET HOME

Kemp and Bentley parted from their pleasant acquaintance at Waterloo station with a promise to meet him a day or two later and dine with him at his club. He turned out to be a well-known North of England sportsman, and, moreover, had been at their old school. When he mentioned his name they recognised him as a one time captain of the cricket eleven, and a bat who had done duty for England on more than one occasion.

"Fancy running up against him," Kemp said. "Now, what are we going to do? Have you got anything in view, Gordon, before you come along with us?"

"Not I," Gordon said. "Of course, I must go to my bank, and I want to see my solicitor. As soon as that's done I am entirely at your service. And of course I shall have to pack a bag with some clothes. I suppose we shall be allowed to get out of these uniforms for the time we are here?"

"I don't see why we shouldn't," Kemp said. "These clothes are all very well, but they are not the sort of thing to dine in. Now, the first thing I'm going to do is to go along to my club and have a Turkish bath and get a change of linen."

"Do your people know that I am coming?" Gordon asked.

"Really, it doesn't matter whether they know or not," Kemp said. "As a matter of fact, they don't. You needn't look so astonished. They don't know we're coming at all so far as that goes. Bentley and myself thought it would be a pleasant surprise. We'll just drop down after tea and take them unawares. When we have had a change and a wash I vote we go and have lunch at the Imperial or some other place up West. Won't it be strange to sit down to a table again to a civilised meal!"

There were other things that struck the trio as strange besides the luxurious luncheon they enjoyed a little later on. Somehow London appeared to be different. There were the same crowds in the street, and the shops looked much as usual, but there was an extraordinary absence of young men everywhere. Kemp pulled up in Regent-street and remarked on the fact.

"Where are all the boys?" he asked. "I didn't think they'd all joined the army. And yet, with the exception of the men in the shops, and the clerks, I can't see any of them."

Almost as Kemp spoke the traffic in the street drew on one side and down the road came a battalion connected with some new regiment, swinging along with their heads up and fully conscious of the impression they were making. It was quite evident that these recruits were new to their khaki, and they were without rifles or side arms, but there was no mistake about their physique. They were young for the most part, men between twenty and thirty, but as to their quality there could only be one opinion. They had been in training long enough to be welded together, and, despite the fact that they had no band, they swung along in perfect step, as fine a twelve hundred as it would be possible for any country in the world to produce.

"That's ripping good stuff," Bentley said. "Some of our Territorials out yonder are all right, but they are not quite so fine as those chaps yonder. Who are they?"

An elderly man looking on gave the desired information.

"Kitchener's army," he said. "I don't rightly know what regiment they belong to, but they come from the north, and they have been training in one of the parks here. Makes you feel proud of your fellow-countrymen, doesn't it? And they're not the pick of the basket, either. There are millions like 'em. Mean to say you haven't seen them before?"

"We haven't had a chance," Gordon said.

"Oh, I see, you're just back from the front, are you? Well, when you return you can tell the men out yonder what you've seen. Say that, good as French's army is, better is coming. Say that in three or four months' time we are going to send you something like three million of the same pattern as those fellows in the road there. Most of them are steady married men, who have left their wives and families to fight for the flag. When I see a sight like that I forget all my doubts and fears, I forget about the slackers and the fools who prate about peace with Germany, because I know it's all right."

The speaker jammed his hat firmly on his head and went his way.

"That's very comforting," Bentley said. "I'm glad I saw that every third man we meet is wearing uniform. This is still the good old England that we're all so proud of, and it's evident that the heart is in the right place still. Come on now, I shall enjoy my luncheon all the better for this."

They lunched luxuriously with a zest and appetite such as neither of them had ever known before. Then they passed the afternoon at a matinee, and just after dark made their way by taxi down to the Keep House.

The place was one mass of lights, and every room appeared to be occupied. As they entered the hall Dorothy Kemp came out of what had been the drawing-room with a tray in her hand. She nearly dropped it when she saw them standing there.

"Harold!" she cried. "And Ronald, too! This is more than a surprise. What does it mean?"

"It means that we have been good boys, and the head-master has sent us home for a holiday," Kemp explained. "And, what's more, we shall be here over Christmas. I suppose you can find room for us somewhere? This is our friend, Ian Gordon, one of our company. He hasn't anywhere to go to, and I told him that you would be glad to see him here."

There was no occasion for Dorothy to say so, for Gordon could read a welcome in her shining eyes and in the pressure of her hand. A moment or two later Mrs. Bentley and Nettie also appeared. There was not much said, for the occasion did not call for words. There was not much room for them, either, for the house was full of wounded, but, as Kemp said, any place would be good enough for them; they could shake down in the garage or the stable, either of which would be luxurious quarters in comparison to what they had been accustomed to.

"I don't think it will be as bad as that," Mrs. Bentley smiled. "We read in the papers that occasionally some of the men at the front were allowed to come home, and we prepared a bedroom at the top of the house for you two, and also for a friend or two. You will find everything you want up there. And I don't suppose you will mind dining with us and the nurses. We are very busy and very happy here, more like brothers and sisters than anything else. And when I tell you that Royalty has been here you can imagine how proud we are of our work. Every nurse is a friend of one of the girls, and they are working splendidly. You must come round and see our patients presently."

It was comparatively late in the evening before Bentley got a chance of a few quiet words with Dorothy. There was a little room at the end of the corridor used as an office, and there they sat alone.

"It's good to be back here like this again," Bentley said. "I can't tell you how glad I am to see you. To-morrow I'll tell you all about our adventures, but I don't want to talk about them tonight. I want to forget everything except that I am back here. You are happy in your work?"

"Oh, indeed I am," Dorothy said. "Really, I don't know what we should have done without it. It enables us to forget all the worry and anxiety, and when night comes we are too tired to do anything but sleep. We are all friends here, too; there are more than a dozen of us who a few months ago thought about nothing but amusement. And I'm glad to say there isn't one of my friends who wouldn't take her share in the good work."

"A fine work," Bentley exclaimed. "How fine, I don't believe even you people realised."

It was little that the returned Musketeers needed in the way of amusement or recreation just now, for it was only when the bow was relaxed that they began to realise the strain which they had gone through. The mere fact that they had nothing to do was in itself a luxury after all that they had gone through. It seemed strange, too, to sleep the night through and wake in the morning to luxury and comfort. Indeed, at first, this had been rather a difficult matter, but at the end of two or three days they were getting into it, and it was only then that they began to discuss their past experiences. After all, there seemed to be nothing to say, and the things that Nettie and Dorothy followed with breathless interest had become to them the mere commonplaces of everyday life.

"You see, there are so many of them doing it," Bentley told Dorothy. "If our men out there were properly rewarded the Victoria Cross would be as common as the Iron Cross of Germany. Occasionally some incident stands out more brightly than the rest by reason of its dramatic surroundings. Then it gets into the papers and everybody begins to talk about it. But the lucky man himself knows perfectly well that he is merely one of a crowd, and takes it all for granted. Now, I'll tell you a little thing that happened to me that did not get into the papers, and never will now. It was about two months ago, when we were being hard pressed one night. The Germans were absolutely on the top of us, indeed they were in our trench, and had they been properly supported I should not be here telling you this story at the present moment. Those chaps had taken us entirely by surprise; they had badly cut up some of our fellows the day before and they were wearing our uniform. They were led by a man who spoke excellent English, and we were all utterly deceived. It was not till they were absolutely in the trench that we discovered what was going on. Just before they charged they threw about a dozen hand grenades into the trench, and it was that that gave them away. One of those grenades lay right at my feet without exploding, and I had no idea that it was there. But the man next to me stooped and picked it up and stood there with the beastly thing in his hand. If it had exploded then it would have blown him all into little bits. And no one knew that better than himself. But he waited with it in his hand till a dozen or more Germans appeared on the edge of the trench and then he threw the grenade in the middle of them. A second or two later there wasn't one of those Germans left. The man I am talking about, and one other, drove them back with their own bombs, and about ten minutes later we had their trench instead of them having ours. This doesn't sound much in cold blood, but if you'll think it over you will see that it wants some doing."

Dorothy's eyes gleaned as she listened.

"I should like to meet that man," she said.

"You have met him," Bentley said quietly. "He was one of the wounded we sent over here a month or two ago. He was the hero of that football match I was telling you about, and he is commonly known amongst us as George. You remember him."

"Oh, I do," Dorothy exclaimed. "I remember all of them. I hope some time we shall see them again."

"I tell you this just as an ordinary instance of the things that happen every day out yonder. And I can tell you another story of a man who regarded himself as a coward. As a matter of fact he wasn't anything of the kind, but he thought he was because he had the most vivid imagination. He was a chap who couldn't sleep and couldn't eat, the type of man who crouches down every time he hears a shell. But he wasn't a coward, and all of us knew it, though he must have undergone the tortures of hell every time he went under fire. Take it one way and another perhaps he is the bravest man I ever met. He was a gunner. Well, one night his gun managed to blunder right into the German lines and was abandoned there. It was left in a barn, and the Germans were shelling the barn all the time. The driver had been killed and one of the horses too. In the early dawn that man forced himself to go back to the barn under heavy fire and managed to bring that gun away. He was wounded in two places, but he got back to our lines all right. He is somewhere in England to-day, and I hope that we may meet again."

All these things and more Bentley told Dorothy as they sat in the little office discussing the future. Only four or five days remained of the holiday now, and they were making the most of their time. Kemp was somewhere with Nettie Bentley and Gordon had struck up more than a friendship with a little golden-haired girl who was assistant to one of the nurses.

"I like your friend, Mr. Gordon," Dorothy said. "And I am so glad you brought him here. It seems a shame that a nice man like that should have no friends."

"He seems to have one now," Bentley laughed. "Like most quiet, self-contained men, he has a good deal of feeling, and I am much mistaken if most of those feelings are not concentrated upon your friend, Miss Nellie Somers."

"So you've noticed that?" Dorothy asked.

"I should have been blind if I hadn't. I never saw a man more hopelessly smitten. He went down before those blue eyes at the first glance. She's a dear little girl, too, and will make any man a good wife. But what's the use of a fellow thinking about that kind of thing just now? Of course I know its the fashionable thing to do. I know that hundreds of officers have married recently and gone to the front after a few hours' honeymoon. But is it right, is it fair to a girl? You see, so many of them will soon be widows; indeed, a lot of them are widows already. It doesn't strike me as playing the game to marry a girl and leave her to her fate, so to speak, with all the future before her. But, of course, there must be two sides to the question, and people might say that I have no right to speak seeing that I am in no position to keep a wife myself. Don't you agree with me Dorothy?"

Dorothy looked up with a demure light in her eyes.

"I don't think I do," she said. "It may be romantic perhaps, but I think there is something fine in the idea of a girl giving herself to a man who is fighting for his country. Even if he gets killed, as so many of them will, she has always the consolation of knowing that she married a hero. And as to not being able to keep a wife, that is rather a commonplace argument, especially in a case like mine where I have a good deal of money of any own."

Bentley caught his breath sharply.

"Do you really mean that?" he asked.

Dorothy met his glance steadily.

"I do, Harold," she said. "It may sound audacious on my part, but I do mean it. If this war was over to-morrow you would marry me almost at once. It matters nothing that you have no money; what can it matter when I have enough for two?"

"And you would be happier if I made you my wife before I went back to the front?"

"Yes," Dorothy said. "I may be wrong, but it seems to me the right thing. There never will be anybody else but you. And there are other questions I cannot discuss. I know, too, that Ronald is going to ask Nettie to marry him, and if Mr. Gordon is in earnest we might have three weddings. Are you very angry with me for making the suggestion? Does it strike you as being bold and unmaidenly on my part?"

CHAPTER XLVII - BACK TO THE FRONT

Exactly how the whole thing came about it would have been difficult for any of the three friends to say. It seemed to be the most natural thing in the world, and there was not a nurse in the house who did not regard it as the proper thing. Indeed, the little girl with the golden hair frankly declared that she had gone out of her way to propose to Ian Gordon, a suggestion that he repudiated with great indignation. But the fact remained that he and Nellie Somers were engaged, and that they had made up their minds to be married before the all too brief holiday was over. It would take a day or two to procure the special licences, and this would just permit a few hours' honeymoon, which they had decided to spend on a short motor trip to Brighton. There was only one of the trio who had any doubts about the wisdom of the step, and that was Harold Bentley. The other two were rich, and could please themselves. He, on the other hand, had no money, and from the worldly point of view was doing exceedingly well. But he was very much in love, the glamour of the situation was upon him, and there was nothing for it but to fall in line with the rest.

There had been a good many romantic marriages since the beginning of the war, but these three looked like being something out of the common. To begin with, there would be three of them under one roof, and the fact that all the brides were actively engaged in nursing the wounded, and were working a hospital of their own, added to the glamour of it. The local papers got to hear about it, and the story was told far and wide. Some of the wounded were sufficiently recovered to attend the ceremony, and this added picturesqueness to a ceremony which otherwise was practically private. It was over and done with at length, and, the newly-married couples went their way in pursuit of a honeymoon which would have been regarded as something a little short of madness a few months ago. But the war had changed all that; the war had changed a good many things and swept away many traditions that would never be worshiped again.

Meanwhile matters at the front were dragging slowly along. The wet winter had set in, days and weeks of rain, during which the opposing forces sat down doggedly before one another, waiting with what patience they could for the spring. For all practical purposes the great German offensive was broken. So far had they gone that it began to seem impossible that they could go any further. The foe could bring up men, and yet more men, guns, and yet more guns, but they had a solid force opposite them now, and though occasionally they tried one of their mad rushes, and exhibited their usual recklessness with regard to human life, the front was firmly locked against them.

Great things were promised for the spring, but so far as the real peril was concerned Germany had shot her bolt. She might, and probably would, call out every available man she possessed; but even a country that has been preparing for war as Germany had done for the best part of half a century could not possibly keep up this high tension for ever.

And meanwhile England was getting stronger and stronger as the Germans began to grow weak. Not that they were really weak, but no country can lose over two millions of the flower of her manhood without suffering from this terrible loss of blood. It was as if some athlete in the full flood of his powers had taken on some big task at a moment when he was already engaged upon a labour that had taxed him to the uttermost. And all the time that Germany was waiting there face to face with the allies in the trenches, Britain was gathering her forces from all parts of the globe. She already had something like three million men under arms, and all these would be ready in the summer.

Bentley and Kemp and Gordon discussed the situation one sunny morning at the end of December as they sat out on the Brighton front. They had only another 24 hours of their holiday left to them; early in the morning they would be off to join a troopship sailing from Newhaven, and it had been arranged that their three brides should go back to London by motor.

"It seems to me," Kemp said, "that we haven't begun yet. What price the fools who said that the war would be over by Christmas and that Germany could not stand the strain for longer than that? We have had some pretty tough fighting so far, but nothing in comparison with what is to come."

"We shall have some good stuff," Bentley said. "You've only got to look about you to see that."

Brighton was full of troops. They swung along down the front, they filled the promenades; the men in khaki seemed to be everywhere. For the most part they spoke in a tongue which was not familiar to the south, though they were getting used to it now. There were mill and factory hands, sturdy miners and dockers, all of whom had come down from the north at the first sound of danger, to be led later on by French and his generals in the advance on Berlin. They were eager and excited, and keen to get to work, but men like Kemp and his friends, who had had four months' experience, knew only too well that many weary months would elapse before the great forward movement could take place. There was nothing in the papers day by day except accounts of occasional skirmishes or the taking or losing of a trench, and certain sections of the British public were beginning to ask themselves questions. At first it had been assumed lightheartedly that the advance on Berlin was only a question of weeks. Few people regarded Austria seriously; she was not ready for war; had been no better prepared than France and England; and as for Turkey, she would be speedily wiped off the face of the map of Europe. It was impossible, incredible, therefore, that Germany could hope to hold out for long against the combined forces of England and Russia and France.

There were three men, however, sitting on the Brighton front that bright December morning who knew better than that. They were by no means blind to the danger, and it would be something in the nature of a miracle if the three of them came back safely at the end of the war.

They sat there for a long time, each man absorbed in his own thoughts. It was Kemp who rose at last and shook the feeling of depression from him.

"Come on," he said. "Let us go across to the hotel and join the girls. This is our last day, so let's make the best of it. Who knows when we shall have another opportunity? We have our work to do, and they have theirs, which in its way is quite as important as ours. We ought to be proud of what they are doing. Now come along."

The following afternoon the trio were dropping out of Newhaven harbour on their way to Dieppe. It was no time for repining, no time to think of anything else except the stern work in front of them. Here were fresh troops going to the front, together with men who had recovered from their wounds, and seasoned fighters returning from their holiday. They were all in the best of health and spirits, and all of them eager to get back to the firing line.

Two days later they found themselves once more in the old familiar trench behind the ruined castle, with the canal in front and the Germans just across the water.

Ginger and the rest greeted them heartily.

"We're all glad to see you back," he said. "We're dull enough, goodness knows, and likely to be as far as I can see. Why didn't you say as you was goin' to get married? We read abaht it in the pipers, and wished you all good luck."

CHAPTER XLVIII - NEUVE CHAPELLE

The short days and long nights dragged on in the trenches; the heavy rains had poured down, flooding the whole of the dreary country far and wide, and yet the British were holding their lines with a dogged tenacity as marvellous in its way as their more brilliant feats of arms. In all the work the British army has done in the course of its long career there has really been nothing greater than that dogged patience turned against the German front during all those terrible months before Ypres. It was different from anything that Tommy had ever done before. Hitherto he had fought to conquer; he had learnt how to fall back doggedly when disaster threatened; but to sit quietly down month after month, up to his knees in water, frost-bitten and starving, was a new experience to him.

But he stuck it, stuck it in a way that the pleasure-loving section of the people at home leading their lives just in the ordinary way will never know, and will never appreciate if they do. But all this was coming to an end now. The floods were drying up, and life was gradually becoming endurable. So far our small army had borne all the heat and burden of the day; so far it had been a stone wall against which the flower of the German army had flung themselves in vain. Now it was felt that the tide had turned, and it was for the British to make the advance, though the Germans had not realised it as yet.

It was Wednesday, March 10.

To all outward seeming it was much the same as any other day—a heavy morning coming up sullenly through the clouds. But behind the British lines things were moving at last, and all through the night long lines of men had marched down the roads leading to the German position through Laventie and Richebourg St. Vaast, heaps of ruins which had been smiling villages only a few months ago. Here they came, regiment by regiment, the Indians, dark and mysterious, Sikhs these, and farther down the road the Gurkhas, and with them the Leicesters and Territorials of the Royal Fusiliers. Here could be seen the silver crosses of the Rifle Brigade, followed by the Black Watch and the Lincolns, these in their turn supported by the Northamptons and the Worcesters, who, amongst others, had covered themselves with glory at Ypres.

French was ready for his first advance.

The essence of the whole thing was its complete surprise. Everything promised well for its success. For some strange reason the German airmen had been comparatively idle during the last few days, and so far no information had leaked out as to what General French and his staff had in the back of their minds. The main idea was that the Germans were to be battered with artillery and their lines rushed before they could recover from the shock of the big guns. And in bringing about this surprise French's men had a good clear 36 hours before them. It was calculated—a calculation that was perfectly sound—that this much time must elapse before the German line, weakened by the terrible weight of high explosive shell, could rush up their enforcements. And to ensure the enemy being held down to the right and left, an attack was planned north and south of the main advance simultaneously with a great thrust on Neuve Chapelle.

It is not necessary to say much of the marvellous tenacity displayed by the British troops in their pinning down attacks at La Bassee whilst the great main fight was going on. The main attack on the whole German position was entrusted to the Indian corps on the right and the 4th Army Corps on the left, and also in the centre. But this could not be carried out until the whole of the barbed wire entanglements had been swept away by the concentrated fire of our artillery. It was up to them to prepare the way for the great assault on Neuve Chapelle. An hour or so before dawn everything was ready, and exactly on the stroke of half-past seven the most deadly concentration of fire of guns of all calibres began that the world's wars have ever seen.

Without a word of warning the deep boom of the first British gun struck on the ears of the waiting troops, all strung up for the coming fray. It was for this moment that they had been waiting for months, for this moment that they had patiently endured the mud, the frost, and the cold. They were going forward now; they were making the first stride in the direction of Berlin. They were well fed, and in spite of the cold many of the regiments had already discarded their overcoats.

Close up against the Sikhs what was left of the Musketeers was standing to. They had had a hot supper the night before, and coffee had just been served out, though not a man amongst them had a thought for breakfast. Every passing moment seemed like an hour as they lay there waiting for the guns. They knew perfectly well that their time had not come yet. Before they advanced the assembled guns would have to send their message, and for at least an hour the deadly rain of shell would continue.

Then it broke loose—not one gun, but hundreds. The men in the front trenches were deafened and dazed by the roar of the field guns pouring out their shells at almost point-blank range, and cutting through the German barbed wire entanglements as if they had been so much paper. The range was so short and the trajectory of those shells so flat that in many cases they passed only a few feet over the heads of the men who were lined up in the British trenches. In some cases the troops were deluged in dust and dirt and spattered with blood from the fragments of human bodies blown high in the air. It was a horrible thirty-five minutes, and then the shells began to burst further ahead as the gunners lengthened their fuses for the purpose of dropping their shots on to the village of Neuve Chapelle, and thus leaving the road open presently for our infantry to come in and finish the work that they had begun.

"Something like a fight, this," Ginger murmured. "This is wot I come out for. I wouldn't 'ave missed it for worlds."

But nobody was listening. Every man was watching the effect of the artillery fire. And then as suddenly as it had begun the roar of the big guns ceased, ceased at least for the time being. After that the whistles began to blow and the British hurriedly scrambled out of the trenches into the open. It was going to be a soldier's battle if ever there was one, a Tommy's fight with officers and men side by side; indeed, the officers, wearing overcoats and carrying rifles with bayonets, looked like the rank and file themselves. From the centre of the attacking line the assault was originally pressed home.

The big guns had done their work well. What half an hour before had been a well-defined line of apparently impregnable trenches was blown out of all recognition, and had become no more than a row of pits in the ground dotted with dead and red with blood. As for the barbed wire, it had vanished as completely as if it had been no more than a handful of rags. The Berkshires and the Lincolns led the way, closely followed by the Musketeers, and their orders were to swerve respectively to the left and right as soon as they were into the first line of trenches, and thus clear the way for the Royal Irish Rifles and the Rifle Brigade to rush the village.

There were, of course, many Germans still left in the other trenches too dazed to fight, which is no reflection upon their courage, considering what they had gone through, and these were only too glad to surrender. The Musketeers were opposed just for a moment by a couple of machine guns served by two German officers fighting with the courage of despair.

CHAPTER XLIX - THE EARLY MORNING

It was an annoying incident, one of those little things that happen in war, and for a second or two the Musketeers hung back before the deadly concentration of that fire. Another minute, and they might have been wiped out altogether, for the experience of the war shows that one machine gun well served may hold a whole brigade, as indeed has happened more than once in the present campaign. There was not a man amongst the Musketeers who failed to recognise the fine work those two German officers were doing. But even the finest feeling of chivalry has to give way at moments such as these.

"We shall have to shoot them," Bentley murmured. "Can't they see that it is quite hopeless? Why, good Lord, they're all by themselves!"

"They ought to be English, sir," Ginger put in. "They're wasted in the German army. Somebody's got to do it, so here goes! That's got 'im, I think."

The two heads behind the machine gun dropped out of sight, and the Musketeers moved forward again. This little interlude had cost them something like 30 of their men. Even in the mad excitement of the moment, when every man was strung up to the highest tension, it was still possible to note every incident clearly. And it pleased Bentley and Kemp to see that those two German officers were not killed, but merely wounded.

"Let 'em off as easily as I could," Ginger said. "I didn't mean to do 'em in, an' I'm glad of it. 'Ere, wot's the gime now?"

The regiment next to the Musketeers had swung round sharply to the right, following up the 34th Garhwalis, who, on the right, had taken their trenches with a rush, run over them, and were pelting hard in the direction of the village. And this even though the artillery behind had not yet finished its work. They had to pause for a moment while the Berks and the Lincolns were told off to assemble the prisoners who were now trooping out of the trenches in all directions.

For a moment or two the Garhwalis were actually standing out there in the open, laughing and joking amidst the terrible din made by the huge shells and the rattle of machine guns all along the line. And then the native regiment went on headlong to what they knew would be the bloodiest work of the day. It was up to them to capture Neuve Chapelle at the point of the bayonet, and to do the foe justice they were fighting with a grim tenacity beyond all praise. They knew only too well that in close hand-to-hand strife like this no quarter would be given, and none was asked. For in individual resistance, haphazard and here and there, it is impossible for attacking troops to discriminate. They must go through their deadly work with all the ruthlessness that war entails. And they were fighting now hand to hand and so close to the foe that it was almost impossible at times to get the bayonet to work. And there was another thing to think of. The enemy's resistance was not broken yet, and the British had to think of the snipers and the chance of being enfiladed from hastily-prepared strongholds at a score of different points.

The village was a sight never to be forgotten. A devastating earthquake could have caused no greater disaster than that wrought by our big guns. The very lines of the streets were obliterated. It was indeed a scene of desolation into which the first of the British made their way. Apparently this honour belonged to the Rifle Brigade. Of the church only the bare shell remained; the little churchyard was a mass of ruin amongst which the very dead had been plucked from their graves. Of all that once pleasant village only two things appeared to remain intact, a pair of great crucifixes, one in the churchyard and the other close to the chateau. The din and confusion were beyond words. A thick pall of shell smoke lay like a cloud over the village, and every time the veil drifted a little the Germans could be seen on all sides crawling, dazed and confused, from their cellars and dugouts holding their hands above their heads and slinking round the shattered houses, whilst others, with the courage of despair, were firing from the windows of the ruined houses and even sheltering perilously behind the few surviving tombstones. Even yet the work had not been finished, for a perfect tornado of machine gun fire was still pouring from the houses on the far side of the village. From a cellar presently there emerged a huge German, his fat frame quivering with fear and his hoarse voice screaming entreaties in excellent English that his life might be spared, as he was a married man. This little note of comedy in the midst of that welter of tragedy and death was the sort of thing that is never lost upon an English Tommy in whatever part of the world he may be. So the Territorial standing before him lowered the point of his bayonet with a retort, "The old missus won't thank me for sending you home," and spared his life. Close by a subaltern in the Rifle Brigade tripped over a sandbag into a German trench and scrambled to his feet to find two officers, mere boys, with their hands above their heads. They were horribly white and shaken, but one of them managed to stammer out in quite good English the words, "Don't shoot, we are from London also," and that was the way in which their hour of trouble came to an end.

Immediately on the outskirts of the village there happened one of those little incidents that can only befall those who know service with the British army all over the world. It came about that the Rifle Brigade, smeared with dust and blood, came in contact, quite by accident, with the 3rd Gurkhas, with whom they had at one time seen service in India. The little men were equally dirty and grimy, but their faces were wreathed in smiles, for they had just been doing work after their own heart. With their knives in their hands they had just rushed a block of houses across the road and destroyed a large party of Germans who had been strongly entrenched there with a large number of machine guns. Just at that moment there was a lull in the fighting, and the riflemen and Gurkhas stood there like long-lost brothers, just reunited, each cheering the other hoarse. This is the sort of thing that one smiles at in fiction, but which happens every day in actual warfare.

But meanwhile the Germans had been taking a terrible toll, as they had done all through the campaign, by reason of the superiority of their machine guns. It is not that the German machine gun is a better weapon than ours; as a matter of fact, it isn't half as good. Where they excel is in the number of them. It was at the point called Port Arthur, and the heroic regiment was the 11th Garhwalis, who had covered themselves with so much glory earlier in the day.

They had leapt from their trenches at the first blast of the whistle, to be almost instantly withered by the devastating fury of the machine guns. The German trench in front was untouched, and so was its two hundred yards of barbed wire, But the native regiment never faltered, though every officer of the leading companies was killed in front of his men. But, though the battalion staggered under the blast of fire, they did not waver, and after fierce fighting with knife and bayonet rolled headlong into the German trenches. At the same time the Leicesters on their left had gone through with a rush which was equally fierce. Their work with the bayonet that day is spoken of still, even though there is so much to speak of; they fought so well that after the fight the divisional general visited their billets and specially congratulated them. But more of this presently. It was barely 9 o'clock in the morning yet, and so far the fringe of the work was barely touched.

CHAPTER L - THE GOOD YOUNG STUFF

The day was beginning to draw on, and there were thousands there who had had enough of it. It was not that there was anything the matter with their pluck, or that fear was gnawing at their hearts, for even the youngest of them had long since got over that numbed feeling which comes to every soldier, however stout his nerves may be, when for the first time he finds himself under fire. It had become a sheer case of physical endurance now, and the battle would go to those that were the best equipped to meet it. And that was where the British outdoor life, the hours in the playing fields, and sport which is second nature, were telling against the foe.

There were points here and there, of course, where the attack hung fire. In so big an engagement this was inevitable. On so wide a field, trenched to the last inch, and fortified with barbed wire entanglements, it was inevitable that even the intensity of our artillery fire must miss some part of these defences. This happened more than once, holding the attack up awkwardly, and causing unnecessary loss of life. For instance, there was a place near the centre of the line where our troops seemed to linger much to the uneasiness of those directing the attack, for it was vital that there should be no gap in the line, and that no trench should remain untaken.

"What are they doing?" Ginger muttered as his company were pulled up and more or less delayed by a detachment of the Seaforths immediately in front of them. "This ain't the way they gets goals. An' they're bringing up their machine guns again. Look at the blighters there on the right."

Bentley and Kemp stood anxiously waiting. So did the others, for they could not understand the delay, and they were drawing machine gun fires from more quarters than one. Then, like magic, the Seaforths wheeled away to the right under orders to attack some German trenches on the flank, and it became plain what was the cause of the delay. Right in front of them lay three rows of barbed wire entanglements, which miraculously had remained untouched by the heavy fire of the British guns early in the day. From just inside the Seaforths came a battalion of London Territorials, the 3rd regiment, probably their first time under fire, and some of the older hands watched furtively to see how they acquitted themselves. But there was no cause for uneasiness. They may have lacked the machine-like steadiness of regular troops, but the force and fire of their attack left nothing to be desired. From that point of view they might have been war-worn veterans. They came with bayonets well down, cheering and singing over ground which was strewn with their own dead and the dead of their comrades. They dropped men, of course, as they plunged forward, but they seemed little to heed that. Not for one moment did they forget that that fine charge of theirs was being carried out under the eyes of the very cream of the British army. On and on they came, to the edge of the German trench, without halt or pause, and then the regulars on their right burst into loud and ringing cheers as they swept right over the trench, driving the surviving Germans like chaff before them. It was a fine thing, finely done; moreover, the gap in the line was filled and the regulars on their flank could advance once more.

"Did you see that?" Bentley cried. "You know who they are, don't you?"

"They're Territorials, like us," Ginger, burst out. "An' wot's more, they're made o' the same sort o' stuff. I knows 'em. They comes out o' the gutter an' off the cab ranks and out o' the banks, an' there're scores of 'em as used at one time to think o' nothin' else but their tennis an' their golf on a Saturday afternoon. You ask them German chaps, and they'd say as our boys weren't soldiers at all. But I don't know as it matters wot you call 'em. It's all the same with that lot. An' there's about three million more of 'em to come."

But no one was listening to what Ginger was saying; it would have been impossible to hear in any case. Kemp was looking anxiously ahead. So far as the Musketeers were concerned, there was nothing more to be done until the barbed wire was out of the way. The right hand leading company managed to skirt round without serious loss, but 'A' Company standing there in the open, were being cut to ribbons. They were close up against the entanglement, and they tore at it with bleeding hands and broken nails in vain. There was nothing for it for the moment but to lie there under a murderous machine gun fire and a deluge of shrapnel, and wait patiently for the bomb-throwers of 'A' Company, now safely through the defences, to make an impetuous attack upon the trench, which they eventually did. Then the Musketeers deployed to the right, and followed up their comrades with the bayonet, and the danger was over. They were in the trench at length, panting, breathless, and exhausted, but they had won their way through and the trench was theirs. But they knew that so far they had cleared only one obstacle, and that as soon as they were out of their trench again they would be confronted with another of those death-traps, coil upon coil of it, and stout enough to resist anything short of heavy gun fire. There was nothing for it but to lie down again and wait to see if it were possible to send back a message to the effect that the attack was being held up by entanglements, and to see if the gunners could not come to the rescue.

Right out there amongst his men came the colonel of the Musketeers. He was grave and anxious, for he knew only too well the terrible danger that lay before his beloved regiment. He crept forward and asked for volunteers to get back behind the line and convey a message to the gunners. Half of the men leapt to their feet at once, and two of them managed to get clear away. An anxious quarter of an hour passed, and then once more the shrapnel began to fall in front of the Musketeers. Only a few shots, but the barbed wire vanished as if it had been so much hay before a devastating fire. Meanwhile, a volunteer party with bombs had pushed their way forward, and had cleared some of the Germans out of their environments. All this time a mob of the foe had been sniping from some cross roads behind their trench, but directly the attack began in earnest these threw down their arms and surrendered. Some of them, however, commenced their fire again when they realised that the bombing party consisted only of a lieutenant and a handful of men, but nevertheless these continued to push forward until they pushed the traiterous foe into the open, where a machine gun officer was waiting for them with his Maxim. There was no question of surrender after that, for within a minute there was not one of the Germans left.

"That was a pretty close call," the colonel of the Musketeers said, as his men cleared the trench and pushed forward into the open. "I am proud of you, lads. If you had been born to the business you couldn't have done it better. But we haven't finished yet. Our objective is that big orchard in front of us. We've got to rush it if we can, and as quickly as possible, for my instructions are that it is very heavily held."

There was no occasion to say any more, for the Musketeers dashed on as steadily as they had begun, right across the open into the orchard, ready and eager for the fray.

But they had been anticipated. The dark forms they could see there were not those of German troops, but a regiment of the Devons, who had forestalled the attack, and had wiped out the whole of the defending force. They welcomed the Musketeers with a grin on their faces. The Germans lay there in heaps, and not one of them survived to tell the tale.

CHAPTER LI - THE DAY'S WORK

It was a great day for the Musketeers, a great day indeed for all the regiments engaged. On the left the Worcesters and the East Lances and the Sherwood Foresters, and other regiments coming up in support took up the good work and continued the attack. The Worcesters were fortunate enough to find themselves engaged in a little contest all to themselves. They had rounded up a mob of Germans in another orchard and driven them into a farmhouse to the north, which, as it transpired, was about the last stronghold of the position held by the foe. The Worcesters would not be denied. They went into the engagement full of pluck and spirit, and once they got the foe going they hunted them up and down those muddy fields as if they had been so many terriers let loose in a barnyard amongst the rats at threshing-time. They hunted them with the bayonet round and round the trees as if they had been playing some game, and drove them into the farmhouse, where they shot them down in scores. Many of the Germans were so panic-stricken that they attempted to force their way up the farmhouse chimneys, only to be dragged down and taken prisoners. It was strange that that farmhouse, more or less in the line of the German trenches, had escaped the destruction wrought by the heavy fire of the British guns, but so it was, and that the Germans had made good use of it was proved by the fact that every bedroom was lined with sandbags, and every window boasted a machine gun.

It still lacked a few minutes to the hour of 2 when the whole village and its outlying houses were in the hands of the British, and even then the advance had not been quite so quick as anticipated for the reason that here and there certain brigades had been delayed by the barbed wire entanglements. Apart from that, the conditions were all in favour of a further advance towards the ridge. For the Germans were fairly on the run now, and all their iron discipline was lost. It was in vain that their officers tried to rally them: indeed, the mental and physical condition of the prisoners was eloquent testimony to the complete demoralisation which had set in. It is no exaggeration to say that the prisoners were panic-stricken. They were not old men, either, not men past the military age, riot men of the Landsturm or

Landwehr, but fine, well built and nourished young Prussians and Bavarians, well clad and perfectly equipped.

On the whole it was a fine fight, and one that covered the British troops with glory. Throughout those terrible and trying hours there had been no incident that any one amongst them need be ashamed of; there were terrible difficulties in the way, however, physical and natural difficulties, but for which not only the village of Neuve Chapelle but the ridges as well would have fallen into the hands of the all conquering Britons. It was those flat plains, marked here and there with isolated houses, and gashed with a network of trenches, that served to waste the precious time. For here and there the full impetuosity of the British advance was held up by the resistance of handfuls of Germans holding these natural points of vantage with machine guns. These were the die-hards, who fought to the last gasp and died beside their guns rather than surrender, thus rendering their colleagues a service impossible to over-estimate. For the precious moments delayed here and there spelt, not minutes, but hours altogether, and gave the Germans time to rake together reinforcements from all over the district, and, consequently, to organise a resistance, hurried but compact enough, to form a strong line along the road and along the fringe of the big woods.

So it was nearly 4 o'clock before the general advance could proceed. And this was the psychological moment if it had been only possible to grasp it, for it is no exaggeration to say that the opposition was then so paralysed that the British troops were able to form up in the open outside the village before advancing, and not a single shot was fired against them. It was just here, opposite the wood, that our men came out of the trenches and strolled about defiantly and fearlessly. Then the left attacked the road again in strength, but by this time the Germans had hurried up more machine guns, and posted them in the houses; and thus the new attack was checked. It is true that the Gurkhas on the right penetrated into the wood, but they found themselves enfiladed and the advantage was lost. From 4 o'clock in the afternoon till dark practically no further progress was made. Then the firing began to slacken down, and the troops slept where they dropped. It had been a costly day, but the reward was great.

The victory of Neuve Chapelle is not to be measured by the trenches gained and the amount of yards lost by the Germans. It is not to be measured, either, by the standard of bygone campaigns. There was a time, and that not long ago, when the battle of Neuve Chapelle might have ranked amongst the decisive conflicts in the history of warfare. By comparison with other battles in this war it was a matter of outposts. But its moral effect is far reaching. It matters nothing what the German point of view may be: to the British Tommy, the child of the cottage, or the son of the palace, it came like a glorious tonic to a man who has long lain sick and weary and who has almost given up hope of feeling his strength and manhood again. It proved to him that he had lost nothing of his pluck or his fine patriotism during all those long and drab months in the trenches. It came to him as a sign that the nation was as sound and as true to the core as it ever had been. It mattered nothing to him that the dawn would bring up enormous German reinforcements, and that the pride of the Teuton would not permit him to lie down without doing his utmost to wipe out the humiliating smart of that disastrous day.

That night, at any rate, the Musketeers, like the rest of them, slept on the ground that they had won. They had had their suppers, they had had their smokes, and they were looking eagerly out for the morrow.

"Well, this ought to have satisfied even you, Ginger," Bentley smiled. "Do you mean to say you haven't had enough yet? We have been wonderfully lucky. So far as I can see, not one of our little lot has been touched."

It was even as Bentley had said. There was himself and Kemp, together with Garton and George and the rest of them, all huddled up together, absolutely worn out, and yet too excited to sleep.

"It was just fine," Ginger said. "Lor' bless yer, I could jump now an' 'owl front pure delight. I feel like a chap wot's just come out o' gaol, I mean like a chap wot's 'ad five years an' then gets loosed out by them chaps as calls themselves the Court of Appeal. You see, I didn't realise as we wos 'arf so fit as we are. If anybody'd told me as we could 'ave gone through a dye like this after all them months in the trenches I'd 'ave laughed. But I didn't see a single bloke as fell out; at any rate. I'm sure it weren't one o' the Musketeers."

"Better work than caddying golf clubs," Kemp suggested.

"Don't you get remindin' me o' that," Ginger replied. "I wants to forget it. An' if it wasn't for you gentlemen I might be carrying on that same gime still. It was you two as made a man o' me an' a good many others, you an' the war between you. An' if you only know 'ow grateful I am—"

But Ginger was talking to the air. He realised that his companions were all asleep. Then he turned over on his side too, and slept the sleep he had so justly earned.

CHAPTER LII - THE NEXT DAY

It was just before dawn next day that the Germans made their initial attempt to recover the ground they had lost at Neuve Chapelle. This first counter-attack was promptly driven off with heavy loss, and the retreating Germans were pursued until they fell back on their machine gun strongholds in the farmhouses on the Pietre-road. It was a costly proceeding for the Germans, especially for the reinforcements, which were shelled heavily by our artillery as they advanced through the wood; indeed, for days afterwards the enemy were observed bringing out their dead from the undergrowth and burying them in the field behind. All that day, too, the Germans heavily bombarded the British lines, but altogether without effect. During the whole of that day and the following night the foe was gathering reinforcements, mainly consisting of Bavarian and Saxon regiments.

Dawn had not broken on March 9 when once more the British line was deluged with high explosive shells, a sure forerunner of one of those massed attacks which are so dear to the German heart, and which from first to last has cost the foe upwards of two million men on the different frontiers. They came on light-heartedly enough, blinded and fooled by their leaders, as is ever the German way. For these doomed troops had been told that there had been a slight accident, and that a handful of English troops had blundered into Neuve Chapelle, and that it needed little to turn them out again. So they came on in their usual dense formation, marching like men on the parade ground to one of the most hideous slaughters of war. Apparently the attack had been badly timed and planned without heed for the future. These Bavarians and Saxons had not expected to find the British so far advanced. In front of our men the attacking party progressed like men on a route march, their officers mounted for the most part, with drawn swords in their hands. At one place, at any rate, a non-commissioned officer was seen driving his men along with a whip as if he were rounding up a flock of sheep.

A minute later the British rifles and machine guns opened their deadly fire. It was not a fight; it was a hideous, revolting slaughter. Right in front of one of the English brigades the German infantry, jogging along at an easy double, came almost up to the muzzles of the score of machine guns in front of our brigade. The onslaught was so great that the advancing file had no time to fall back or steady themselves; they were absolutely wiped out of existence. In less time than it takes to tell, a yelling, cheering multitude of men, full of life and courage stood before the machine guns, and then a huge heap of bodies stilled the advance. But the machine guns tired not, the British rifles never ceased to speak, and when the grey dawn came the corpses lay so deep as to form a rampart behind which the few that survived snatched an insufficient cover.

By the time it was really daylight the attack was no more. But, on the other hand, it was impossible for the British to advance any farther, and so for the moment they had to content themselves with what they had won.

But nothing could detract from the moral effect of the victory. It gave to our men the impetus that they so sorely needed, it restored them at once to a fine offensive force, all the more delighted and inspiriting after the long weary drag of the winter and the dull monotony of the trenches. And so they held on day by day and week by week, waiting and hoping that the glorious day might be repeated. But that time was not yet; many a day was to elapse before the triumph of Neuve Chapelle would prove to have been the forerunner of other victories in the same region.

Meantime the Germans were hurrying up their reinforcements until they had massed something like ten army corps, with a corresponding weight of artillery, in front of Ypres. It was evident that the Kaiser was by no means discouraged by his futile attempts to batter a way to Calais, and that he still held the prize cheap at treble the price of the five hundred thousand men already lost. So here were the British, hard held again, once more fighting on the defensive in that blood-stained region, and clinging on as grimly as they had done in the previous winter. Day after day they climbed to their trenches, despite the fire of those terrible mortars, and sticking to them with a dogged tenacity that nothing could tire and nothing overcome.

Perhaps never in the course of history has the British infantry displayed such high qualities as those manifested during those terrible days, more particularly on April 25, when the bombardment reached a crescendo which marked the maximum of effect. The whole line of our trenches was kept under a fire so continuous and searching that it even destroyed the telephone communications between the trenches and the batteries.

But, despite all this, despite the fact that our trenches were blown to atoms, not one of them had been vacated, and the Germans hurrying to the attack, under the impression that their artillery had done its work, and that our defences were pulverised, found, not once, but invariably, that the British trenches were occupied, and that the machine guns were still ready to do their deadly work.

And here it was that the Territorials once more came out into the limelight. Two regiments of these had been brought up with other reinforcements to straighten the Canadian position. Again and again they were brought under the most merciless fire, but they stood as solid as if they had been frozen there. Their orders were to hold the line at any cost, and they did so. It was another battalion of the same regiment that behaved so magnificently in front of Zollebeke, at which point the German shell fire was absolutely continuous. This shelling had begun at daybreak, and was continued so incessantly that it was next to impossible to bring up reinforcements, and, indeed, it was only when the German guns slackened for the purpose of allowing their infantry to advance that our troops were enabled to gain cover and so help their stricken comrades. It was here that the Royal Fusiliers dashed forward in gallant style and brought their machine guns into action so swiftly that the foe were forced back as if some unseen giant hand was holding them in check. And there were other Territorials to reckon with as well, fine, well-set-up fellows from the north. Northumberlands, Durhams, and Yorkshires, who were called upon to advance right across the open in the teeth of a tremendous machine gun fire to make good the retirement of the French on the left of our line.

In the circumstances it was a big thing to ask, but the Durham Light Infantry were in sore need, as were also the famous Fighting Fifth, who lost their general, who had come in person to keep in contact with his men, which he was forced to do in consequence of the fact that every telephone wire had been destroyed. It was a great advance that the Fighting Fifth made, and it will never be forgotten by those whose privilege it was to see it. It was to make good the gaps caused by these losses that the Territorials were called into action, and right gallantly they responded. There were regiments amongst them absolutely denuded of officers, and in a great many instances it was only a subaltern or two who led back the remains of the battalion under cover of the welcome darkness to billets. And so it went on day after day, until the German attack weakened, and it was borne in upon the foe that once again they had lost their hopes of a triumphal march to Calais. And there for the present we will leave it—leave the line locked and barred more securely than it ever has been before.

CHAPTER LIII - AND AFTER?

For perhaps the last time the German phalanx had hurled itself regardless of cost on that small piece of ground near the town of Ypres. That spot will never be forgotten, but will go down to posterity as the most costly piece of ground ever struggled for in the history of the world. Month after month Germany has struggled for it, had shed the best of her blood and lost the bravest of her first line of troops, to say nothing of a kings ransom expended on ammunition in a futile struggle for what appeared to be no more than a mere heap of ruins. The Kaiser has set his heart upon Calais, just as Queen Mary did, and with much the same result; and it may be that when history comes to pronounce its verdict it will be found that a madman's wild ambition was the cause of his downfall.

This had been going on now for months—one magnificent regiment after another had been flung headlong against the British trenches only to be driven back or wiped out altogether, and yet wearily dragging months saw the eagles no nearer the end of that terrible journey. And it was much the same too in whatever direction the greedy bird of prey turned his bloodshot eyes. He had his successes here and there, no doubt, but each of these was at a cost that no country can repeat many tines and live. And so it was at Ypres, until the foe fell sullenly back, never perhaps to attempt another advance, or, on the other hand, to recommence the hideous slaughter which hitherto had been in vain. For May was passing, and June was at hand, and England's great armies that had been slowly gathered together since last summer were getting ready. Indeed, hundreds of thousands were ready now to come out and help those gallant fellow countrymen who had done so much during all those terrible months. And goodness knows they had earned their rest; goodness knows they had paid a big enough price to save Europe from the fate which had threatened it.

Some time perhaps we shall know the real inwardness of the magnificent task that the first British army set itself to accomplish. What we should have done without them one shudders to think. What would have become of France? Would France have been a second Belgium? Would the heel of the conqueror have been pressed on the neck of Paris? It is difficult to say, but the probabilities are that all these things would have happened. But our armies saved all that; we may not yet have broken the back of the dragon, but we have cut his claws and we can see the blood streaming from between the scales of the monster.

Daily the German assaults at Ypres grew less and less; daily it became apparent that he reckoned himself beaten. And hourly England and France were growing stronger. Hourly England was pouring her troops into France, and Australia and New Zealand and Canada were hurrying up their sons to the front. And, meanwhile, though Germany was still battering at the ruined walls of Ypres and struggling fitfully in the direction of Warsaw, the whole nation was as much in a state of siege as if it had been imprisoned behind the walls of a fortress. It was all very well to argue that they held a portion of France and Russia and the whole of Belgium; in reality this merely meant that they had managed to extend the size of their cage before the iron bars were actually driven home. It means a little more time, a little more patience, and the loss, no doubt, of many more gallant lives, but really these only spell delay of the inevitable.

Then, on the top of all this, another foe has raised its head, another foe not to be despised, a splendid and united nation with some four millions of men behind it, determined to uphold the right and shake off the fetters which Germany and her miserable ally had hoped to forge about her feet. It is early yet to prophesy, but Italy will do her part. And there may be others yet, so take it all in all we have no reason to complain about the outlook for the future. But the men at the front, such as the Musketeers, live wholly in the present; they have their work to do, and they are doing it splendidly.

A week or two later, after the last German dash for Ypres had been finally smothered, what was left of the Musketeers went back to their billets. They had been fighting incessantly now for six weeks. They had had no rest night or day, and human nature has its limits. There were fresh regiments now by the score to take their places, and they were looking forward to what, by comparison, they would call a holiday.

For the most part the group in which we are interested had come out of the fray with hardly a scratch. There were rumours abroad to the effect that they might be sent home before long either to recuperate or to remain there until the battalion was at full strength again, and many wistful eyes turned longingly in the direction of the coast.

"Do you think there is a chance of getting home?" Kemp asked his captain at the first opportunity. "Of course we can go on fighting if necessary, but for the present I think we have had as much as we can stand. They might give us a chance now that so many of the new army are here."

"I think it's very likely," the captain replied. "I can quite understand people at home feeling rather nervous at first as to how the young troops would behave. But when day after day we have been watching Territorials fighting with all the zest and keenness of old soldiers, I don't think there is any cause for anxiety. By Jove, fancy what a reception a regiment like ours would get today if we marched through the streets of London! And I can't imagine anything better for recruiting. The regiment has done its work well, and we are all proud of it. But we are tired, and there is no getting away from the fact. I don't want to boast, but I've been out here now since the first week in September, and I must confess that I should like to see London again. Mind you, I don't say that we shall go, but we must have some troops at home, and what could we have better than seasoned men like ourselves, who have been all through the campaign from the beginning? But don't count on it, and don't be disappointed in any case."

There were others, on the contrary, who were quite sure that they were going back again. Ginger, for instance, had come to regard it as quite a settled thing.

"I don't want to leave it altogether," he said. "I don't think as I could go back to the old life now, an' I don't know as I'm good for anything but soldiering. If I 'as any luck, an' Lord knows I've a 'ad my proper share since September, I'll be a sergeant-major one of these days. I sha'n't never do better than that, along o' my defective education. But, Lor', that's good enough for me, good enough for any chap as didn't 'ope a year ago to be nothin' more than a pore devil of a golf caddie or a cove wot sells pipers in the streets. It seems almost impossible to imagine as I've got a fair chance to finish up with twenty-five bob a week or more, an' a thoroughly good pension when I'm done with. But I ain't thinkin' o' that just now, Mr. Kemp. Wot I wants is to see London again, to 'ear the noise of the streets an' the roar of the traffic, an' find myself a chap wot people looks at when I goes by an' to realise for the first time in my life as I've got money in my pocket an' more to come. D'you know, sir, as I aven't drawn a penny o' my pay since we cone out? An' it makes my 'ead fairly swim when I think of the sprees I've got before me."

"You wouldn't do anything foolish," Bentley suggested. "You've got a fine future before you, Ginger, if you don't abuse it. It would be a thousand pities if you did anything silly now. Now, listen to me, and be advised."

"I ain't goin' to do anything foolish," Ginger muttered. "But if a chap wot's gone through wot I 'ave ain't entitled to a good spree, I don't know 'oo is. One nice little spree along o' my pals, just for a couple o' days, an' then to settle down to respectability afterwards. But I don't want to go unless they can spare me. If the good ole commander-in-chief takes it to 'eart, or if 'e feels as 'e can't whop those bloomin' Germans wifout Ginger Smiff, then 'e's only got to 'old up 'is 'and, an' I'll take on a Staff job without a murmur."

"You will always be the same, Ginger," Kemp smiled. "I don't believe anything would change you. But if I were you I wouldn't reckon too much upon going home. Nothing has been settled as yet, and we may have a disappointment."

"Don't you want to go, sir?" Ginger asked.

"I couldn't tell you how much," Kemp responded. "I hardly like to think about it. But we've got to play our part and go through it all without murmuring. I know Tommy's a born grumbler; there are times when I believe he would mutiny if he wasn't allowed to grouse. But there are some people who smile and do nothing, whilst there are others who grouse and grumble and work like blazes, Tommy's one of the last. It will always be the same as long as the British Empire lasts."

And with this epitaph on the British soldier we can leave the Musketeers, battered and weary and war-worn, and waiting anxiously and patiently for the holiday they have so richly deserved. We can leave them and their fellows either to go to the front again, or to come back, knowing that, whatever there fate is, they will work till they drop and fight till they die. We can leave them to struggle on as they have from the first, never knowing when they are beaten or what it is to taste the bitterness of defeat. And we can leave the womenkind to watch them and pray for them, doing their work at home cheerfully and uncomplainingly; leave them in the hospitals, women like Nettie and Dorothy, doing a noble work with a patience that is divine and a steadfastness which is beyond words.

For the end is not yet; the final victory is still hidden in the clouds and smoke of war.

Truly, it is a "Long, long way to Tipperary—"

FRED M WHITE – A CONCISE BIBLIOGRAPHY

NOVELS (A-Z)

Ambition's Slave (1916)
The Argus Eye (1919)
Blackmail (1902)
The Blue Daffodil (1934)
The Brand Of Silence (1911)
A Broken Memory (1929)
The Bubble Reputation (1908)
By Order Of The League (1886)
The Cardinal Moth aka The Accused Orchid (1903)
The Case For the Crown (1918)
Claxton's Mill (1912)
A Clue In Wax (1930)
The Corner House (1905)
The Councillors of Falconhoe (1922)
Craven Fortune (1904)
A Crime On Canvas (1909)
The Crimson Blind (US title: The Mystery Of The Crimson Blind) (1905)
A Daughter Of Israel (1892)
The Day: Or The Passing Of A Throne (1914)
A Deal In Letters (1923)
The Devil's Advocate (1924)
Dropped From The Fast Express, or A Daughter's Sacrifice (1911)
The Edge Of The Sword (1907)
The Ends Of Justice (1906)
A Fatal Dose (aka Behind the Mask) (1907)
The Fight For The Child (1925)
The Five Knots (1907)
"Found Dead" (1930)
The Four Fingers (US title: The Mystery Of The Four Fingers) (1907)
A Front Of Brass (1910)
The Garden O' Dreams (1909)
A Golden Argosy (1886)
The Golden Bat (1924)
The Golden Rose (1909)
The Green Bungalow (1923)
The Grey Woman (aka Sinister House) (1928)

The Happy Exile (1920)
A Harbour Of Refuge (1918)
Hard Pressed (1910)
The Honour Of His House (1920)
The House Of Mammon (1913)
A House Of Sorrows (1911)
The House Of The Schemers (1906)
The House On The River (1925)
In Trust (1892)
Jim Crowshaw's Mary (1911)
The King Diamond (1927)
Lady Clara (1913)
Lady Edna's Awakening (1920)
The Lady In Blue (1915)
The Law Of The Land (1906)
The Leopard's Spots (1920)
The Lonely Bride (aka The White Bride) (1907)
The Lord Of The Manor (1907)
Love, The Foe (1910)
A Maker of Millions (1909)
The Man Called Gilray (1911)
The Man Who Found Christmas (a novelette) (1915)
The Man Who Knew (1932)
The Man Who Was Two (1921)
The Man With The Vandyk Beard (1925)
The Midnight Guest: A Detective Story (1907)
A Mummer's Throne (1910)
My Lady Bountiful (1905)
The Mystery Of Crocksands (1923)
The Mystery Of The Ravenspurs (aka The Black Valley) (1911)
The Mystery Of Room 75 (1922)
Naboth's Vineyard (1889)
The Nether Millstone (1906)
Netta, The Story Of Sin (1909)
New Century Calendar Clue (1948)
Number Thirteen (1914)
The Old Secretaire: A Christmas Story (novelette) (1887)
On The Night Express (1930)
The Open Door (1907)
Paul Quentin (1908)
Paul, The Sage (1910)
The Phantom Car (1929)
Powers Of Darkness (1912)
The Price Of Silence (1925)
The Psalm Stone (1905)
Queen Of Hearts (1930)
A Queen Of The Stage (1908)
The Riddle Of The Rail (1926)

The Robe Of Lucifer (1896)
A Royal Wrong (1913)
The Salt Of The Earth (1918)
The Scales Of Justice (1908)
Secret Of The River (1934)
The Secret Of The Sands (1911)
A Secret Service (1913)
The Seed Of Empire (1916)
The Sentence Of The Court (1913)
A Shadowed Love (1905)
The Shadow Of The Dead Hand (1926)
The Silver Stream (novelette)
The Slave Of Silence (1906)
A Society Jezebel (1917)
The Sundial (1908)
Tregarthen's Wife: A Cornish Story (1901)
The Turn Of The Tide (1923)
The Weight Of The Crown (1904)
The White Battalions (1900)
The White Bride (aka The Lonely Bride) (1910)
The White Glove (1910)
The Wings Of Victory (1919)
The Yellow Face (1906)

SHORT FICTION SERIES

THE MASTER CRIMINAL (1897-1898)

A series of 12 short stories featuring Felix Gryde, who describes himself as "a really clever soldier of fortune."

The Head Of The Caesars
At Windsor
The Silverpool Cup
The "Morrison Raid" Indemnity
Cleopatra's Robe
The Rosy Cross
The Death Of The President
The Cradlestone Oil Mills
Redburn Castle
"Crysoline Limited"
The Loss Of The "Eastern Empress"
General Marcos

THE LAST OF THE BORGIAS (1898)

A series of stories featuring Professor Victor Colonna, a vigilante physician who murders undesirable people with undetectable poisons.

The Scrip of Death
The Crimson Streak
The Holy Rose
The Saving Of Serena
The Varteg Necklace
The Three Carnations

DRENTON DENN - SPECIAL COMMISSIONER

Drenton Denn is a tough newspaper reporter on the payroll of The New York Post. His hallmarks are a straw hat, a Norfolk jacket, a perennial cigar, and a terrier by the name of "Prince."

The Yellow Moth
The Red Speck
Dust
The Fire Bugs
The Great White Moth

THE ROMANCE OF THE SECRET SERVICE FUND (1900)

This series features Newton Moore, the top agent at The Secret Service Fund.

By Woman's Wit
The Mazaroff Rifle
In The Express
The Almedi Concession
The Other Side Of The Chess Board
Three Of Them

THE DOOM OF LONDON

This sci-fi series of six stories describes a variety of catastrophes which ravage London.

The Four White Days
The Four Days' Night
The Dust Of Death
A Bubble Burst
The Invisible Force
The River Of Death

THE SAGE OF TYBURN (1905-1906)

Each of these stories was preceded by the header The Sage Of Tyburn.

No. 1 - The Chronicle Of The Yellow Girl
No. 2 - The Chronicle Of The Blue-Eyed Syndicate
No. 3 - The Chronicle Of The Inconsequent Princess
No. 4 - The Chronicle Of The Elderly Adonis
No. 5 - The Chronicle Of The Libelled Velasquez

THE DRAGON-FLY (1909)

Six stories about an impecunious but brilliant amateur criminologist, entomologist and ornithologist by the name of Horace Daimler. Each of the stories was preceded by the header The Dragon-Fly.

No. 1 - How Horace Daimler Got His Name
No. 2 - The Three Red Rats
No. 3 - [title unknown]
No. 4 - [title unknown]
No. 5 - A [illegible] Crime
No. 6 - The Mirror Over The Fireplace

REAL DRAMA (1909)

A series of stories published under the subtitle "Being Some Leaves From The Notebook Of A Late Theatrical Agent."

His Second Self
An Extra Turn
"Not In The Bill"
The Plagiarist
The Man In Possession
A Pair Of Handcuffs

THE TELEPHONE STAR (1912)

A series of stories about Keith Marrit, a star journalist working for a fictitious newspaper called The Telephone.

No. 1 - The Case Of El Hamid, The Seer
No. 2 - The Case Of The Genuine Counterfeit
No. 3 - The Case Of The Yellow Car
No. 4 - The Case Of Lord Wintercotte
No. 5 - The Case Of The Rusty Nail
No. 6 - The Case Of The One-Eyed Chauffeur

GIPSY TALES (1903-1916)

A series of stories describing the adventures of a wily British navvy with Romany roots, who is known only as "Gipsy." In his fantasies Gipsy portrays himself as a playwright, and tries to stage-manage the dramatis personae and the situations that feature in the stories.

A Matter Of Kindness
A Liberal Education
A Stranger In Bohemia
Drops Of Water
The Unpremeditated Curtain
Mere Details
Out Of Season

THE DIARY OF A LONELY SOUL (1915)

The Diary Of A Lonely Soul - Story 1 [title unknown]
The Diary Of A Lonely Soul - Story 2 [title unknown]
The Diary Of A Lonely Soul - Story 3 [title unknown]
The Diary Of A Lonely Soul - Story 4 [title unknown]
The Diary Of A Lonely Soul - Story 5 [title unknown]

AN A-Z OF OTHER SHORT FICTION

According To The Statute
The Ace Of Hearts
Adventure (aka A Trick of Fate)
After Reynolds
Alias "James Jones"
An Ally
And This Is Fame
Anonymous
The Apple-Green Plate
Applied Mechanics
The Arms Of Chance
Art Critics
At Short Notice
Aunt Mary
Autumn Manoeuvres
The Azoff Diamonds
A Bad Cold
The Balance Of Nature

The Barrister At Bay
Below Zero
The Better Way
Big Fish
The Big Thing
Billy's Xmas
A Bit Of Egypt
The Black Admiral
The Black Cat
The Black Narcissus
The Black Prince
Blind
Blind Chance
The Blindworm
A Block Of Marble
A Bootless Errand
Brayton's Secret
The Broken Lute
A Broken Sceptre
The Broken Trail
The Buff Gauntlet
Burglar Bill's Pupil
By Grace Of His Majesty
By Wireless
A Call On The Phone
A Captious Critic
The Case For The Prisoner
The Charlatan
A Christmas Bride
A Christmas Deputy
Christmas Cards
The Christmas Carol
A Christmas in Peril
A Christmas Star
The Clock Struck Twelve
The Colonel's Christmas Pudding
Compounding A Felony
The Convict
Coralie And The Pearls
A Corner In Elephants
The Courage Of Despair
Crossed Swords
The Dancing Shadow
The Daughters Of The Moon
A Daughter Of Nature
The Dawnstar
A Deal In Diamonds
Denny

A Derelict In Clover
The Desert Ship
A Dog's Life
The Doll's House
The Dormer Window
A Dose Of Quinine
The Doubting D, or, A Cranky Cryptogram
A Draught Of Life
Early Closing Day
An Eastern Princess
The Eavesdropper
The Ebbing Tide
The Egg Of The Little Auk
The Emsdam Dispatches
The Empty House
An Error Of Judgment
The Evidence For The Prisoner
Excess Profits
An Eye For An Eye
The Eye Of The Camera
The First Stone
The Foil
Forget-Me-Not
For Love's Sake
For Once In A Way
For Value Received
A Foster-Father
Found!
The Fourth Man
Free Labour
A Friendly Call
From Information Received
Full Fathoms Deep
Gabrielle
A Gamble In Love
A Game Of Draughts
A Garden Of Pearls
Gentlemen Of The Jury
The Gates Of Ramshi
The Grey Bat
The Grey Raider
The Guiding Star
The Half-Crown Princess
The Hand Invisible
Hardy's Big Coup
The Heart Of The Anarchist
Heavy Metal
The Heels Of The Dawn

Her Christmas Dawn
His Christmas Gift
His Majesty's Mails
A Hole In The Net
The Hospitallers
Ice In June: A Playwright's Story
Icky Of Oluk Lake
Imperial Preference
In Black And White
In Rosemary Lane
In The Dark
In The Fog
In The Pit
Introducing Mr. Pentsymon
The Joinville Tunnel
Judgment Reserved
Karma
Kindergarten
The Kingmaker's Token
Lady Mary's Bulldog
The Language Of Flowers
The Last Drive
The Law Of The Jungle: A Tale Of Mean Streets
The Leather-Pushin' Private
The Left Hand
The Lesson The Ants Taught
The Livery Of Death
The Lonely Furrow
The Long Arm Of Bronze
Love In Aether
The Luck Of The Game
Made In England
The Man Himself
The Man Who Got Through
The Man Who Rang The Bell
The Man With The Eyeglass
A Masked Battery
The Master's Voice
A Matter Of Habit
'Merica
A Message from the Flood
The Midnight Call
The Missing Blade
The Missing Note
The Mistletoe Bough
Moray The Traitor
More Than Coronets
The Morning Glory

Music Hath Charms
A Musical Treat
The Mystery Of Room Five
Natural Selection
Nerves
The Night Express: The Story Of A Bank Robbery
The Northern Light
Not On The Records
An Object Lesson
The Odds On Zero
One Day With A Working Ant
One Foggy Night
One Of The Old Guard
On Peace Night
The Onus Of The Charge
The Orpheusia
Ostentation
The Other Man's Story
The Pardon
A Parrot Cry
The Path Of Progress
The Pawn And The Rook
Pearls Of Price
Photo By Lesterre
Pictures In The Snow (a Christmas story)
A Place In The Sun
The Platinum Chain
A Popular Novelist
Poste Restante
A Prize Crop
Proof Positive
The Purple Terror
A Queen In Hiding
A Question Of Money
Rachel's Seventh Year
Rawhide Science
The Real Dramatic Touch
A Record Round
Red Petals
Rob Peter—Pay Paul
A Rope Of Snow
Rose Of The Desert
A Royal Bag
The Royal Train
The Salmon Poachers
Santa Anna
A Satisfactory Reference
Saviour From The North

The Second Chapter
Second In The Field
The Shebeeners
A Single Hair
Sir Jeremiah's Big Shoot
Sister Louise
The Sixteenth Chapter
A Sleeping Partner
Sleeping Partner
A Sound In The Night
"Special" To The Telephone
A Stolen Interview
The Straight Game
The Stranger Within The Gate
Sub Rosa
The Substitute
The Superman
The Supreme Test
The Sword Of Justice
A Table Tragedy
The Thirty-Seventh Month
This Little World
A Thrilling Exit
The Throat Of The Wolf
The Ticket
To Be Let Furnished
Treasures Three
The Two Bon-Bons
Two Of Them
The Unbelieving Eye
Unbidden Guests
The Unexpected
An Unrecorded Crime
The Vital Spark
The Vital Spot
War Ribbons
The Waterwitch
The Western Way
When The Moon Set
The White Geranium
The White Spot
White Wings (1922)
The Wings Of Chance (1922)
The Witness (1920)
The World Next Door (1916)